LISTEN TO THE DRUMS

An African Odyssey

BARBARA OLIVE SMITH

LISTEN TO THE DRUMS

An African Odyssey

To SARAH

With all good wishes.

Barbara

Listen to the Drums
Barbara Olive Smith

Published by Aspect Design 2015
Malvern, Worcestershire, United Kingdom.

Designed, printed and bound by Aspect Design
89 Newtown Road, Malvern, Worcs. WR14 1PD
United Kingdom
Tel: 01684 561567
E-mail: allan@aspect-design.net
Website: www.aspect-design.net

A copy of this book has been deposited with the British Library Board

ISBN: 978-1-908832-87-0

For Susie, who believed in me.

CHAPTER 1

February 1949

Heather leaned over the ship's rail and stared down into the oily black water. A sluggish bow-wave seemed too lazy to leave the side of the vessel as she nosed through the narrow harbour gap, slow-motioning her way towards the bustle and noise of the crowded dock. Ropes snaked through the air, were caught by strong hands and wound round iron bollards to hold the ship fast. Orders were already being shouted from ship to shore and greetings were loudly exchanged between passengers and the crowd waiting below in the full glare of the sun.

The air was heavy, sultry with a blanket of tropical heat as Heather raised a hand to shield her eyes. An aromatic potpourri eddied up from the busy panorama of the dockside; it was hard to define the mixture of oranges, lemons, spices, and smoke, overpowered by the pungent scent of sweat. She looked round at the other passengers leaning over the rail on either side of her. They were mostly wives of Colonial Service Officers like herself, whom she had met for the first time on this journey from England. They seemed to know everything there was to know about West Africa, its climate, customs and people. She was just a raw recruit – and felt it.

The women had been eager to share their experiences and to warn her of the pitfalls ahead; laughingly scaring the living daylights out of her about the snakes, scorpions and spiders. Some of them were counted as 'Old Coasters', having spent many tours of duty living in outlandish places under primitive conditions, and this showed in their tell-tale leathery skin, while their voices rang with the tone of those used to dealing with servants.

Heather asked herself, Whatever possessed me to come to this part of the world?

It was a question she was to ask again and again in the months to come.

But of course she'd had no choice. She loved Edward and wanted to be with him, so where he went, she would follow, even though she'd heard Africa referred to as 'the white man's grave'.

Her eye was caught by a commotion on the dock as a huddle of African market women in brightly coloured mammy cloths squabbled noisily over precarious mounds of red, yellow and green fruit stacked high on a layer of palm fronds spread over the dusty ground. She turned from the scene to search for Edward among the crowds gathered along the harbour. It was three months since she had seen him. They had been married less than a month before he was posted to Facriwa. Although the war was over, food rationing and clothes coupons were still the order of the day and her wedding gown had been hired to save precious coupons for dresses for her new life in the tropics. Suddenly it all seemed a long time ago.

The scene before her bristled with movement; nothing seemed to stand still. A bevy of scantily clad black children, their feet bare and bellies distended, zigzagged between the throng of people waiting to meet passengers from the ship. They stretched out skinny arms to beg for money, anything that was edible or could be sold. Laughing, singing and chattering, they fought together like noisy magpies over anything that was thrown to them.

And then she saw him. A sun-bronzed man, dressed in khaki shorts and bush shirt, waving up at her. This was an Edward she hadn't seen before, almost unrecognisable – and somehow better than the pale counterpart she had kissed goodbye in the pelting rain at Temple Meads railway station in Bristol. Her heart warmed at the sight of him, so different from Edward in grey flannel trousers and tweed sports jacket. She waved back and blew a kiss, her cheeks flushed as she rubbed the sweat from her brow with the back of her hand.

Today would be the beginning of a new life for both of them.

A tall African joined the crowd on the dock and edged his way over to where Edward stood gazing up at the ship. He spoke briefly to Edward, who nodded and smiled at him before pointing up to the deck where Heather stood. The ebony giant turned and looked directly at her. Even from this distance his stare was impelling; she felt as if she were being drawn towards him. She broke the eye contact, turning away to shake off the sensation of being pulled somewhere against her will. Like a leaf caught up by a gust of wind, the disturbing impression left her, and when she looked back down at the dock, the man had disappeared. A shout from one of the crew overtook the episode, but a question mark remained in her mind.

Heather's introduction to her African home was spectacular, coinciding as it did with a deafening thunderclap as Edward drove the car up the laterite drive to the small bungalow. There was no time for him to carry his wife across the threshold as, laughing and gasping, they ran hand in hand through a deluge of needle-sharp rain along the path which had already turned into a slippery quagmire. Soaked within seconds, their clothes stuck to their bodies like steamed pudding cloths, and once inside the bungalow they did indeed steam, for the downpour had done little to bring the temperature down.

They shouted at each other above the racket as the rain hammered a noisy tattoo on the corrugated iron roof, standing in puddles, still laughing as the rain dripped to the floor. Edward fetched towels and they dried their hair as he yelled, 'Don't worry, it won't last long.'

Then he threw down his towel, took her in his arms and gave her a long hungry kiss. She leaned against him, wanting to prolong the moment. This was where she should be, this was her new home and everything was going to be all right.

'I don't care how long it lasts – I've been waiting for this for weeks,' she said. She held her towel across the lower part of her face like a yashmak, her brown eyes inviting, teasing him.

'You brazen hussy,' he said, pulling her back into his arms, and he was about to kiss her again when the door was pushed open by a muddy bare black foot and a houseboy appeared carrying a tea tray. His white drill shorts and shirt were sodden, his skin showing through in brown patches where they stuck to his body. Tributaries of rain trickled down his face and dewy patterns clung like cobwebs in the short fuzz of hair on his head. Grinning broadly at Heather, he set the tray down on the table with a crash and wiped his face with the flat of his hand.

'This is Sammy, our houseboy,' Edward introduced him.

'Welcome, Madam. I hope Missis be plenty happy here in dis place.'

'Thank you, Sammy. I'm sure I shall,' Heather replied, crossing her fingers as she surveyed the room.

It was stark, functional, and devoid of any personal touches to give away anything about the person who lived here. The only thing to show that this was Edward's home was their wedding photograph in its silver frame, standing like a bleak landmark on an enormous desk pitted with cigarette burns and circle stains where glasses had rested. The furniture was solid, heavy and practical and made locally, Edward told her later, by carpenters in the Public Works Department. The upholstery was grubby, pock-marked with stains both ancient and modern, and in several places the kapok stuffing escaped through ragged holes. The cement floor had been treated with dark red tile paint and had a network of cracks giving it the appearance of a large ordnance survey map.

Heather removed the wet, month-old Daily Telegraph which acted as a makeshift cover over the tea tray and poured the tea. A cracked saucer with a few biscuits and a plate holding a huddle of small bananas were on offer.

'How far did Sammy have to come with this?' she asked, discarding the soggy newspaper and regarding the trail of muddy footprints left by the houseboy.

'I'll show you as soon as the rain's stopped. The kitchen is over on the far side of the compound.'

Heather detected a faint note of apology in Edward's reply, and felt vaguely apprehensive as she bit into a biscuit. It was soft and tasted mouldy.

When the rain had almost given up, Sammy brought her dripping cases from the car and stood them in the middle of the bedroom floor.

Heather looked at the single beds pushed together, feigning double bed status, and at the mosquito net suspended from a hook in the ceiling, covering the sham like a lacy white umbrella. She bent and pressed her knuckles into the nearest mattress. It was brutally hard. Edward noted her action and remarked, 'It doesn't do to have a soft mattress in this climate, love, it would only make you hot and sweaty.'

A full-length mirror with a crack across the middle mocked Heather with a distorted picture of herself. After the soaking, her hair was damp and bedraggled, her make-up had been washed away and she felt barely presentable, but Edward still looked at her as if she was beautiful. She gazed back at him, feeling vulnerable, and he drew her close.

Later, Heather had time to assess the room. She was dismayed; it was gloomy, musty-smelling and anything but an ideal love-nest. The bathroom was equally daunting with its monstrous rust-stained iron bath. The cold water tap had a pipe leading from it, but the hot tap was a fraud and led nowhere. Out of devilment, Heather turned the tap and it came off in her hand.

'That one's only for show. Sammy heats the bath water in kerosene tins on the kitchen stove. They call them "debbi cans" here,' Edward told her, and again Heather detected a hint of apology.

The lavatory was even worse and Heather giggled as she surveyed the square wooden box with its hinged seat. Edward explained that it hid a bucket which was emptied every morning by the sanitary boy by way of a door in the outside wall of the bungalow, with luck replacing it with a clean bucket before anyone was caught short. The primitive arrangement brought back Heather's memories of the outside privy at her uncle's farm where she had been despatched during the school holidays. Honeysuckle and ivy had grown in abundance over the low roof, and inside, squares of newspaper threaded on string hung from a nail on the back of the door.

She was brought back to the present as a large shiny brown cockroach scuttled past her foot and vanished through a gap between the box and the floor. Suppressing a shriek, she grabbed Edward's arm, thankful later for her restraint when she discovered that this particular specimen was but a midget compared with those resident in the kitchen and store room.

As they sat drinking cold beer by the light of a Tilley lamp on that first evening, Heather gave Edward all the news from home and told him about her voyage out from England. In exchange, Edward was enthusiastic in telling her about his work with the African farmers. He was responsible for a large area and each village had to be visited regularly to inspect their crops and livestock. He gave advice on everything from soil erosion and plant diseases to fertilizers and crop spraying. He was brimming with optimism and plans. Heather listened attentively as she watched flying termites committing suicide round the lamp and drop into a bowl of water on the ground beneath.

'Sammy will collect them and fry them for his breakfast in the morning,' Edward told her. Naively she thought her leg was being pulled until she saw a pile of termites in the frying pan a few days later. She could see that Edward had settled happily in the months spent here on his own and accepted that it was now her turn to adapt to these strange surroundings.

Once the storm had passed the air was sweet and warm and when they went to bed, the room seemed changed, set for a romantic liaison. The soft glow of the bush-lamp dismissed the previous gloom, giving it a welcoming intimacy. The bruising rain had teased a seductive scent from tropical blossoms which worked its own magic masking the musty smell that had pervaded the room earlier in the day.

Their loving was passionate, full of an ardour that had not been present on their snatched honeymoon spent in a drab, unheated hotel bedroom in Cornwall during a miserably bleak week in October before Edward's hurried departure for West Africa. Heather nestled into the crook of his arm, thinking of the jokes she'd heard on the ship about the fierce passions aroused by sultry seductive tropic nights. She smiled and snuggled closer, thinking that perhaps there was more than a grain of truth in the ribald stories. Long after Edward had doused the lamp, she lay listening to the drums beating out in the satin blackness beyond the compound. There was a primitive urgency about the drumming that disturbed her.

'It's only the local news being broadcast,' Edward assured her. 'You'll soon get used to it. News is being passed from village to village by the talking drums.' He ran his hand along the curve of her thigh and pressed his lips to her bare shoulder. 'It's a sort of Morse code used to exchange the gossip of the day. All the villagers for miles around will know by now that the new Madam has arrived.'

Heather wondered how long it would take to get used to being addressed as Madam or Missis.

'Who was the tall African man who spoke to you on the dock when I arrived?' she asked Edward.

'That's Kovina. He's the son of the chief in one of the villages just north of here,' Edward said. 'It's in my area and Kovina has helped me when I've had problems explaining things to farmers up there. His mother used to be a teacher at the mission school. You'll like him, he's a nice chap, and better educated than most in this part of the world.' Edward was quiet for a minute before adding, 'I suspect he's got himself involved in local politics.'

'Is that bad?'

'Could be. Time will tell.'

The drums were still throbbing their messages far and wide as Heather's thoughts drifted back to the dance at the Victoria Rooms in Bristol where Edward had proposed to her. The war had ended nearly two years earlier, but she was still recovering from the shock and grief of Martin's death. Her fiancé's plane had been shot down over Germany. Life had seemed full of trouble; the aftermath of war was loath to lose its grip on misery and hardship. Her world seemed drab and empty with little to look forward to and only an aching memory left of her love for Martin.

Her feelings for Edward were strong and sincere, but she hadn't thought she loved him with the same depth of feeling she'd had for Martin. Or was it simply that first love always seemed the strongest, she'd wondered. If she married Edward he would provide her with the means of escape from this post-war austerity. The vision of starting a new life in Africa held many attractions. Edward had sailed from Liverpool on the MV Apapa two weeks after their wedding.

Heather's imagination had painted a picture of palm trees silhouetted against a bluer-than-blue sky, vibrant colours of flowers, exotic fruit and spectacular wildlife. She had reckoned without tropical downpours, the persistent whine of hungry mosquitoes and sharing her home with cockroaches, lizards and numerous other tenants.

Now she tossed and turned on the horsehair mattress which sent prickly spines through the sheets, defying her to find a kind spot, until she fell into a troubled sleep long before the drums had finished sending their messages.

CHAPTER 2

As Edward had predicted, news of Heather's arrival had reached all the surrounding villages by morning, and soon after he had left the bungalow for his office, Sammy came to tell her that someone was waiting to greet her. Several African women sat on the bare earth by the back door, each bearing a gift to welcome the new Madam. They had brought mangoes, paw-paws, and scrawny live chickens hanging upside down, their feet tied together with lengths of dried grass. One old crone with sparse wisps of greying hair and few teeth handed her a straw nest containing four small eggs.

Heather thanked them for their gifts and wondered what to do with the mangoes and paw-paws. She had never seen them before and asked Sammy how they should be cooked. The houseboy's eyes widened and he chuckled as he explained that they should be eaten raw. Later, she saw Sammy's wife holding her sides and shrieking with laughter as he told her of Madam's ignorance.

Over the first few weeks, she set about putting her stamp on the bungalow, making it more of a home with pictures and personal things she had brought with her from England. But as time passed, she became bored and began to miss her family and friends at home as she had no white neighbours within several miles. Her African visitors from the surrounding villages were a welcome distraction and she soon picked up the local pidgin English spoken by most of them. She asked Edward for a long wooden bench and this was placed by the back verandah steps, and soon became a meeting place for villagers who sat patiently waiting, gossiping noisily until Sammy caught sight of them. Depending on his mood, he either ignored them or chased them off, until Heather found out and ticked him off.

One morning she found an old man sitting cross-legged in the dust at the foot of the steps. He spoke no English so she called Sammy to find out why he had come.

'Dis man, him be called Kanisi. Him get bad leg. It hurt him plenty. Him want Missis look-see him leg.'

Heather greeted the little man, dressed only in a ragged loincloth. His wizened walnut face was wasted, his back bent and his scarred body emaciated. She unwound the rag which served as a bandage and was assailed by a sickening stench before the festering ulcer was exposed. She guessed it was yaws, which she had read about in Edward's copy of Manson's Tropical Diseases, and knew it was contagious. She was doubtful about treating it, yet couldn't bring herself to send the old man away and felt duty-bound to try to ease his suffering. Her stomach churned as she washed and cleaned the wound and then applied a little of the sulpha powder her doctor had given her before she left England. He had been giving her a typhoid injection and became interested when she told him she was going to West Africa. He told her he had worked in a research laboratory in Nigeria for a few years and gave her a large jar of sulpha powder.

'You'll find this stuff useful if you get any cuts or insect bites that won't heal,' he'd advised her.

When she had put a fresh gauze pad on Kanisi's leg and bandaged it, the old man held her hands between his twisted leathery fingers, bowed ceremoniously and backed away with a toothless smile of thanks. Warmed by his gratitude, Heather could only hope her efforts had done some good.

Kanisi returned three times to have his leg dressed and on each occasion she was pleased to see that the ulcer looked clean, less angry, and was beginning to heal. Word spread quickly and before long every morning the bench by the verandah steps accommodated villagers waiting for her to tend their various ills. Worried by her lack of knowledge, Heather pored over a family healthcare book she had brought with her from England, anxious as to whether she was doing the right thing. In the end she figured that in most cases, it was simply a matter of relying on common sense and basic hygiene, and when she was stumped by anything she called Sammy to tell the sufferer to go to the Mission Clinic. As this was some distance away, she suspected many of them wouldn't make the effort.

Sammy interrupted her one morning as she sat working at her sewing machine.

'There be big black man come to see Madam,' he said. 'And him come to the front door,' he added, wishing to impress. Heather knew this was unlikely to be one of the local villagers and opened the mosquito netting door slowly, curious to see who the visitor could be.

It was Kovina, the tall African she had seen talking to Edward on the dockside when she had first arrived; the man whose stare had such an uncanny effect on her. He stood with one hand resting on the verandah wall, wearing the standard government officer's khaki shirt, shorts and long socks. He didn't hear Heather's approach and she was able to observe him for several seconds, absorbing every detail of this man who had provoked such a curious response when their eyes first met. He had a small scar above his left eyebrow, high cheekbones and thin straight lips. She thought she detected petulance or aggression in those stern lips and the arrogant set of his jaw. She noted his hands; the long sensitive fingers were not those of a labourer, the skin lay over the bones like oiled leather.

'Good morning,' she addressed him quietly and formally. 'My houseboy tells me you wish to see me.'

The man straightened and held out his hand, his reply equally formal.

'Greetings to you, Mrs Greenwood. Welcome to Facriwa.'

'Thank you. I believe you are Kovina? My husband has told me a little about you. I understand you help him sometimes?'

He smiled his pleasure at her recognition and the smile took the hardness from his mouth.

'Yes, I am Kovina Owusu, and you are right. I have sometimes worked with Edward when he's been in my father's district. Most of the farmers in that area speak only limited English.'

'Please come in and let me get you a drink,' Heather invited. 'Would you prefer tea, coffee or something cold?'

'Coffee, please.' He stood in the doorway for a moment, and looked round the room, taking everything in.

'It's easy to see signs of a woman's touch in here,' he said. 'I can see you've been busy.'

Heather blushed, both pleased and surprised that he should notice her attempt to brighten up the soulless room. Newly appointed young agricultural officers like Edward received salaries which didn't allow their wives to indulge in spending sprees on house improvements. Heather had bought cheap cotton prints at the local village store to make cheerful cushions and bright curtains, which had transformed the sitting room, bringing life and colour into the austere colonial-style bungalow.

She rang the bell to summon Sammy, and as she asked him to bring coffee, she couldn't help but notice the look that passed between her servant and this unexpected guest. Their silent communication ended in a barely perceptible nod, giving the exchange an air of conspiracy. She felt uneasy, wanting to know the reason for the telepathic link between the two men.

'It's kind of you to come and welcome me,' she said briskly. 'I come from quite a large family of brothers and sisters and I'm finding it a bit lonely being stuck out here at the back of beyond with no neighbours.'

Kovina raised an eyebrow and hesitated before he replied, and she had the uncomfortable feeling that he was trying to read her thoughts.

'Yes, I can imagine the days must seem long when you're far from your family,' he said, looking round the room again, 'but it is apparent that you have kept yourself occupied.'

'There's a limit to what I can do to improve this place,' she said, 'and if it were not for the villagers who call in the mornings, I would see no one to speak to all day except my houseboy, Sammy.'

'Time must hang heavy at the moment but before long you will find other expatriates will treat this as a stopping-off place, a watering hole on their way into Sekari for supplies.' Kovina frowned and changed the subject. 'I understand that you have been treating some of your visitors who are sick, and it is partly that which has brought me to see you.'

'How on earth did you know that?' Heather asked, then a thought occurred to her – of course it must be the talking drums. She laughed; 'Surely your bush-telegraph has more important gossip to pass on?'

'You'd be surprised. Any news travels fast in this country, no matter how trivial it may seem,' he said, and noting her cynicism, he added, 'We may be backward and we may have few telephones, but very little gets by without it being reported. Being a newcomer, you'll be the subject of interest for quite a while.'

Sammy padded in on his bare feet and placed the tray of coffee on a small table between them.

'You seem to be acquiring quite a name for yourself as the new Madam Witchdoctor, and apparently—'

Heather handed him a cup of coffee and butted in before he could finish his sentence. 'I should explain: I have no medical training, but when people come to my door begging for help, what am I supposed to do?' She stirred her coffee vigorously. 'It seems only right, only human, to treat their sores and fevers to the best of my ability. I can't turn them away when they show me their horrible ulcers covered in mud and leaves.' Warming to her subject, she waved her coffee spoon at him to make a point. 'It's no wonder they don't heal. For the most part all they need is straightforward guidance in cleanliness and hygiene.'

Kovina looked thoughtful but made no comment and Heather continued. 'Fortunately, I seem to be having some success.'

The African shook his head. 'The mud and leaves are probably not what they seem. It's likely that this so-called mud is made from a mixture of ground-up bones of snakes, monkeys or other creatures.' Seeing Heather's horrified expression, he went on: 'Even the bones of dead relatives are kept by proper witch doctors, not only for healing purposes, but for use in many of our tribal rituals.'

The emphasis was not lost on Heather.

'Are you joking?' she asked, laughing in disbelief, sure that he was exaggerating just to see her reaction. He was trying to shock her.

'Certainly not. I can assure you it's quite true. Witch doctors also use the roots and leaves of many plants just as your pharmacists use many herbal remedies.'

'That may well be so,' Heather said. 'I have no doubt that they can be very effective in many cases, but I think you must agree, my orthodox method of using sulphonamide powder and clean bandages appears to bring better results than any of your witch doctor's potions.'

'I won't argue with you. You may be right, but you have a lot to learn about this country and you should tread carefully. What you consider orthodox in England may be far from acceptable here in Facriwa.' Kovina placed his coffee cup on the table with slow deliberation. 'Our local healing man, Komfo, is very powerful. He has great influence over tribes for miles around and he could cause trouble if he considered you were undermining his authority. Most of the village elders respect him, though it is only fair to say that many also fear him. I advise you to be cautious.' He took a handkerchief from the pocket of his khaki shorts and wiped his mouth, never taking his piercing eyes from her face. He frowned.

'Mrs Greenwood, I don't wish to frighten you, but people who go against him have an unfortunate habit of dying suddenly for no apparent reason, or they simply disappear.'

Heather was taken aback and, for several uncomfortable seconds, did not reply.

'Oh, come on now, surely you're exaggerating,' she said finally.

'No, I'm afraid not.' He stood up, preparing to leave, and then the serious expression left his face and he smiled as if to clear the air. But his smile was not sufficient to break the undercurrent of tension that had built up between them, and as Kovina looked at her, Heather felt again that strange sensation of being pulled towards him. Shaking herself free of the invisible cord, she turned away from him. Kovina gave her a sideways glance.

'Is something the matter?' he asked.

'Oh no...' she shivered. 'Just someone walking over my grave.'

'What a curious thing to say!'

Of course, Heather told herself, it must sound odd to an African who had never heard the expression before. And come to think of it, she thought, this imposing African was himself decidedly odd.

'It's just an expression we use in England,' she explained, 'and it doesn't really mean anything.' Out of courtesy, she asked him to stay and tell her more about the customs of his country, and was relieved when he said that he had to attend a meeting. He didn't tell her what it was for and she wondered if it could be of a political nature. Edward had said something about Kovina being involved with one of the political parties that were springing up all over the country now that talk of independence and self-government was in the air. The young men of Facriwa were thirsty for the opportunity to run the country in their own way, and some were getting impatient.

CHAPTER 3

Edward arrived home late from work that afternoon, and kissed Heather as if she were very precious. He was thankful to have her to come home to after weeks of returning to a bungalow with only Sammy to greet him. Knowing that she would be there waiting for him made all the difference to his day. He flopped into a chair, easing off his muddy shoes, wriggled his toes, and waited to hear news of her day.

Heather told him of Kovina's visit.

'Oh yes, and what did you think of him? Big chap, isn't he? What did he have to say for himself?'

'He came to welcome me: or so he said, but I think he came to warn me off treading on the witch doctor's toes,' Heather told him. 'It seems that this man, Komfo, I think he called him, is not best pleased with me treating his patients.'

'I'm not surprised. He'll be missing the dash he gets from them.'

'Dash?'

'It simply means giving a tip, a gratuity if you like. Sometimes a dash can be a form of bribe.'

'Good God! That's not fair. These people are poor – they can't afford to pay for a dollop of mud and a few leaves. How on earth are they expected to get the money?'

'True enough, but don't be deceived by appearances. Some of the market mammies are quite wealthy. They save every penny to send their sons to school. More and more of them are making it to university. It's a good investment. Once qualified as a doctor or a lawyer, the son is expected to provide for his parents and other members of the family for the rest of his life,' Edward explained. 'And as for paying the witch doctor, the poorest members of the tribe pay him in yams or chickens, or even by working on his land, bringing bales of grass for his stock, chopping firewood.

Anything is currency here and you can be sure no one gets away without paying.'

'So what d'you think I should do?'

'I think you should stop holding your morning clinics for the time being. There's no point in asking for trouble,' Edward advised.

Heather gave a defeated nod.

'Where did Kovina get his education?' Heather asked Edward. She had become so used to speaking pidgin English to the village people that Kovina's command of English had surprised her, even though Edward had told her his mother had been a schoolteacher. 'At the Catholic Mission where his mother taught. Then I think he went away to a college somewhere.'

'What does he do now?'

'He works in the District Commissioner's office in Sekari. I've no idea what post he holds, but I imagine it's pretty high in the ranks. He seems to travel about quite a bit so it may be that he has to visit villages and gather information about matters under dispute. Why d'you ask?'

'Just curiosity.' She couldn't bring herself to tell Edward about the strange effect the African had on her. She wondered if he had some hypnotic or psychic power. She'd heard of such people, and there must be some cause for the disturbing feeling of being drawn to him. She shook her head, hating to admit that the man had the power to upset her, and tried to push the disquiet to the back of her mind. She would try to avoid further meetings with Kovina.

Sammy seemed ill at ease at breakfast the following morning. He kept looking over his shoulder, his hands were shaking and he dropped things. Watching him, Heather saw the beads of sweat on his forehead and wondered if he had malaria. Finally, when he sent the milk jug flying off the table, she asked him if he was feeling ill. Sammy shook more than ever and rolled his eyes, but he didn't answer her question.

'I think there's something wrong with Sammy,' she remarked to Edward when the boy went back to the kitchen for more milk. 'D'you think he's got malaria?'

'No, there's more to it than that. I'll have a word with him presently.'

After breakfast, Edward followed Sammy into the round mud hut which served as the kitchen. It was built on the far side of the compound and had a thatched roof which caught fire on a fairly regular basis and had to be replaced. The kitchen housed a large iron Dover stove, a wooden table, a rickety chair and a small cupboard used to store sugar and flour. The legs of the cupboard were paddled in old baked bean tins filled with kerosene to prevent ants and cockroaches from trespassing. A pile of logs was stacked to dry out against the wall nearest the stove, and above this, two lop-sided shelves held a collection of battered pots and pans, a large kettle and two heavy flat irons.

Sammy was standing by the table, gripping the edge with both hands. His eyes were closed as he rocked from one foot to the other. Perspiration ran down his face as if he had a high fever. He made a low moaning sound which rose and fell, ending in a whimper. His eyes flew open when Edward addressed him and he jumped as if he'd been stung.

'What's the matter Sammy? Are you sick?'

'No, Massa, I am well.'

'Come on now, tell me what's up.' Edward spoke slowly and quietly. 'Has something happened to frighten you?'

The houseboy didn't reply, but shook his head and pointed to a patch of ground outside the open door of the hut. To the side of the entrance some small lines and circles had been scratched into the red earth and alongside these symbols two pebbles and two large twigs lay in a small indentation scooped out of the powdery soil. Sammy pointed again.

'Komfo make big juju for me, Massa. Him make bad trouble for all people in dis place if Madam use dat magic medicine powdah again,' he said, shaking violently.

'You no fear, Sammy. I go make palaver with the chief. Madam no use powder again. You savvy?' Edward's voice was stern with authority as he tried to calm the terrified servant. He was not sure how Heather would react if he told her about the warning sign left by the witch doctor or one of his cohorts. There was no sense in frightening her, so he simply told her that Sammy had received a message that the witch doctor was displeased because she was treating the villagers and was afraid of what might happen to him and his family if they become implicated.

'But that's plain stupid,' Heather said, hackles rising. 'Why didn't the silly man send a message to me? I'm the one involved.'

'There's no knowing, but I'll have a word with the village chief,' Edward assured her. 'He's the one to sort it out, and I have to see him today anyway, about vaccinating stock owned by some of the farmers. I should be able to raise the subject with him without causing too many ripples.'

'Can I come with you?'

'No. You wouldn't be welcome. It wouldn't be considered proper,' Edward said. Seeing her disappointment, he added: 'It takes quite a time to have a palaver with a chief.'

'Why? What d'you mean?'

'There's a protocol that has to be followed. These meetings can't be rushed,' Edward explained. 'One of my field officers will have to see an elder of the village who will make the purpose of my visit known to the chief. Then, if the chief agrees to see me, there's a further diplomatic procedure to be observed before I can broach the subject I've come to talk about.' Edward packed a sheaf of papers into a folder and tied it with red tape.

'That looks most appropriate,' Heather said, pointing to the tape. Edward ignored the interruption as he continued.

'I have to ask after the chief's health, the health of his wives and children, the state of his crops, the well-being of his stock and whether his maize has been beaten to the ground by that last storm.'

Heather interrupted again. 'What a rigmarole. No wonder your work takes so long!'

Edward laughed and put his arms round her shoulders as they walked out to the car. 'That's not all. The chief then calls one of his wives to bring a bottle of gin. He pours a libation on the ground to ensure the blessing of the gods and his ancestors, and finally we get to drink a little gin before settling down to the purpose of the meeting.' Tenting his fingers, he intoned: 'Here endeth the first lesson in diplomatic approach to palavers with African chiefs, aaaaaamen,' and grinned at Heather. 'You soon get used to it, and although it takes up a lot of time, you often hear words of wisdom and useful bits of gossip which may come in handy, so it's seldom a waste of time.'

'I like the drinking of the gin bit best,' Heather said.

Edward dropped Heather and Sammy off at the Paradise Store and then drove out to the experimental farm where his office was tucked between an animal feed store and a starkly whitewashed room used by the veterinary officer. He would give his headmen their instructions for the day, hear any complaints from the labour force and then go to the village chief.

Paradise Store was on the edge of Tegey village and just within walking distance of their bungalow, provided the day was not too far advanced and the sun not too fierce. It was a long low wooden building with a sagging corrugated iron roof and a covered verandah which ran the length of its ramshackle structure. Bush-lamps, tin kettles, battered straw hats, umbrellas, hoes, machetes and an assortment of other goods, all covered in a thick layer of red dust, hung from hooks screwed into the undulating overhang of the roof. At the bottom of the steps leading up to the verandah, a man sat hunched over a Singer sewing machine, his bare feet flapping up and down as they worked the treadle. The clanking machine cried out for oil, but battled on, shaking the notice board propped against its rusty stand: shirts made in half an hour, it lied. A skinny brown and white dog wobbled on bony haunches, scratching half-heartedly as it shifted the flea population from one part of its anatomy to another and loosening an engorged tick which fell from its torn ear.

Heather and Sammy mounted the uneven steps to the verandah and stood a few seconds as they entered the store to allow their eyes to get accustomed to the dim interior. A cluttered army of dishevelled sacks of flour, rice, sugar and salt were drunkenly stacked against the walls. Tins of kerosene, packets of misshapen melting candles, boxes of hard yellow soap and the ubiquitous tins of red floor polish used in all Government offices and expatriate bungalows stood around in gangs. Bolts of mosquito netting, white shirting and sheeting rubbed shoulders with rolls of garish cotton prints to form a bright pyramid at one end of the scarred wooden counter.

'Good morning, Pius,' Heather greeted the store-keeper who leaned against the counter cleaning his teeth with a chewing stick. It was hard to tell his age; his face was pock-marked and deeply lined and was topped with coarse grey hair which looked as if it had just been permed into thick corkscrew curls. The whites of his eyes were flecked with brown spots and his cheeks bore deep tribal marks. Heather had asked Sammy about these scars worn by so many people.

'Him get him face cut when him piccin. Den dey fill de cuts wid wood-ash from de cookin' fyah. Dat stop dem mending propah,' he informed her.

Pius shifted the chewing stick to the corner of his mouth with his tongue and grinned at Heather. He always seemed pleased to see the white Madam who had moved into the agricultural officer's bungalow a few months ago, and as she gave her order, they chatted amiably in pidgin while Sammy put her purchases into a woven grass basket. When this was finished the storekeeper rummaged in his thatch of coarse hair until he located a pencil stub which he licked before totting up the amount in a grease-stained school exercise book.

Some African customers wandered into the dark little store but as soon as they saw Heather they backed out quickly without a word. She recognised two of them as visitors to her morning clinic and felt surprised and hurt at what appeared to be a deliberate snub. She shrugged off their odd behaviour, but just as she was about to leave, a young girl arrived carrying a baby strapped to her back in a mammy cloth. Heather had spent a long time trying to help Comfort, the young mother who was barely more than a child herself, so when the girl turned on her heel and left as soon as she saw her, Heather called after her, 'Comfort, wait. What's the matter? Why are you running away?' and made to follow, but Pius stood in the entrance, barring her way.

'Best you let her go, Missis. She frightened too much. Komfo tell her she not have palaver with Madam again.'

Shaken and upset by the incident, anger welled inside Heather. She had done her best to befriend the child bride. What could the witch doctor have against her for showing compassion?

Sammy picked up the shopping basket and they left the store without another word, scattering a handful of scrawny chickens clucking and scratching in the dust along their path. The sun was already high as they made their way up the bush road towards the bungalow. Heather flicked at the flies pitching round her eyes, nostrils and lips, seeking every available drop of moisture. A truck rattled past, spraying them with choking clouds of thick laterite dust. The short walk home seemed like a ten-mile trudge.

She sank thankfully into a chair as soon as they reached the bungalow, perspiration running down her face, its salt stinging her eyes as she put up a hand to wipe her forehead. Her cotton dress stuck to her body and she kicked off her sandals, her bare feet making moist footprints on the concrete floor. Suddenly a wave of nausea swept over her and she leaned forward, feeling giddy and light-headed. She held her head in her hands, telling herself it was the shock and hurt of Comfort's rejection that was upsetting her. But in her heart she knew; all the signs were there, these sudden attacks of sickness had occurred for several days now. Closing her eyes, she leaned back against her bright new cushions and waited for the nausea to pass.

CHAPTER 4

Edward put his foot down as soon as the doctor at the Mission Hospital confirmed Heather's pregnancy. There was to be no more treatment given to her African friends, the risk of picking up an infection was too great, he said. Heather guessed he was all too thankful for just such an excuse to put a curb on her activities to avoid the possibility of reprisals from Komfo and his followers.

She was amused by Sammy's obvious delight when Edward told him the news. The houseboy's expressive face showed his pleasure by his broad white grin. His eyes widened and he clapped his hands like an excited child. Edward issued him with some instructions though he harboured little hope that they would be carried out.

'Now that Madam is going to have a piccin, Sammy, you must see that she doesn't carry heavy bags when you go to the market and make sure those pye-dogs of yours don't bark their heads off every afternoon while she's resting. You savvy?'

'Yes, Massa. I tell my missis she must keep dem damn dogs quiet propah. I go beat her plenty if she let dem shout,' Sammy said, happily shifting the responsibility and grinning even wider, for they were all well aware that there was precious little chance of him beating his wife. Milah was a heavily built woman with bulging muscles from years spent hoeing their small plot of land and carrying heavy calabashes of water from the stream. When so inclined, she could floor Sammy with a single well-aimed swipe, as had been demonstrated on more than one occasion when he wove his way unsteadily back to their hut after spending a night with his brothers in one of the bars in Tegey village.

The houseboy's relief was apparent when Heather told him she would no longer be tending people from the village, and that he should tell them to go to the Mission Clinic. He brightened visibly, knowing that he was unlikely to have any more of Komfo's threatening ju-ju tokens left outside his door.

'But if that young girl, Comfort, should come back with her piccin, I want to see her. You understand, Sammy?'

His eyes rolled, and the corners of his mouth drooped in disapproval and dismay. He could see big palaver ahead. Why couldn't Missis savvy the trouble that awaited all of them if she went against the wishes of the witch doctor?

'It's all right, Sammy.' Heather smiled her reassurance. 'I won't give her any medicine. I only want to talk to her. Surely Komfo can find no fault with that.'

But the houseboy shook his head, full of doubt – he knew Komfo and his ways better than Madam.

In an effort to find a new pastime to fill the long lonely days, Heather set about creating a garden in the dusty patch of dried-up earth surrounding the bungalow. She rose early every morning to get tasks finished before the heat and flies made work outside impossible. She soon became absorbed in this new hobby and drew up plans for flower beds and a rockery. Attempts had been made by previous colonial wives to cultivate the barren compound and Heather patterned her imagination with their ghosts, dressing them in long skirts, buttoned boots and the wide-brimmed double-crowned felt terai hats as they supervised their staff.

She laughed as she decided they must have had parasols and fans. Of course they wouldn't soil their hands and would wear long white elbow-length gloves. They would have had garden boys to dig and weed and water, and later on, as her garden grew and flourished, she too would employ a garden boy. Evidence of past endeavours could be seen in the stunted hibiscus, bougainvillaea and franjipani which still struggled for existence in the rock-hard ground. Determined to succeed, she pored over the botanical books she had borrowed from the British Council Library in Sekari.

Edward was pleased that she had found a new interest, but was sceptical and warned her not to be too ambitious.

'You should know by now, love, this is a cruel climate,' he said one late afternoon as they walked arm in arm round the compound. 'The only water we have is rainwater, and that's too precious to use for watering the garden. We can go for months and months without a drop of rain.'

Heather knew that their only water supply came from rain collected from the bungalow roof during the wet season and held in storage tanks, but she frowned at Edward's lack of enthusiasm.

'I've got to have something to do. It's all right for you – you're out at work all day and meeting people, I'm marooned here with nothing to do but read and write letters home. I get bored stiff and I must find other interests. I want to create something, don't you see?'

'Yes, my dear, but I don't want you to expect too much and then be disappointed when half the things you plant just curl up and die because the sun scorches the living daylights out of them.'

'Don't be so pessimistic, Edward. I'll put a mulch round everything so that it doesn't dry out,' Heather retorted, vaguely remembering how her mother used to put grass cuttings round tender young plants during warm summer droughts at home in her Somerset garden.

Sammy was sweeping the verandah when he heard of Madam's crazy idea. He leaned on the yard-broom and offered half-hearted encouragement.

'Plenty bugs, plenty big bugs will come and eat Madam's t'ings,' he predicted, shaking his head at the stupidity of this new venture. To Sammy, spiders, mosquitoes, cockroaches, termites and indeed any creeping, crawling or flying insect came under the one heading: they were all bugs, and Sammy hated bugs, unless they happened to be edible.

He unbent sufficiently to assist in plans for the task of saving water for Heather's embryo garden. Every drop of washing-up water from the kitchen, the suds from the bath when he had laundered the clothes, the bath water at night, were all to be saved and poured into a large oil drum Edward had discovered lying in a clump of tall grass at the edge of the compound. This soon rendered homeless a large assortment of bugs who had made their homes inside it, including an indignant scorpion which vented its annoyance at being disturbed by stinging the hapless houseboy on his foot and sending him hopping round cursing and hollering. The episode only served to convince him still further of the foolhardiness of starting a garden.

'For goodness' sake, get a move on,' Heather urged her plants, 'and don't expect any more water today, you've had your ration.' She was kneeling on an old blanket, forking round the base of the stems, willing them to do as they were told. As she worked, a shadow fell across the ground, startling her into rocking back on her heels. She looked up to see Kovina's smiling face above her, his eyes mocking as once again she felt their curious hypnotic power.

'I heard that you've become a gardener,' he laughed, 'but no one told me you hold conversations with your plants.' His eyes strayed to her long shapely legs beneath her blue cotton shorts.

'Hardly a conversation,' she replied shortly, put out by his mirth. 'They don't answer back, you know, but I can assure you all the best people do it. It is a recognised fact that plants thrive on verbal encouragement.'

'The way you were ordering them about, I'm surprised they didn't have something to say for themselves,' he said, trying to keep a straight face.

Heather pushed back her wide-brimmed straw hat and wiped the sweat from her forehead with the back of her hand, leaving it streaked with gritty soil. Kovina put out a hand to help her up. He held on to her arm rather longer than necessary and although the hesitation was not lost on Heather, it made her vaguely uneasy.

'I suppose the bush telegraph informed you of my horticultural activities?' she asked, the question bordering on sarcasm. She bent to retrieve her watering can and relented. 'Come on in, it's about time I stopped for the day.'

They sat on bamboo basket chairs on the verandah while Sammy brought them cold drinks on a brightly coloured tin tray advertising the local beer made at Sekari Brewery.

'I brought you these,' Kovina said, delving in the breast pocket of his khaki bush shirt and handing her a fistful of old envelopes. 'I asked the garden boy up at the Mission to save you some seeds from the school gardens.'

'That's very kind of you,' Heather responded, surprised at his thoughtfulness and feeling guilty at the sharpness of her tongue. She shook some of the seeds on to the palm of her hand and examined them. 'I don't recognise some of them, you'll have to tell me what they are.'

'I can only help with a few of them. You must persuade Edward to take you up to the Mission to have a chat with Musah, the garden boy. He loves his plants and I'm sure he'd welcome the chance to show it off to you. He knows what all the seeds are, and I know you will like him.'

'Do you have a garden?' Heather asked.

'Hardly what you'd call a garden. My wife grows a few vegetables and of course we have a few paw-paw trees, bananas and a lime tree. Grace is a very practical person, she's not interested in flowers – you can't eat them! She was a nurse at the Mission Clinic before we married, but now the children keep her busy.'

'Children? How many?'

'Three. Two girls and a boy. My son is the eldest.'

Heather took a while to digest this information; she hadn't pictured him as a family man. Kovina was looking at her expectantly, and she said the first thing that came into her head, thinking it best to keep off his personal affairs.

'Oh, by the way, Edward has asked me not to treat any more of my sick visitors.'

Kovina raised a quizzical eyebrow, puzzled by the sudden change of subject.

'I think that's very wise,' was his only comment. Nonetheless, he was surprised; he hadn't expected her to be so easily intimidated by Komfo's hostility, and was thoughtful later as he left the bungalow.

Comfort was waiting for Heather when she went into the garden early the next morning. Her baby was asleep, strapped to its mother's back with a mammy cloth. Heather retraced her steps, inviting the girl to follow. The girl looked doubtful, wary. Taking a quick look around to assure herself she wasn't being watched, she quickly scuttled up the steps like a frightened animal and went inside the bungalow.

Although neither of them mentioned the witch doctor, it seemed to Heather that Comfort was trying to make amends for her hasty departure from the Paradise Store a short while ago. Heather was pleased to see the baby was making good progress and held the tiny infant in her arms while she advised the young African girl about the need to boil the water she gave to the baby.

'The water you bring from the stream is not clean and it could make the piccin sick,' she explained. Comfort nodded her understanding but tried to explain her dilemma.

'The mother of my husban', she be old woman. She very wise old woman. She tell me not to boil de water. She say she never make de water hot for her piccins. She say it bad ting to boil de water. My husban' go beat me if I no do what his mother tell me.'

'But you see, Comfort, I expect she was able to breast feed her piccins. You can't do that so you have to use powdered milk and the water you use to mix it must be boiled. You savvy? If you don't believe me, ask the nurse at the Mission clinic.'

The girl nodded miserably and Heather guessed there was scant chance of the girl going against her husband's wishes. She would certainly receive a beating for such disobedience. Heather wished she could persuade Comfort's partner to come and see her, but that wouldn't work because he would lose face with the other men of his tribe if he were seen visiting the house of the white woman who was already in Komfo's bad books.

Within three weeks, Sammy brought Heather the news that Comfort's baby was dead. Edward would not hear of her going to see the girl.

'We have no idea what caused the baby's death. If you contracted dysentery or some other illness through visiting her, you could have a miscarriage and lose our baby.'

Heather had to admit the sense of this and asked Sammy to try to find out more about how the baby died. He reported back after a few days.

'De piccin get plenty pain for him belly,' he said, 'den he be sick and him shit too much. Den him dun go die.' He stated all this matter-of-factly, all too accustomed to the high death rate among infants.

It may have been dysentery, and it may have been caused by contaminated water, and if so, it could have been prevented – Heather would never know, but her distress was made greater when she discovered that the blame was laid firmly at her door. Komfo had wasted no time spreading the story round the villages that the white woman possessed evil powers and she had used them to bring about the death of Comfort's baby.

Heather knew that Comfort had already lost one baby soon after birth and grieved quietly, disheartened by the knowledge that she had been unable to prevent the death of this second child. She fumed at her inability to help the girl, knowing only too well that Comfort would soon be pregnant again. No doubt her husband would buy another wife before long. one who was able to breast feed her babies, and Comfort would just become the family drudge, fit only to do menial tasks. The futility of it all made her want to shout for all the world to hear, but she could only remain silent.

As her own baby grew, Heather found it increasingly difficult to work in her garden and so Edward dropped her off at the Mission School one morning to meet Musah, the garden boy Kovina had told her about and who had sent her the envelopes of flower seeds. She was hoping that he would be able to tell her if one of the students at the Mission would be willing to come and help in her garden to earn some pocket money.

Musah lived in a large round mud hut with a thatched roof tucked away in a corner of the Mission compound. Heather walked down the laterite path and peered into a roughly built lean-to tacked on to the hut. It was home to a few primitive tools, a collection of old cigarette tins and jam jars containing seeds, home-made watering cans made from kerosene tins with wooden handles nailed across the top, and several pieces of matting made from woven palm fronds. The latter, she noted later as she walked round the plant nursery, were used as shade mats to protect young seedlings from being scorched by the blazing sun.

Musah turned out to be anything but a boy, and in his long earth-brown robe, he looked as if he had walked straight from the pages of an illustrated bible. It was difficult to tell his age; it seemed to Heather that Africans showed their years far sooner than white people and this she put down to the sweltering climate and the harsh life they had to endure. She looked at Musah's short stubbly hair and dry parchment-like skin drawn tightly over high cheekbones and guessed him to be a few years older than herself. This is some 'boy', she thought as she introduced herself to the tall slim man. His skin was lighter than most of the Africans in the area and his nose not as flat or his lips so full, and she was fascinated by his clear bright expressive eyes.

After a tour of the extensive Mission gardens, the unlikely pair sat side by side on a couple of upturned beer-bottle crates beneath the shade of a large poinciana tree. Heather looked around her at the shrubs and trees surrounding the tidy compound, the well-kept flowerbeds with their borders ruler-straight and edged with white painted stones, and congratulated Musah on the variety of the plants and the neatness of the gardens.

Soberly, he nodded his thanks and chuckled as he explained: 'When the children have been up to mischief in school they are given the task of painting the border stones and keeping them as straight as the path of an arrow.'

Heather had been feeling low when she arrived, but this man's impish sense of humour lifted her spirits. His air of fun was infectious and despite herself, she was soon laughing with him. She asked him where he had learned to speak English so fluently, and when he saw that she was genuinely interested and not asking out of politeness, Musah told her his story.

'I do not know the year of my birth, I can only guess,' he said. 'I was born in Northern Nigeria and my mother already had too many mouths to feed, so she sold me when I was still very young, to an Arab trader who travelled the coast of West Africa selling ivory, ebony carvings and crocodile and python skins. He brought me here to Facriwa. I was his slave and he beat me and had me castrated,' he said, with little sign of bitterness or rancour. 'He watched me like a hawk watches its prey and at night my hands and feet were tied with rope. I was obedient and worked hard until he finally relaxed his guard and then I planned my escape.' Musah reached into the pocket of his long brown robe and brought out a primitive leather pouch, from which he drew a short slim blade. 'It took me many weeks to make this. I had to work on it in secret and hone it in such a way that the cutting edge was limited so that when I held it between my teeth to cut through the thongs which bound me during the hours of darkness, I would not cut my mouth. I made my escape at night, and ran as fast as I could to put many miles between me and my master. During the day I slept under bushes or in caves and I ran as far and as fast as I could every night until the food I had brought with me had all gone. I thought I would beg a lift in one of the passing mammy lorries once I left the bush and reached a wide main road, but I was exhausted and fell into a culvert at the side of the road. I was discovered there by a white missionary and his wife and they brought me here to the Mission. They gave me food and shelter and when I was strong again I worked in their house to pay for their kindness. They let me stay and gave me decent clothing and encouraged me to attend the classes at the Mission School. They had no children of their own and treated me like a son. When they were recalled to England they arranged for me to stay with the family who came to replace them. I was saddened by the loss of the only people who had ever shown me true kindness. I became restless and wanted to explore, to find out if I could fend for myself.' Musah stopped and looked inquiringly at Heather.

'Please don't stop, Musah,' she responded, 'your story is fascinating, almost unbelievable.'

'There is not a great deal more to tell,' he replied. He cleared his throat and continued. 'I travelled all round the country finding work wherever I could, never stopping long in one place. I worked as a clerk in a bush clinic, as a caretaker in a government rest house, as a laboratory assistant at a botanic research institute,' he grinned, 'and also as a prison warder. I met many people and learned many things, but I always came back here for a few weeks every year. You see, I think of this as my home. The Mission was extended a few years ago and I was offered the job of head gardener. It suits me well and gives me plenty of time to think and read.' He let his hands rest quietly in his lap as he finished.

Although the hardships of his early life showed in Musah's face, Heather marvelled that he still retained an enviable optimism. They talked of many things, and the identification of the seeds was overtaken by numerous other interesting topics. Not only had Heather found a good storyteller in this gentle, quietly spoken man, he was also a patient listener, quick to attune to the mood of anyone sharing his company.

Reluctantly, she rose from the hard beer crate and shook the folds of her cotton dress free from her sweat-dampened legs, thanking him for turning the pages of his life for her and for showing her a new facet of Facriwa and its people. As she was about to leave, Musah asked, 'What troubles you?'

The question took her by surprise and she was tempted to brush it aside, but his look of concern coaxed her to reply truthfully, albeit hesitantly.

'Nothing. Nothing really. Well, it's…it's just that one of the village girls has lost her baby and I am being blamed for its death.'

'And who is blaming you?' Musah asked sharply, though he seemed to anticipate her answer, and nodded thoughtfully when she replied.

'Komfo, the witch doctor.'

'That man is evil. He and his juju have a great deal to answer for. I have known several witch doctors from several tribes, each with different customs and beliefs. They have mostly been good men with special wisdom and often have awesome powers that others cannot understand,' he said. Scratching deep marks in the powdery red earth at his feet with a bamboo cane, he continued: 'Witch doctors have much knowledge passed down from their ancestors. They know which leaves and roots can heal, bring relief from pain, or cause you to sleep so deeply that you appear to be dead.' He pointed toward Tegey village with his stick, 'But that one is a sham, a fake. He will try to prey on your mind. Do not let him. Shut the door on your thoughts of him. It is important that you do not let him possess your mind.' With that, Musah sat down heavily on the beer crate and rested his chin on his hands, still clasping the bamboo cane. He closed his eyes. Their meeting was at an end, but as Heather was about to turn away, his eyes opened and he smiled, then slowly, he winked.

CHAPTER 5

The man lay on the floor in a pool of blood; Kathy stared down at the body in horror.

Kneeling beside him, she touched his hand. It was cold. She fell across his body as a fusillade of bullets ricocheted on the wall above her head.

Heather closed the book with a snap and put it on the bedside table.

'That's enough of that – if I read any more I'll have nightmares,' she said, yawning widely. She leaned across Edward and kissed him lightly on his forehead. 'Goodnight, love.' The words had barely left her mouth when a crash came from outside, quickly followed by the sound of breaking glass.

'What the heck was that?' Edward shouted. He pushed the mosquito net aside and leapt out of bed. As he ran to the door, he called back to Heather: 'Stay there, love. Don't come out until I've found out what's going on.'

Across the road, opposite the drive leading up to the bungalow, a car was lying on its side in a shallow storm-drain. The headlights were still on and steam hissed from the smashed radiator. It appeared to have been driven off the road, crashing into a tree on the far bank. Edward peered inside the wrecked vehicle; the driver seemed to be the only occupant. He wrenched open the passenger door and climbed in beside the man, who showed no obvious signs of injury. His head lay back against the seat, his eyes closed as if he slept. Must have had a heart attack or fallen asleep at the wheel, Edward thought. He slid his hand under the driver's legs and put an arm round his shoulders, edging him gently across the seat. As Edward carried the man to the side of the road Sammy shuffled up and stood watching, rubbing sleep from his eyes.

'What happen, Massa. Who dat man?'

'I don't know, Sammy. Give me a hand with him.'

As they lay the man on the coarse stubble of dusty grass at the verge of the track, his head rolled towards them and they caught sight of the hole in his forehead. And when Edward drew his arm away, he felt warm blood smear his wrist.

'Oh my God! He's been shot!' Edward said, his voice low. 'He didn't just crash the car. The poor devil's been shot!' He looked towards the trees shadowing the far side of the road, the obvious direction from which a gun would have been fired. The dead African was smartly dressed in a suit, white shirt and tie. Standing beside the body, Sammy stood with a tattered strip of coloured cloth around his loins, while Edward wore white underpants and a pair of flip-flops. Set in the moonlight like a black and white photograph, the motionless characters made an odd tableau. Edward was the first to move. 'You stay here with him, Sammy. I'll get dressed then I'll drive him to Sekari Hospital. Not that it'll do him any good, the poor chap's beyond help.'

His head shaking, Sammy rolled his eyes and backed away from the corpse.

'Yes, Massa,' he said, visibly unhappy at the prospect of being left alone with the body. He rocked from one foot to the other and as Edward moved away he called after him, 'Massa, you no be gone for long time, huh? Massa be plenty quick, huh?'

Edward dressed hurriedly as he told Heather that a car had hit a tree and that the driver was a bit dazed.

'I'll drive him to the hospital, I won't be long. You get off to sleep. I'll be back as soon as I can.' He saw no point in scaring her with the true details at this time of night, but before he could stop her, Heather had grabbed her dressing gown and run out on to the road as quickly as her ungainly pregnant body would allow. She knelt beside the still figure and an image of what she had just been reading in her book flashed into her mind. She put her hand to the man's forehead to comfort him, then caught her breath and screamed.

'Edward! Edward, why didn't you tell me it was Sammy?' she shouted. Edward reached her side in seconds, and stared down at the body, nonplussed.

He looked up and down the road, trying to penetrate the shadows thrown by tall trees bordering the track. He tried to shake off the feeling that this must be some crazy dream, he must be in the middle of a stage farce; this sort of thing just didn't happen in real life. Sammy moaned and turned his head slowly from side to side. His eyes flicked open and shut, then opened again quickly as if to make sure he was still alive.

'What happened, Sammy?'

A swelling was rapidly appearing on the houseboy's head. The bump reached from his cheekbone up into the tightly curled black hair growing low on his temple. He grimaced and propped himself up on his elbow, trying to bring his eyes into focus, wincing as he raised a hand to his throbbing head.

'I don't know, Massa. I jus' sit by dat man like you say.' He turned and pointed to where the body had been, but now there was nothing to be seen except an indentation in the grass. 'Eek! Where him done go?' His voice squeaked the question as his eyes mirrored his terror, and his jaw dropped as if worked by a puppet string. No answer came to his question and he gulped, trying to collect his wits and contain his fear as he continued: 'Somet'ing done hit my head. It done hit my head propah, Massa.' He raised his hand to demonstrate the blow, flinched, thought better of it and leaned back on his elbow once more.

Heather pulled her thin dressing gown more closely round her heavy body. The night was warm and humid but she shivered and her teeth chattered as she looked from Sammy to Edward.

'D'you mean to tell me there was another body here?'

'I'm afraid so, love.' Edward's voice was sheepishly apologetic.

'But that's ridiculous. Where's it gone? Bodies don't just disappear into thin air!'

'This one appears to have done so,' Edward said, helping Sammy to his feet, where the boy stood swaying a little.

Heather folded her arms to stop them shaking.

'I simply don't understand what's going on,' she said. Edward put his arm round her shoulders and started to lead her back to the bungalow, but before they had gone more than a few steps, a dark figure parted from the shadow of the trees at the side of the bush road and came towards them.

They didn't recognise Kovina straight away. A dark brown and fawn coloured cloth was wrapped round his body and thrown over his shoulder in the manner of the village elders. He appeared to glide towards the trio, his sandaled feet making no sound on the dusty road. He signalled briefly to Sammy, saying a few words in the local dialect. The boy was still gingerly dabbing at the swelling on his head, but he nodded and padded off unsteadily in the direction of his own quarters. Kovina's presence and the few words he had spoken seemed to have reassured him.

When Sammy was well out of earshot, Kovina spoke.

'It is best that you forget what you have seen here tonight. It is a political matter and has nothing to do with you. You would be wise to blot it from your mind. It will be taken care of by those concerned.' His words were delivered with an air of authority.

Taken aback, Edward could barely contain his surprise at what almost amounted to an order.

'Good grief, man! The driver of that car had been shot. I saw the bullet hole in his head. I didn't dream it. Surely you don't expect me to forget what I saw?'

Heather's sharp intake of breath at this exchange was audible, but Kovina continued.

'You may find it difficult to forget, but you mustn't get involved. Believe me, I'm not trying to be melodramatic, your lives could be in danger.'

Kovina had been speaking quietly, but now he lowered his voice still further and took a step closer to them. 'You must be aware of what is going on here in Facriwa. Some factions are demanding self-government now, they are not prepared to wait for decisions to be made by your bowler-hatted men in Whitehall who know little about our country. They are hungry for power and won't hesitate to kill anyone who stands in their way.'

Edward shook his head.

'Be that as it may, Kovina, I would be neglecting my duty if I failed to report tonight's events to the District Commissioner. I'm sorry, but I can't ignore what I've just seen.'

'You need have no worries on that score. I can assure you, the DC will know what has happened before sunrise. I beg you, Edward, let the matter rest for your own safety. It will be dealt with by those concerned.'

'Tell me who he was – the man who was shot. Who removed his body, and where has it been taken?'

'You ask too many questions, my friend. I can't disclose the dead man's name, and you'd be none the wiser if I did. Suffice to say that he was one of Komfo's men, making it all the more important that you deny all knowledge of what happened here tonight.' Kovina looked directly at Heather, his face stern. 'You must understand that it would be unwise for either of you to become implicated.'

'Are you telling me that Komfo is involved with politics?'

'I have already said enough, and—' Before he could finish the sentence, the sound of a car starting up beyond the trees reached them. Kovina raised his hand in salute, turned on his heel and walked away towards the bend in the road.

As soon as he was out of sight, Heather gripped Edward's arm.

'What the heck's going on? Tell me, Edward. What was that all about? You lied to me, you told me a man had been hurt in an accident, you said nothing about anyone being shot. How did Sammy get mixed up in it?' Her voice was sharp and her eyes warned Edward that she would not be put off by more lies.

'I didn't want to worry you. I knew you'd be upset, and there was no point in worrying you unnecessarily. Can't you see – we can do nothing about it. Kovina is right, and I didn't want to take any risks.'

'It upsets me far more to know that you lied to me. I'm not a child.' Her voice rose in exasperation. 'For goodness' sake stop treating me like a schoolgirl. You must have some idea what's going on, so why won't you tell me?'

Edward sighed and steered her towards the bungalow.

'Let's go in and I'll tell you what little I know, but really Kovina hinted at it all just now.' Once inside, he put a match to the Tilley lamp and poured a couple of stiff drinks. 'As far as I can gather,' he said, passing her a glass, 'it's all wrapped up with this mad rush for independence. It's not our problem and there's nothing we can do about it. We should heed Kovina's warning and not get involved.' He sipped his whisky and continued: 'A few hotheads have formed themselves into small political groups and are stirring up trouble, and they're best left for the police to deal with.'

'What sort of trouble?'

'According to one of my headmen, they're going from village to village up and down the country trying to drum up support and threatening anyone who opposes them. Apparently there have been riots in some of the bigger towns.'

As Edward talked, his mind raced ahead trying to gloss over the worst of the incidents related to him. He excused this ploy by telling himself that half the stories were probably exaggerated or rumours spread to create further unrest. His strained face didn't go unnoticed by Heather, but she was determined to find out what was going on and did nothing to make his task easier. She waited for him to continue, convinced that the truth was being kept from her.

'I'm sorry, love, he said, 'but that was another reason why I didn't want you to go on treating people from the village. From what I hear, our witch doctor friend is involved in politics in a big way.' He patted her hand as if placating an upset child. She shook his hand away.

'Don't do that, Edward. I don't want to be mollycoddled. It's not fair,' she said sharply, ignoring his look of concern at the outburst. 'Why didn't you tell me this before? Haven't I the right to know?'

'Why? What can it do but worry you? Can't you see I was trying to protect you?' Edward retorted. Heather finished her drink and stood up to face him, hands clenched.

'If you ever lie to me again, I'll leave you.'

They lay in their beds for the rest of the night with an uneasy silence like a shutter between them; neither able to sleep and neither able to find the right words to repair the damage.

Heather knew she had to accept the fact that Edward was the sort of man who would skirt around trouble; he wouldn't court disaster and would avoid confrontation whenever possible. He would go out of his way to shield her from the harsh reality of what was going on in this country, where men felt the need to take the reins and steer its destiny. She should be thankful for his concern and protection, but she resented being overprotected. Until her marriage she had lived the sort of rough and tumble life usual in a large family, and often felt nostalgic for the good-natured bullying and teasing she had suffered from her elder brothers. They had taught her to stick up for herself and to fight her own battles and as a child she had always been happier playing cowboys and Indians and climbing trees with the boys than playing with her dolls. She was unlikely to change now and was not afraid to accept a challenge. Edward would have to accept that she was no shy timorous woman who needed to be guarded from the knocks of the world.

Edward was perplexed by Heather's attitude. An only child, born to elderly parents who doted on him, he followed his father's pattern of kindly, gracious behaviour towards his mother; this was not so much a deference as a deep love. It came naturally to him to safeguard Heather and to treat her as something precious. He felt she should be cherished, and warding off any possible danger or risk to her would inevitably remain a priority. Physical violence had always been abhorrent to him, though he was by no means cowardly. Many times had his nose been bloodied at school for sticking up for younger, weaker boys when they were bullied, though he would prefer the diplomatic approach rather than resorting to the bull-at-a-gate method.

Tentatively, he reached his hand across to touch Heather, and felt a surge of love as she grasped it and held it to her lips.

By morning, all signs of the night's activities had vanished. The wrecked car was no longer lying against the tree, there was no evidence of the shattered glass from the windscreen and the bloodstains had dried, blending in with the red dust of the road.

Sammy had also disappeared. When he failed to arrive at breakfast, Heather went to his quarters at the far end of the compound to investigate, fearing the blow to his head had affected him more seriously than they had thought. His wife, Milah, shiny faced and ample, came to the door of the hut, a baby suspended in a mammy cloth on her back and an older infant balanced comfortably astride her hip.

'Him done go, Missis,' she said in reply to Heather's question.

'Where him done go, and when him done come back?' she asked.

'I no savvy where him done go an' I no savvy when him come back,' Mila replied. She swung the child from her hip down to the ground where it flopped over into the dust, then she folded her stevedore arms across her pendulous bare breasts, making it all too clear that this was all she had to say about her missing spouse.

Heather returned to the kitchen and eyed the big iron stove. She got the impression that it challenged her with gleeful malevolence. Ever since her first encounter with the monster when she had tried to bake a cake, she knew it held a grudge against her.

Hands on hips, she addressed it:

'Let's get this straight – I'm not standing any nonsense from you,' and taking up the long heavy iron poker, she thrust it between the bars and waggled it amongst the ashes, still warm from heating last night's bath water and cooking the dinner. 'So don't imagine you'll be allowed to play me up again.' The dying embers should soon be coaxed back into life, but Sammy hadn't stacked logs by the stove to dry out ready to feed the brute.

'Drat that boy,' she fumed, and committed the cardinal sin frowned upon by all white madams when it was practised by their cooks. She put a generous dollop of wax floor polish on to one of the logs, heaved up the front grating of the oven and threw the log inside. She stepped back as the fire roared into life, belching out thick pungent smoke as the heat hit the wax. Coughing and choking, she started stacking logs beside the stove to dry out. If Sammy took his time about returning, she had to be prepared with more fuel to cook the rest of the day's meals, boil the drinking water and heat the kerosene tins full of bath water.

A sudden sharp pain shot through her; she drew in her breath and leaned back against the wall, holding her swollen belly in both hands. She closed her eyes as the perspiration ran down her face, and waited for the spasm to pass. After a minute or two she continued preparing breakfast, thankful that Edward hadn't witnessed her in mid-twinge and praying that it wouldn't return.

She put fat into the heavy frying pan, and suddenly an overwhelming homesickness for her mother's spotless kitchen in England overtook her. There, every gadget behaved itself impeccably at the flick of a switch. She pushed a wayward lock of hair from her damp forehead with the back of her hand and continued to prepare breakfast.

The baby was not due for another two weeks and the pain, although it didn't alarm her, made her uneasy. She dare not mention it to Edward – he would immediately fuss around her like a mother hen and would be too worried to leave her to go to work. She laughed; they were alike, she and Edward, each trying in their own way to shield the other from worry and stress.

Breakfast over, Edward held her close to him, told her to leave all the work and household chores until Sammy came back, and made her promise to get a rest in the afternoon, then he left for work and Heather returned to the kitchen. She had used the last of the bread to make their breakfast toast and would have to make dough now and leave it to rise in the warm room. She sieved the flour, picking out the weevils, grubs and other livestock, remembering that when she first arrived in Facriwa this necessity had filled her with disgust, but now it was just another routine which was carried out automatically. She had accepted that the large bags of flour from the Paradise Store housed many active tenants.

Heather kneaded the dough in the hot-house atmosphere of the stuffy little kitchen while the beads of sweat that gathered on her forehead trickled down to form dewdrops at the end of her nose and chin. She wiped them away with floury knuckles, stopping her exertions to lean against the wooden table to remember her childhood, when the baker's boy arrived at the back door of her parents' house. His squeaky old bicycle had a large wicker basket full of crusty loaves, still warm from the ovens at the back of the High Street bakery. She recalled her mother's smile at the small teeth marks in the crust where she and her brother had nibbled the loaves before putting them on the scrubbed table in the stone-flagged kitchen. She longed to sink her teeth into a thick slice of that bread right now, spread thickly with farmhouse butter and home-made raspberry jam. So many mouth-watering memories of such simple fare. No butter here, and the oily melted margarine in tins from Paradise Store just couldn't match up.

The sharp pain returned without warning and she hooked the wooden chair forward with her foot and sat on the hard seat. Leaning her head back, she rested her shoulders against the whitewashed wall and stared up at the smoke-grimed ceiling where hornets were coming and going with their catch of paralysed live insects, storing them in their nests in the corner to feed their larval offspring. When the pain had passed she covered the dough-filled tins with a cloth to keep the flies off and left the bread to rise. She riddled the hot grey ash from the stove and fed it with two more logs before returning to the bungalow to splash her face with water. She lay on her bed and slept fitfully for a couple of hours until another searing pain held her in its grip. She rubbed her swollen belly with the palms of her hands. 'What's the rush?' she asked her baby. 'I'm not ready for you yet.'

But the unborn infant had other ideas.

CHAPTER 6

Heather had no idea when Sammy would return; the bungalow had no such luxury as a telephone and there were no neighbours near enough to call for help. She walked out to the kitchen, rubbed a mixture of egg and milk on the top of the well-risen dough and put the baking tins into the oven. She stood in the doorway looking across the compound towards Sammy's quarters. If the worst came to the worst she would have to call on Sammy's wife to act as midwife, a thought which filled her with apprehension. No sound came from their hut and the place looked deserted, and then she remembered: it was market day, so they would be away in Tegey village until nightfall.

It would be too much of a risk to walk that far in the heat of the day when the sun was at its most merciless, she could pass out on the side of the road. She would just have to sweat it out as best she could. Edward seldom managed to get home at lunchtime – if only he would come home today when she needed him most. If only he would come home, if only Sammy hadn't disappeared, if only she were back in civilisation with her mother close by, if only…if only…

She talked to herself; the sound of her voice was oddly comforting. She didn't feel quite so alone. 'Best to keep going until teatime. Must keep myself occupied, time will pass quicker that way.' She unlocked the door to the storeroom where the packing cases, tin trunks and travelling cases were kept. One wall was lined with shelves stacked with tins of kerosene for the Tilley lamps, candles, matches, insecticides, mosquito sprays and floor polish. There were enough tins of food to last until the next shopping trip into Sekari to replenish their stocks. They did a shopping trip every five or six weeks, driving through a dust bowl during the long dry season and through a sea of thick cloying mud during the rains. They always bought extra supplies during the rainy season in case the roads became flooded or a bridge should be washed away. Shortages could sometimes be made up from Paradise Store, but at double the price and the goods were often old or damaged.

Heather pulled a small suitcase from the pile stacked against the wall and took it back to the bedroom where she packed it with the things she would need for herself and the baby. She fingered the tiny baby garments and held them to her cheek, enjoying their softness. A surge of emotion swept through her. Tears welled and spilled over as her body shook with a mixture of pent-up sobs and another searing pain. She felt no strong maternal instinct and took it for granted that it was something that arrived with the baby, a pre-ordained emotion that came as part of the deal. Now she just felt tired, frightened and completely at odds with this unkind thing inside her. She lay on the bed and clamped her teeth round the corner of a pillow as pain took over once more. When the contraction had passed, she sat up on the edge of the bed and tried to remember what she had intended to do that day; she must do something to steer her mind away from the inner attack being made by her impatient offspring. The mosquito screens at the windows – that was it, she was going to clean them, but would she manage to wield the heavy brush? It was really Sammy's job but he always missed the corners where most of the cobwebs and dust collected with an assortment of crisp flies. She had remonstrated with him on several occasions, always with the same result; he grinned broadly and waved a dismissive hand.

'Yes, Missis. I clean 'em propah nex' time.' But he never did. Dust-laden corners with dead tenants didn't exist for Sammy, and although Heather knew she should stand over him and make sure he did the job properly, it was quicker and less aggravating for them both if she did the job herself. Sammy was cheerful and willing and she hadn't the heart to scold him for skirting tasks which he considered to be a waste of time. The day she had found him cleaning one of her wedding presents, an antique silver candelabra, with an abrasive metal saucepan scraper, was a different matter, she had flown into a temper and shouted at the houseboy.

'What on earth d'you think you're doing with that, you stupid boy?' Her voice, spiky with anger, had frightened Sammy and in his agitation he had dropped the candelabra on to the concrete floor.

'I done clean 'em propah, Missis,' he defended.

'That's not cleaning it, it's ruining it,' she barked at him. 'This belonged to my great grandmother!' She picked it up from the floor, now dented as well as scratched and unpolished. It was a sorry object. 'Look, can't you see these scratch marks?' she held it out to him but he stepped back, hung his head and looked down at his feet, the picture of contrite misery.

'Sorry, Missis,' he mumbled. She dismissed him to the kitchen and minutes later heard him singing happily to himself, the incident already forgotten and forgiven as far as he was concerned. On reflection, Heather had been sorry she had lost her temper. It was not Sammy's fault. No one had ever shown him how to clean silver, he had no idea of its value and was simply doing his best. She was the one at fault, she should have had the common sense to teach him before the damage was done. It was just another lesson she had learned the hard way – never assume Sammy knew or understood anything. By the time she had discovered him rubbing her brown suede mosquito boots with Brasso, she had become immune and had learned to curse inwardly and accept his transgressions. The result was always the same if she scolded him. Sammy would not look her in the eye, but would stare down at the ground, shuffling his feet like a naughty child caught in some misdemeanour, then he would look up at her wide-eyed and smiling, sure in the knowledge of dispensation.

'I no do dat bad t'ing again, Missis. No. I shuah no do dat bad t'ing again.'

Until the next time.

Heather stood behind one of the high-backed bedroom chairs, holding the wood in a grip that whitened her knuckles as each wave of pain engulfed her. She looked at her watch once again; no, surely that couldn't be right. It must be more than eight hours since she had felt the first warning twinge in the kitchen that morning. It had gone on forever. Her watch must have stopped. She held it to her ear. Relentlessly it ticked away the seconds. It was impossible to relax for long between each onslaught. Her body had been taken over by this agony which twisted, wrenched and stretched her body beyond endurance.

'Oh, Mum! Edward…someone…anyone! For Christ's sake, somebody come and help me,' she screamed at the empty room.

Finally, Edward's car drove up the gravelled drive. Heather was barely aware of his arrival. He stood in the bedroom doorway for a second, stricken by the sight of her gripping the chair with both hands, her teeth drawing blood as they bit her lower lip, her hair wet and dishevelled. He rushed forward as her knees buckled and she sank slowly to the floor.

David was born in the early hours of the morning at Sekari Hospital. Sister Maureen Kelly, the Irish midwife, bullied Edward into leaving her and her patient to get on with it, being firmly of the opinion that husbands were superfluous and more trouble than they were worth at such times. 'You'll just get in the way,' she said, bundling him from the room. She was a breezy buxom spinster, due for retirement, but the thought of spending several lonely years at the vagaries of the Irish climate and divorced from the social life afforded her in Facriwa did not appeal to her. She intended hanging on to her job here in the colony until they saw fit to throw her out, and when that day finally came, she would be sadly missed; not only was she a first class midwife, she also had an advanced sense of humour and was always top of the guest list for all the colonial wives' dinner parties.

She swore encouragement at Heather through the last stages of her labour with all the finesse of a navvy.

'Come on then, girl. Get a move on. Let's get the little bugger out!'

Heather gritted her teeth and grunted back at her. 'I'm doing my best, but it hurts.'

'Of course it hurts. This isn't a picnic. For goodness' sake push. Not like that. For heaven's sake, girl, push as if you mean it,' Maureen urged.

Heather pushed and yelled. 'It's all very well for you – you're not doing the pushing.'

'Stop being half hearted about it. Get your back into it or we'll be stuck here all night.'

'How many babies have you had?' Heather gasped, heaving on the piece of cotton sheeting the midwife had tied to the bedrail for her when she first arrived.

'What's that for?' she'd asked, 'mopping up the sweat?'

'It'll help you to have something to grip when you feel your body's being torn apart. I can't have you tearing up the hospital sheets, we're short enough as 'tis with the laundry boiler broken down again.'

'I've done the tearing apart bit,' Heather wailed, 'now all I want is my baby.'

Sekari Hospital was in the process of having a new maternity wing built, and by some error in planning, the old maternity block had been demolished before the new one was complete. As a temporary measure, a long shed with a corrugated iron roof and an earth floor had been brought into service. The electricity supply was fed into the shack-like construction from a generator by means of a crude arrangement of cables and wires pegged at intervals to the walls and ceiling. A single bare bulb above Heather's bed provided a sickly light until the generator gave up the ghost and breathed its last, plunging the room into darkness a few minutes before Heather's baby made his debut.

The doctor arrived in a mood less than joyful at the birth of a new life, having been called out in the middle of the St Andrew's Night Ball at Sekari Club. Heather was jostled out of a weary stupor and giggled inwardly at the sight of his hairy legs and tartan kilt beneath his white hospital coat.

'I can't see a bloody thing,' he complained, peering through the flickering light of a couple of candles the midwife had placed on the bedside locker. A diminutive African nurse appeared out of the gloom with a small bush lamp, her shadow dancing along beside her on the whitewashed wall.

'De generator be buggered up again,' she informed him. No one answered. This was Facriwa and they were all accustomed to such breakdowns.

Heather held the little white parcel which cocooned her son and looked down at the small pink face. This tiny morsel is mine, she thought, I'm responsible for it, I have to feed it, clothe it, teach it and love it… and it will completely change my life. She was suddenly overwhelmed by the responsibility that had fallen on her shoulders and buffetted by a kaleidoscope of emotions; filled with relief that her ordeal was over and that her baby had the right number of fingers and toes, she wept, sobbing her gratitude that all was well, as a profound sense of pride and protection swept through her like a tidal wave.

Edward arrived at the hospital at the same time as the first blinding flash of lightning, quickly followed by a low growl of thunder. The rain threw itself earthwards with malevolent ferocity, bouncing off the ground and rapidly filling the deep storm drains at the side of the road as the sky opened its sluice-gates.

Heather had been drifting towards sleep on cotton wool clouds, and Edward's kiss brought her back to the world. She opened one eye to see him standing in a puddle as rain dripped from him, his hair plastered to his head as if he had just stepped out of a shower.

'Thank you for my son, darling.'

'Who told you it was a boy?' Heather was now wide awake and aggrieved. She had specially asked the midwife and doctor not to tell Edward whether he had a son or a daughter. She knew he wanted a son and had savoured the moment when she could tell him. She had been robbed of a precious moment.

'The watchman in the car park told me. He heard it on the drums, so everyone knows by now, even out at Tegey village.'

'That's not fair. They all knew before you did.'

But Edward didn't care. He pushed the mosquito net aside and lifted his son from the cot, cradling him in his large hands, rocking him gently. The baby opened his eyes, yawned hugely, stuffed his small fist against his mouth and sucked vociferously.

'The poor little chap's starving,' Edward said, glowing with the special pride of a new parent as he studied his son. 'My son,' he said quietly, testing the words, 'My son,' he said more loudly. He thought it sounded good. Very good.

'I couldn't get here earlier,' he said. 'There's been a spot of bother in the centre of Sekari town and the police have cordoned off some of the roads.'

'What sort of bother?'

'Just the usual political hoo-ha. Nothing to worry about. The District Commissioner was there sorting it out with someone from the radio station. Apparently news of the unrest in this part of the world has trickled through to London and it's been blown up out of all proportion.'

Heather looked at him and thought, it's all very well for you to tell me there's nothing to worry about, but I am worried. After the recent murder outside their bungalow, she felt she had every right to feel worried. Stories of the trouble brewing in Sekari had filtered through to even the smallest of outlying villages, and until now it had seemed too distant and remote to be of any consequence. She could do nothing about it and it had nothing to do with her, but for the first time in her life she felt grown up. She had responsibilities now; a child to protect, and once she was out of hospital she would find out more and try to understand what was going on.

On one of Edward's visits to the hospital some days later, Heather asked if Sammy had turned up after his disappearing act.

'Yes, and he was very cagey about where he'd been, but I suspect he was away at one of Kovina's meetings. According to the gossip amongst my headmen, Kovina is trying to calm things down in our district. He's aiming to put a stopper on Komfo and his gang who are trying to terrorise local government workers and expatriates' servants into going on strike,' Edward told her. 'Sammy was almost in tears when I told him you were in hospital with our new son, and since then he's been frantically rushing about trying to make amends for being away when you needed him.' Edward laughed. 'He must be feeling guilty – he's been chopping a mountain of wood, cleaning the windows and polishing the floor until it's as treacherous as an ice-rink.'

Heather smiled. 'That won't last long,' she said.

Edward didn't think it wise to mention that Sammy had also dropped a tray, smashing a cup and saucer and their only teapot, and had burned a hole the shape of a flat iron in one of the pillow cases Heather had painstakingly hand-embroidered. But he did have some other news. 'Oh, by the way, that gardener chap from the Mission called with some bulb things. He said he'd promised to bring them for you.'

'Bulb things?'

'Yes, he said you'd know all about them. Apparently he dug some up in the bush and the others he found growing at the side of the road, so I imagine they're wild.'

'Good old Musah, bless him. He is kind. They'll be the gloriosa superba corms,' Heather said. 'You know the ones, those lovely scarlet and yellow lilies. Remember? They look almost like orchids.' She was touched that Musah had remembered her remarking that she would like to plant a big bed of them at the foot of a shade tree in the garden.

'They looked just like yams to me,' Edward remarked.

For the first few days after her return from hospital, Heather busied herself getting used to a new routine. Time passed more quickly now that she had the baby to keep her occupied, and all of a sudden other expatriate wives called, keen to see the new arrival and glad of an opportunity to take a break from the monotonous routine of living in remote back-of-beyond territory. Agricultural stations were often two or three hundred miles apart so that socialising usually turned out to be quite an event, not lightly undertaken as the rough roads linking them were likely to be full of axle-breaking potholes.

Dick and Mary Forwood were stationed at a poultry farm in the north of the territory and were the first to call on Heather and Edward. Passing through Tegey on their way to Sekari for a shopping expedition, they were bursting with news of the rioting in villages all around their area.

'I had no idea there was trouble so far north,' Heather said in some surprise.

'My God, yes! There was a chap killed by a spear a couple of weeks ago and only yesterday the DC was called to look at a body found in a culvert at the side of the road. The man who reported it said the victim had been strangled, but the DC told me it looked as if he had been tied to the back of a car or lorry and dragged along the road by the rope around his neck.'

'How awful,' Heather said. 'How on earth could anybody be so cruel?'

'That's nothing,' Dick continued, 'according to news on the grapevine, the whole population of one small village was mutilated. They had their hands cut off and their tongues cut out. The few who survived ran away and hid in the bush, and when all was quiet, they were too terrified to report the event.'

'But that sort of thing can't go on. What are they doing to stop it?' Heather asked.

'A couple of men have been arrested, but there must have been a whole gang of them involved and until someone comes forward to say what happened, there's little the police can do,' Dick said.

Heather turned to Edward as she handed coffee to her guests. 'Did you know anything about this?'

'No, not really, though there have been rumours. It's hard to know what to believe. None of the reports I've heard have been substantiated,' he replied. 'The trouble is, everyone is too frightened to talk in case they are the next to be found with a spear through their guts.'

'We passed a group of about twenty young men on our way here,' Mary told them, 'and we thought they belonged to a gang repairing the road, but they were brandishing pangas and shouting "Freedom for Facriwa". We had to slow down to get through them and they started banging on the car roof with sticks and shaking their fists. It was a frightening few minutes and I was relieved when we left them behind.'

Dick interrupted: 'The police and army are putting up road blocks but that's a fat lot of good unless the troublemakers are in cars or lorries. All they do is walk a few yards into the bush at the side of the road to bypass the duty patrols, who are often drunk anyway.'

'Don't the leaders know that talks are going on here and in London about granting independence?' Heather asked.

'No doubt some do, but most of them are scrabbling for power in preparation for the takeover. Things aren't moving fast enough for them and now they're shouting for a general strike, and if they're successful the country will be in a proper mess.' Edward shook his head and put his coffee cup on the table. 'The trouble is, the more upheaval and bloodshed they cause, the longer the talks will take. It hasn't occurred to them that the British Government will become even more convinced that Facriwans aren't yet capable of running their own country.'

'It's a shame, really,' Mary joined in, 'because in the remote villages they haven't the foggiest idea what it's all about. They're happy to go on as they've always done, leading their own quiet lives and not bothering a soul, but now they get beaten up if they don't attend these subversive meetings tucked away in some secluded clearing in the bush. And of course it's an ideal cover for the hardened criminals to infiltrate and blame any unpleasant outcome on the young political hotheads.'

It was on the tip of Heather's tongue to tell Mary and Dick about the shooting incident outside their bungalow, but Edward caught her eye and shook his head. Indignant, she was about to ignore his signal when she remembered Kovina's warning that night: It is best that you forget what you have seen. Your lives could be in danger.

She couldn't afford to take any risks now that she had David to think of, but it dismayed her to accept that she was being intimidated just as surely as the poor ignorant frightened people in villages up and down the country. An unseen finger of fear was pressed against her temple, ensuring her silence, but it was time someone spoke out – and next time she saw Kovina she intended asking him a few straight questions. Edward was certain to be ratty with her if he found out, so she would keep it to herself.

CHAPTER 7

Sammy seemed strangely preoccupied when serving dinner. He tripped over the step into the dining room, spilling soup all over the floor, and attempted to serve their chocolate pudding before the chicken casserole.

'Something make trouble for you, Sammy?' Edward asked eventually.

'My missis and piccins be sick. Dey get plenty belly palaver,' came the reply.

'You want to take them to the Mission Clinic?'

'I see if dey better for morning time. If dey still be sick I take dem to Komfo. He done get plenty good medsin for belly palaver.'

Heather's shocked expression was not lost on the houseboy, and he hastily added: 'It be too far to take dem to de Mission Clinic.' He didn't look Heather in the eye as he defended his course of action, preferring to fiddle with a tea towel, stare down at the floor and shuffle his feet.

'I'll drive you up there in the morning if you like, Sammy, but I shan't have time to wait until they've seen the medical orderly. You'll have to walk back or get a lift on a mammy lorry,' Edward offered.

'No, Massa. It best I go see Komfo. Den he be plenty pleased wid me and he no put juju on me again.' He could not have made it more plain that he wanted to get back in Komfo's good books. He had been scared almost witless by the warning signs left outside his hut by the witch doctor, and Edward could see that it would be pointless and probably unwise to try to persuade him otherwise.

'What was all that stuff about Komfo putting a juju on him?' Heather wanted to know as soon as Sammy had left the room.

'You know what he's like, I dare say it was all in his imagination,' Edward fibbed. 'Most of these people's lives are ruled by superstition.'

'Where did you put those Gloriosa superba corms Musah brought me when I was in hospital?' Heather asked the following morning. David was lying on the bed between them, blowing bubbles while Edward tickled his toes. He adored his little son and spent every spare minute with him, noting with pride the baby's every new development.

'They were wrapped up in a bit of old newspaper. I put them on a shelf in the storeroom,' he said. 'Just look, Heather, look at the way he's smiling at me.'

'It's most likely wind,' Heather said in the worldly wise know-it-all way of a new mother.

She searched the storeroom shelves for the corms, but they were nowhere to be seen. Tins of food and bags of sugar often went missing and she knew Sammy's piccins pilfered from the store whenever they got the chance to slip in and out quickly without being caught. Because of this, she was in the habit of giving them a few sweets and biscuits from the big glass jars in the store every Saturday morning, in the hope that it would deter them from stealing. It did not, but she couldn't bring herself to do anything about it because they had so little, and she figured she was partly to blame for forgetting to lock the door. Puzzled by the disappearance of the corms, she stood in the middle of the small room and took a last look round the shelves, loath to believe Sammy's children had been up to their tricks again. She frowned, and then recalled Edward's remark: They looked just like yams to me. Of course, that explained it.

She found Edward.

'I can't find those blessed things. I think Sammy's kids must have pinched them, thinking they're yams, and they're poisonous, you know.' They looked at each other as the truth dawned. 'If they've eaten them, it's no wonder they're ill!'

'But Sammy wasn't sick,' Edward pointed out.

'I know, but he often eats with his cronies down at the Okay Bar in Tegey village. Chances are, he was the only one who didn't eat any.'

'Well we can't do anything about it now, they've already gone off to see Komfo, so we'll just have to wait until they get back. That witch doctor will have a field day if he finds out what's happened,' Edward grinned at her. 'Shall I call you Lucretia, dear?'

Heather threw a tin of peas at him, but missed.

Sammy returned later in the day carrying an old margarine tin containing a revolting-looking muddy brown potion concocted by the witch doctor. He sounded faintly apologetic as he informed Heather that his family had been given some of Komfo's cure before leaving his compound and they were feeling better already. He coughed and surveyed his toes, before adding that the witch doctor had told him that she was responsible for his family's belly palaver and had used white man's juju to poison them.

Heather seethed at the allegation. Edward's prediction had been right, and when she had simmered down, she asked the houseboy about the missing corms, but he denied that his children had anything to do with their disappearance. Heather recognised his unease and knew that he was well aware that they had ended up in his wife's cooking pot. He avoided her eyes as she questioned him, staring miserably down at his feet – the picture of guilt.

Heather told Edward the outcome when he arrived home from work.

'If they did take the wretched things, perhaps it will have taught them a lesson,' he said, adding: 'trust the wily old Komfo to implicate you again. It was an opportunity too good to miss.' He laughed. 'And I suppose I'll have to watch my step if you've taken to using white man's juju. For all I know, it could be my turn next. Will you turn me into a frog?'

'I might well do so – if I thought you'd turn into a handsome prince when I kissed you!'

'Touché! Aren't I handsome enough for you as I am?' Edward croaked. 'By the way, in a couple of weeks I've got to survey a new area not far from here. It's a place I'm thinking of using as an experimental plot for a new variety of maize. Would you like to come with me? We could go just before teatime when the sun has worn itself out a bit, then it won't be too hot for David.'

'Mmm. Yes, it's time your son got to know something about what his dad's up to, just in case he wants to join the Colonial Service one day.'

Edward digested the idea for a moment. 'Wouldn't it be wonderful if we could afford a farm of our own in England? Then all our sons could help as they grow up. Just think of them all, ploughing the land, milking the cows, bringing in the harvest.'

'Hey, wait a minute. What's all this "all our sons" talk? How many are you banking on? Don't I have any say in the matter?' She reverted to her grandfather's Wiltshire dialect: 'An' what about the muck spreadin', clearing them ditches an' sweepin' the slurry from the yard? I notice you don't mention any of the dirty jobs around the farm in this dream world of yours.'

'Oh, I should think half a dozen lads should be enough, and as for the dirty jobs, we'll leave those to you and the girls.'

A cushion whistled passed his ear.

'I've been meaning to take a look at this place for some time,' Edward told Heather as they started off in the car for the area to be surveyed. 'But the headman and overseers have kept trying to put me off. They say it's an old burial ground and the spirits of their ancestors shouldn't be disturbed.' He looked at Heather, anticipating an outburst, as he went on: 'You see, my dear, it is sacred ground and holds a very powerful juju.' He was not disappointed.

'Oh no! Not more of this juju nonsense,' she cried in dismay. 'These people have their entire lives ruled by one ridiculous superstition after another.'

'You mean like avoiding walking under ladders, touching wood and throwing spilled salt over your shoulder?'

'Don't be an idiot, that's completely different. You know very well what I mean.'

The car left the dirt road and rumbled up a narrow rough track with more than the usual ruts and potholes, gradually winding its way up towards a flat plateau. Edward stopped the car as patches of scrub and stunted trees prevented them going any further. All around them the ground was studded with small outcrops of rock before it rose steeply, finally levelling off like a table top.

'This looks like it,' Edward said, and took a battered map from the breast pocket of his bush jacket. He opened it out and spread it across his knees. 'I think you and David had better stay here near the car while I go and take a look up there. Don't go wandering off, they tell me there are a lot of snakes in this area. They come here because these rocks retain the heat of the sun when it gets cooler at night.'

Heather threw a rug over a flat rock and sat down with the baby on her lap.

'I won't be long,' Edward said, 'it doesn't look too promising as a trial area with all these rocks scattered about, but there may not be as many when I get up to the top.' He reached for a panga from the back of the car and started hacking his way through the scrubby undergrowth covering the steady incline, and was soon out of sight.

'Mind the evil spirits don't get you,' Heather called after him and buried her face in David's plump bare midriff, sharing the joke with him. The baby gurgled happily, seeming pleased to join in his mother's fun.

Edward was away much longer than Heather had expected and she began to feel anxious. The sun had dipped towards the horizon and darkness fell quickly in this part of the world, giving little time for twilight. Mosquitoes were already active, whining and dancing in erratic flight among the lengthening shadows as she folded the rug and took David back to the car.

A shout, followed by crashing and thrashing high up in the scrub, alarmed her and she got up quickly to see what was going on. David had been fast asleep on his mother's lap and let out a wail of protest at being so peremptorily disturbed. She cuddled him close, calming him as she caught sight of movement in the prickly bushes above, then Edward appeared, slipping and slithering down the slope towards them, dislodging stones, tufts of grass and red earth on his downward plunge. He still gripped the panga in one hand while he tore at his bush jacket with the other. As soon as he reached level ground, he threw down the panga, still tearing at his clothes, ripping the garments off one by one in a frenzy, until he stood before her, naked.

'What on earth are you doing?' she cried.

Edward rubbed and scratched at his body, dancing from one foot to the other.

'It's not the bloody evil spirits that've got me,' he said, panting from his exertions, and still vigorously brushing his arms and legs. 'I walked into a column of driver ants. The blighters were all over me before I realised they were there. I think their leader must have signalled to them "OK, chaps, let him have it" because they all started biting at once as if they'd heard a starting pistol!'

Heather couldn't help herself. She doubled up with laughter, hugging David against her as she shook with mirth.

'And here was I, scared half out of my wits thinking you were being pursued by a horde of angry ancestral spirits,' she chuckled.

'It's nothing to laugh about. Come on! Quick, for goodness sake, get them off my back and places where I can't reach.'

Heather put David on the car seat and brushed the rest of the ants from Edward's body while he shook them from his clothes. He dressed hurriedly, his skin still red and smarting from the painful bites, while Heather tried to suppress her silent laughter.

The car protested noisily as they left the site, bumping and bouncing slowly back down the rough track until they reached the main road once again. They had only driven a short distance when they were overtaken by another car which pulled across in front of them, forcing Edward to stop.

'What the hell…what's that idiot doing?' Edward shouted, opening the car door ready to have a few sharp words with the other driver. Kovina slowly unravelled his long legs from the car in front and walked back towards them.

'Hello,' he said affably, resting his arms on the car roof and looking in the window at Heather. 'What took you up to the burial ground?' He waved back towards the track they had just left.

'I was looking for a place to site a small experimental plot,' Edward replied, rubbing at the angry red blotches on his arms left by the ant bites.

'I'd steer clear of that spot if I were you,' Kovina cautioned. 'It's supposed to be an old burial ground and said to be haunted.'

'Well, it certainly gave Edward a fright. He's just walked into a train of driver ants.'

'Have you been badly bitten?' Kovina asked.

'The blasted things were all over me before I even knew they were there.'

'And then they all started to bite at once?'

'Yes, they certainly did.'

Kovina nodded. 'It's their usual way of operating. If you're still intent on surveying the area, it would be wise to clear it with the village chief. Burial sites are just as sacred here as they are in any other part of the world.'

'I don't think I'll bother.' Edward replied. 'There are far too many rocks up there to make it feasible. It would be too costly to clear the site. A juju grove it may be, but there must be plenty of people not scared off by that.'

'What makes you think that?'

'The whole place is covered with footprints and there are empty beer bottles and other signs of activity up there.'

Kovina frowned but made no further comment, and after a few pleasantries to Heather and remarks on how well David was doing, he left them and drove off in a cloud of dust.

A few days later, Edward dropped Heather at the Mission for another visit to Musah. The gardener greeted her warmly, clearly delighted that she had brought the baby for him to see. He held a calloused black finger out to the infant who clasped it tightly with his chubby hand.

'He is a strong one, this son of yours,' he said, smiling down at David.

Heather nodded and thanked him for the Gloriosa superba corms, telling him of her suspicions as to what had happened to them.

Musah shook his head and chuckled.

'If you're right and they were stolen and eaten, they would have given someone quite a bellyache.'

'Oh, they did that all right! Sammy had to take his wife and children to Komfo for a remedy. Of course he implied that it was my fault, so I am now credited with using a powerful white man's juju.'

'That's just the sort of thing he'd do. You presented him with a fine opportunity to sow seeds of doubt, knowing that Sammy would almost certainly tell other members of his tribe.' Musah tickled David's toes as he continued. 'You must be careful. Always be on your guard against that man. Don't give him the opportunity to implicate you in anything to do with him. He will see to it that he always comes out the winner.' He looked at her sternly like a belligerent headmaster dealing with a recalcitrant pupil. Heather accepted this, believing in his wisdom.

'You caused him to lose face with the people who came to him for treatment. You were able to cure them more quickly than he could, and you didn't expect payment or reward. He'll not forgive you for that.'

The constant warnings about the witch doctor were making Heather feel uneasy and she quickly changed the subject, recounting Edward's clash with the driver ants at the old burial ground. She thought the incident would amuse him but this was not the case.

'It's regarded as a holy place,' Musah said, 'though as far as I know, no one can actually remember anyone being buried there.'

'So it's all conjecture? I mean, if no one knows of a burial taking place at the site, it could all be a myth.'

'That is true. But it is also possible that tales of the graveyard have been passed down from generation to generation along with many other legends down through the years. Africa is full of ancient rituals and superstitions.'

'Don't I know it!' Heather laughed. 'On the other hand, the stories about the burial ground could be recent and may have been made up just to frighten people away. It would be interesting to dig a few pits up there to see if any bones are uncovered.' She shivered even as she offered the theory.

Musah looked beyond her, away into the distance, as if debating whether to divulge some secret. Heather waited as he hitched his brown robe up on his shoulder with a work-worn hand.

'I've seen lights up there many times after the sun has gone down. Although it is some distance away, being on that raised plateau, they are easily seen from here. You may be right, it could be that the story of evil spirits at the burial ground is being kept alive for a purpose. Perhaps someone wants to conceal something from prying eyes.'

Heather was about to tell him Edward had seen lot of footprints there, but hesitated. She had listened to enough talk of evil spirits and juju and suddenly felt sickened by it all. She wanted nothing more to do with it. If she didn't dismiss it from her mind, she might well become entangled in some web she could neither explain nor understand. She was glad when Edward's car appeared, and breathed a sigh of relief as he came along the path bordered with whitewashed stones. It was time to go home and talk about ordinary everyday things: letters from home, the next shopping trip to Sekari and whether to plant pineapples in her new vegetable patch; it was time to forget all about burial grounds, be they haunted or otherwise. But as they were about to leave, Musah disappeared into his hut, emerging presently with a package which he handed to Heather.

'This is for your piccin,' he said. 'It was given to me by my father, who received it from his father before him. It should be handed down to my son. But I shall never have a son, and it is already written that it should belong to David. It will protect him.'

Heather winced inwardly as she took the gift and unwrapped it from folds of yellowing newspaper. Oh God! she thought, not more superstition, not more mumbo-jumbo. I can't cope with it, I'll go mad! What did Musah mean, 'it has already been written that it should belong to David'? Her fingers felt the soft leather pouch suspended from a thong to be worn round the neck. Although crudely made, there was a strange beauty in the intricate pattern of a fish etched into the leather, with a dull red stone for its eye. As she held the talisman on the palm of her hand, a sensation like a small electric shock tingled up her arm. She felt dizzy and closed her eyes. She saw the face of an old man. At first she thought it was Musah, but the man in this vision was very much older. His eyes regarded her with hundreds of years of wisdom burning behind them. She was pillowed in an aura of peace, a sense of complete well-being. She needed to talk to this old man; instinctively she knew he would be able to unlock the door to many mysteries – but a light touch, as of a feather, brushed her senses, and he was no longer there.

CHAPTER 8

Heather's garden was slowly taking shape, repaying her for the hours of hard labour spent every morning before the sun sapped her energy and brought a myriad small fruit flies to feast on the sweat on her brow. Her first intention had been simply to add colour and shape to the barren waste of laterite surrounding the bungalow, but as her taxing work was rewarded, she found she was enjoying the task more and more. Now each month made her more purposeful as new colours and fresh depths of light and shade transformed the once stark outlook of the compound into a garden of which she could feel proud. Her labour also helped to push aside the harsh reality of that other world beyond her garden. Komfo, his complicity and juju were shunted into a siding of her mind as she went about the business of becoming a good mother to David and learning how to turn an arid dusty bare patch into a lush tropical plot. However, some things were too important to set aside – they eroded her peace of mind and were ruining the lives of many African people.

One of the leading political activists had been imprisoned and this led to reprisal killings and countless other atrocities. Those trying to calm the situation, both white and black, were often considered to be cowardly pacifists doing their utmost to hold up progress towards self-government and freedom from the yoke of colonial rule. Bricks were thrown through their windows, their cars were stoned and their pet dogs were found poisoned or with their throats cut. Arms and ammunition were being smuggled into Facriwa from adjoining territories while tension mounted and rumours became increasingly unbelievable and far-fetched. Road blocks manned by police and army patrols sprouted like mushrooms overnight, causing frayed tempers and making journeys twice as long. Most of the bigger towns were subject to curfew, giving rise to further annoyance to the inhabitants and not a little alarm as curfew breakers were imprisoned or shot at by nervous police officers. Some of the incidents contained a comical aspect despite their gravity: a building contractor was fired upon by an over-zealous soldier and received a bullet in his backside when he paid a call to his outside toilet, and a young forestry officer was also injured while taking his dog for a walk in the garden just after dusk. Such episodes were becoming ever more frequent, providing further fodder for the gossip-mongers, as newly-trained young army recruits went about their duties, trigger-happy and often drunk.

Heather fretted when stories reached her of the hostile world beyond her own small boundary. David was growing into a sturdy little boy, already making his first attempts to walk, and she was concerned about his lack of playmates and his safety. As she watched her son stagger precariously round the room, making sudden jerky dashes for the stability of a chair or a table, she dreamed of leave in England and the time when she would be able to show him off to his grandparents.

She sat on one of the basket chairs on the wide verandah and thought how it would be: the doting grandmothers, visits to the park behind her parents' house and David playing on the swings and see-saws. In her imagination, she steadied the boy as he climbed the ladder to the top of the slide, calling encouragement as he made his first perilous journey down the slope. As she visualised her son's excitement when she took him to a big toy shop, she was reminded of all the things they were forfeiting by living in Africa. By now she had become accustomed to the privations, the heat, the fevers, the snakes and so often the sheer boredom and loneliness. Had they been stationed near a town, there would have been other expatriate children and perhaps a nursery school run by one of the wives. If only...she dreamed on. Edward had already served beyond the usual tour of duty and it was beginning to tell on him. He was tired and drained of energy following a bout of malaria, and home leave could not come soon enough for all of them.

Heather aired her worries about David's lack of companions and nursery school to Edward and suggested that she should prolong her stay at home with the boy to give him and his grandparents longer to get to know each other. She knew such a plan would delight her parents, but Edward was horrified at the proposal, blurting out his feelings with an uncharacteristic display of righteous indignation.

'It would be far better if you had another baby to keep David company, and there's nothing to stop you bringing books back from UK so that you can start teaching him yourself as soon as he's old enough.'

'But I don't know a thing about teaching,' she replied. 'It's a specialised job and I wouldn't even know where to start.'

'So now's the time to learn,' Edward argued. 'You say you get bored, and David's still little more than a baby yet, so do it now while you've got plenty of time on your hands.'

She had heard about the Parents National Education Union from another ex-patriate wife who was coaching her daughter until she was old enough to go to boarding school in England, and made up her mind to write for details. Secretly though, she thought she wouldn't have the patience for teaching; it was a vocation and she didn't feel she was cut out for it.

Kovina was a frequent visitor to the bungalow, often arriving in the morning when he must have been well aware that Edward would be away at work. It bothered Heather, though she valued his friendship and was still drawn to him in that strange way which she found difficult to explain, even to herself.

On one such occasion her hand touched his as she handed him a cup of coffee. He put the cup down on a small table and turned to face her. He took her hand in his and started to say something, but she felt the colour rise to her cheeks and withdrew her hand from his grasp, disturbed and confused. She mustn't get caught up in something she didn't understand. She needed to back off from this situation. Abruptly, she asked him if Komfo had been involved in some of the recent disturbances in Tegey village. He seemed unabashed by her action and professed to know nothing about the local incidents. Her mind searched for something to diffuse the situation and she told him what Musah had disclosed several months ago about the lights he had seen up at the old burial ground.

'Oh yes. I know all about that. Edward told me he'd seen tracks up there, if you remember.' He stirred his coffee and deliberately looked straight into her eyes until once again she was forced to look away. She found herself staring down at her feet, like Sammy, as Kovina continued, 'I went up there myself one night not long ago, to see what was going on. Your friend Komfo was there with a couple of men. I don't know what they were up to, but when I questioned him, his excuse was that they go there regularly to gather seeds, roots of plants and some special pods, which he assured me were ingredients needed for his medicines.'

'And do you believe him?' Heather asked, her interest aroused. 'There's bound to be some other reason for nocturnal visits. If they were only at the site to collect plants, surely they would go in daylight,' she scoffed.

'According to the witch doctor, the medicinal potency exuded from the plants multiplies if harvested after dark.'

'What rubbish! That man must take you for a gullible fool!'

Kovina looked more than a little put out by her outburst. 'Yes. Well… I'm inclined to agree with you there, and for that reason I intend to go back and take a proper look when there's no one about.'

'That's daft. It would be asking for trouble. From what I've been told about that nasty piece of work, it could be dangerous if you stumbled upon him and his cohorts while they are in the middle of carrying out one of his peculiar tribal rites.'

Kovina crossed one long leg over the other and listened to her, a half-smile on his handsome face.

'Oh?' was all he said.

'What if you caught him at a meeting with his disciples, egging them on to cause more riots or strikes? It's too risky. You could find yourself in real trouble.' She felt a tension building between them and laughed nervously, saying the first thing that came into her head. 'He might bring some dreadful curse down upon you.'

Kovina shook his head and laughed aloud.

'I doubt whether he'd do that, and anyway, there's no need to worry – when I do decide to go back, I'll not be alone and I shall not go unarmed.' He smiled and gave her one of his sidelong glances. 'But I'm glad you're concerned about my safety. It shows that you care.'

Heather brushed off this last remark, and tried to instil some humour into what could turn into an awkward situation.

'Oh, get away with you. Now, I can't sit here chatting to you all morning – I have work to do and it's time you were off,' she said briskly.

Heather was disturbed by Kovina's assertion that he would go back to the burial ground, even if armed and not alone. She told Edward about it as soon as he returned from work.

'Sounds as if he means to get to the bottom of it, and I suppose it won't hurt to find out what's going on, but I should have thought he'd have had more sense than to stick his head in that hornet's nest,' he said.

'He said he wouldn't go alone,' Heather reminded him.

'That won't make much difference. Whoever he takes would more than likely be scared stiff of Komfo, same as most of the locals, and at the first sign of trouble would be off down that track like a dose of salts.' Edward said. 'Whoever Kovina gets to go with him will no doubt be full of bravado, but if anything untoward happens, you can bet they'd lose their nerve and make a run for it.'

'Oh, ye of little faith,' Heather laughed.

A strident yell from the direction of the kitchen ended the conversation and sent them running outside to investigate.

They found Sammy standing with his back against the kitchen wall, a short stumpy piece of wood gripped in his hand. His arm was raised as if to strike, but he appeared mesmerised by the snake on the dusty floor a few inches from his feet. His eyes were fixed on the reptile as he braced himself, pressing back against the wall, waiting for it to attack. The black cobra was magnificent, its head raised with hood spread ready for its fangs to deliver their deadly venom. It waved slowly from side to side like a hypnotist's medium, its scales shining like wet coal.

Heather and Edward watched in shock from the doorway as Sammy closed his eyes, sucked in a great gulp of air, then slowly, slowly, slowly as if each second held a magic ingredient of protection, his knees buckled and his glistening sweat-covered body slid down the wall leaving a dark smear of fear-sweat on the dry mud-built wall.

Edward stepped forward quickly and grabbed a log from the pile by the kitchen door. He threw it at the snake, hitting it but not killing it. Writhing and twisting, the sheen of its scales dimmed as it thrashed in the dust. Seizing another log, Edward hit the snake again and again until it lay still, then he leaned against the wall, panting from his exertions, perspiration beading his forehead as the log fell from his hand. Sammy opened his eyes, his hand shaking as his own useless weapon dropped and rolled across the dirt floor until it came to rest against the cobra's lifeless form.

For a second everything was still, as if all movement, all sound, all life itself had been switched off, then a burst of chattering, ululating and handclapping broke the silence as Sammy's wife, piccins and friends, their cheerful faces beaming at the conquest, squeezed into the narrow kitchen doorway. The youngest boy in the throng picked up a stick and danced round and round the compound, miming the killing of the snake, delighting his audience until his ragged shorts lost their precarious hold round his skinny waist and dropped to his ankles, bringing him to the ground with a resounding thwack.

Sammy recovered quickly once the racket started and he realised all danger was past. He came out of the snake-induced trance none the worse and brightened still further when Heather suggested he brew a large pot of tea for everyone. She could see that Edward was upset. She knew, from a story he had told her months ago, that his aversion to killing any living thing stemmed from a time when, as a child, he had witnessed a man drowning unwanted kittens in a bucket. The memory of the occasion returned undiminished whenever he saw anything killed. As she followed him back to the bungalow she saw Milah, Sammy's wife, stoop to pick up the dead cobra. It would be cleaned, cooked and eaten before nightfall.

Just after midnight a few weeks later, Heather and Edward were woken by a loud hammering on their bedroom door.

'Massa, Massa. Come quick, Massa!'

Sammy stood in the passage with a small wiry whippet of a man at his side. The stranger was pygmy-like, black as a moonless night, shiny as if rain had fallen on his pock-marked skin. He was agitated and gesticulated wildly as words flew from his mouth accompanied by a shower of saliva as he rushed to tell his story. He didn't speak in pidgin; either he knew none, or what he did know had been overtaken by his haste to be heard. Sammy translated as quickly as he could, his sentences ragged and disjointed as the urgent words spewed from the diminutive messenger.

'Massa, dis man, him say Kovina go for dat place where dey go bury people long time past.' He waved his arm in the direction of the ancient burial ground. 'Him say Kovina be hurt. Him be hurt propah. Some man done go shoot him. He tink Kovina be dead.'

The frightened little man grabbed Sammy's arm, shaking it as he gabbled away, almost incoherent in his agitation, his eyes rolling like those of a cartoon character.

'Him beg you go wid him. Him fear too much to go back dat place by hisself. He say if white man no go wid him, Komfo may shoot him too.'

A fraught silence hung in the air as Edward tried to digest the story. The little man watched, rocking from one bare foot to the other, imploring eyes darting from Edward to Sammy as he waited for a decision.

'Don't go, Edward,' Heather broke in, gripping his arm. 'It's far too dangerous. You know that man is evil. Please, please, Edward, don't go.'

Edward put his arms round her.

'I must, love. You know I've got to go,' he reached for his bush jacket hanging behind the door and took the car keys from their hook. His smile was starched as he kissed her lightly on her cheek and tried to make it seem as if he were just going off to do a normal day's work. 'Try not to worry, I'll be back as quick as I can.'

'Can't someone go from the village? Can't this man get a gang from the village to go with him?' Heather pleaded, still clinging on to his arm. Edward patted her shoulder and shook his head.

'You go and see if this racket has woken David,' he said gently, 'then get back to bed yourself. I'll be back before you know it.' He turned to Sammy. 'You stay here in the bungalow with Madam and don't open the door to anyone until I return. You take care of Madam and de piccin propah, you savvy?'

'Yes, Massa, I savvy. I watch for Missis and de piccin propah.' Sammy was only too relieved to be entrusted with the task. For a while he thought he might be asked to go with Massa and the small stranger to the secret place, the grove full of wickedness, and if all the tales he heard were true, the scene of many sacrificial rites.

David had not been disturbed by the noisy arrival of their late night visitor, but Heather lifted him from his cot and took him into her bed. She needed the comfort of his small warm body close against her. The child's flushed face, a wisp of golden hair curling damply on his forehead, and the very innocence of her son had a calming effect on her and she dozed fitfully.

The wizened little man curled himself into a ball on the passenger seat of Edward's car, shaking and making soft whining sounds of distress. Edward realised why he looked so polished when the smell of coconut oil reached him. The District Commissioner had once told him that thieves and night raiders in Facriwa stripped naked and smeared their bodies with oil or animal fat so that it was almost impossible for anyone to grab hold of them if they were disturbed during a burglary. He wondered briefly if Kovina would also be covered with oil, but no, surely that would be out of character.

The more he thought about it, the more of an enigma the man became. He seldom frequented the local bars, he didn't hunt or fish as did most of the men from his home village. He didn't seem to spend much time with his family. All his spare time appeared to be spent attending meetings in Sekari, the purpose of which he kept to himself, discouraging questions, though Edward suspected they were of a political nature. He had met Kovina's parents when he first arrived in the Colony and was taken on a trek by his predecessor all around the district for which he would soon be responsible. Kovina's father was chief of his village, a good man who was much respected. He had had three wives, the second of which was Kovina's mother, the only one to survive an outbreak of smallpox. She had trained as a teacher at the Catholic Mission where Musah worked as gardener, and although now elderly and almost blind, she was still revered in the tribe by young and old alike for her wise counsel. Edward couldn't imagine Kovina doing anything to bring discredit on his family, yet he couldn't help wondering what the man had been up to now, and what risks he had taken at the burial ground.

He drove quickly until they approached the turn-off, then switched off the headlights and steered the car slowly up the uneven track. They hadn't gone far when his passenger shook Edward's arm and signalled him to stop. He pointed to a narrow gulley between stunted scrub and scattered rocks, opened the car door and slithered from his seat like a snake. Edward took a torch from the pocket under the dashboard and followed him along the shadowy track. He towered above the little man who covered the ground quickly on velvet feet, making no sound as he loped ahead.

The air was still, the eerie silence broken only by faint rustlings in the undergrowth as small nocturnal creatures went about the business of searching for food. A sudden loud cursing churr-churr-churr of alarm startled them as a nightjar took flight from its resting place in a hollowed-out dust bath on the path, its eyes glowing red in the beam from Edward's torch.

They came across Kovina without warning. He was lying with his back against the smooth surface of a dark grey boulder. His eyes were closed, his face masked by a poultice of sweat, dust and congealed blood. Edward took a handkerchief from his pocket and wiped away as much of the sticky mess as he could, to reveal a small flesh wound above Kovina's temple where a bullet had ploughed its way through the thick black hair. He ran his hands over the rough cloth wrapped around Kovina's seemingly lifeless form. They came away tacky with blood where another bullet had entered the lower part of his abdomen. Edward rolled his handkerchief into a tight wad and plugged the wound from which blood was still oozing.

Kovina would have to be moved to Sekari Hospital quickly if there was any chance for him to survive. The pygmy sat on his haunches watching Edward's every move and when Edward lifted Kovina's shoulders, he understood what was required and bent to pick up his feet. Together they carried the wounded man back down the track as fast as they dared for fear of jolting him and causing further loss of blood. They had only gone a short distance when a shrill scream rent the quiet night apart, stretching their taut nerves still further and scaring the pygmy so much that he dropped Kovina's feet and rolled himself up into a tight ball like a hedgehog. It was a good camouflage, Edward thought; with arms and legs tucked away he took on the appearance of a round dark rock, hardly distinguishable from those scattered all around the gulley. The scream died, ending with a rasping, gurgling sob, which was cut off abruptly as if someone had had the life choked out of them. It was followed by an unearthly high-pitched wailing and chanting, hardly human, rising and falling, rising and falling; then the ululations echoed round them, seeming to come at them from all sides, getting sharper in resonance with each passing second, boring into Edward's ear-drums, tattooing inside his skull until he thought it would drive him mad. The appalling sound ceased suddenly as if terminated by the flick of a switch, leaving in its wake a deep black silence and the stillness of death.

Despite the humid night air, a shiver ran through Edward's body. He felt as if he were standing at the edge of a precipice looking down into nothing. He tried to swallow but his mouth was dry and his lips felt like old parchment as he ran his tongue over them. Seconds passed and his heartbeat slowed, his mind came back to reality and he returned to the task in hand. He was thankful not to have had any part in whatever was happening on the ground above, and for the first time was able to understand why so many people lived in fear of Komfo. He prodded the black stone with his foot and the pygmy unravelled. In silence they lifted Kovina's body once more and continued on their way back down the path to the car.

Kovina opened his eyes briefly and spoke to the small African, his voice a hoarse whisper as Edward made him as comfortable as possible on the back seat. Edward understood little of the language but he caught the name Safo before Kovina lapsed into unconsciousness again.

CHAPTER 9

The main road into Sekari was pock-marked with potholes and slanting eroded gulleys where the last rainfall had filled the culverts at the verges, and the journey was anything but comfortable. Edward knew he had to get Kovina to hospital quickly, and reluctantly abandoned all thought of a slower, easier drive for his injured passenger. He turned to the other man hunched up on the seat beside him, his feet tucked up under him, his head thrust forward like a turtle's from its carapace.

'You be Safo, eh?' he asked.

Life came into the leathery features and a toothless grin replaced the worried frown worn by the little African ever since Edward first set eyes on him.

'Yeth. Me Thafo, Matha.' The lisped reply released the strain on Edward's face and his mouth relaxed into a smile.

They sat on a hard wooden bench at the hospital for an hour and a half, steeped in the smell of strong disinfectant, listening to the echoing sounds of squeaky trolleys protesting as they were wheeled into side wards and the snores, grunts and groans coming through the open door of a much bigger ward, until a tall grey-haired man walked down the long whitewashed corridor and introduced himself as Dr Donald Macleod. He told them that Kovina was out of danger. The bullet had done quite a bit of damage but had been removed without any complications.

'He's lost quite a bit of blood,' the doctor said, feeling in the pocket of his stiffly starched white coat for a packet of cigarettes. 'He'll take a bit of time to recover and of course the main thing now is to watch out for infection, but with luck he should be OK.' He propped himself against the wall as he flicked open his lighter and drew on the cigarette. 'You realise this incident will have to be reported to the District Commissioner and the police?' he said, eyeing them with interest.

'Of course,' Edward replied, though he sensed that Kovina would prefer that the whole thing should be hushed up.

'You were with him when it happened?'

'No. Safo, this chap here, came to my bungalow to tell me about the shooting and to ask for help. I think he was probably with Kovina when the shooting took place.'

The doctor turned wearily to Safo, who sat quietly, awaiting his turn. He addressed the half-pint little man in his own tongue and after a few minutes, Safo nodded, turned on his heel and ran from the room.

'I've told him to let the man's wife know what's happened. Some sod has cut the hospital telephone lines again,' the doctor said, shaking his head. 'I also let him know that he'll be called to give a statement to the DC and the police.'

'In that case, I think you can be pretty sure he'll go off into the bush and disappear until things have died down. Afraid of his own shadow, is that one,' Edward said, adding: 'Won't this news have been passed on by the drums by now?'

'I shouldn't think so. It's not the sort of stuff the bush telegraph want to broadcast. This is the fourth shooting casualty we've admitted tonight. Someone's having a party and needless to say, anyone involved in any of the night's activities will swear blind they were a hundred miles away.' He flicked ash from his cigarette into a water-filled jam jar standing on a small side table, and continued: 'And if necessary, will produce a dozen or more witnesses to prove they were where they said they were. As you say, that little fellow – what did you call him, Safo? – will probably disappear off the face of the earth for a few weeks.' He shrugged his shoulders, yawned and ran his hand through his hair. 'I'm off to bed; may as well salvage what's left of good kipping time.' But even as he spoke, the entrance doors burst open and a man was helped in, staggering under the weight of the spear embedded in his shoulder.

The first thin fingers of a misty dawn branched out from a purple horizon as Edward left the hospital. A night watchman squatting by the car stood up slowly on one leg, put his hand to his head in salute, coughed, spat into the dust, scratched under his armpit, then sank back on his haunches again to fill his clay pipe.

As Edward drove through the quiet, almost deserted streets on the outskirts of Sekari township, spirals of smoke rose with all the time in the world as the women poked life into the smouldering embers of yesterday's fires, ready to prepare the first meal of the day. Pye-dogs yapped and squabbled, scratched desultorily and rolled in the red dust to dislodge bloated grey ticks. Cockerels had long since heralded the birth of a new day with their gravel-throated crowing; now they set about the more important task of chasing cackling unwilling hens back and forth between the thatched shacks, in and out of the spindly paw-paw trees and yam patches.

Edward opened the bedroom door quietly and looked at Heather and David asleep on the bed. His wife lay on her side, curled in a crescent with the child fitting within the curve of her body like the last piece of a jigsaw puzzle, neat and complete. A wave of tender emotion swept over him; he wanted to gather them up in his arms and smother them with love. The moment passed, the opportunity was missed as the sound of Sammy's wife bellowing threats at one of her brood bounced across the compound, breaking the spell. He gently lifted the mosquito net and kissed them both. They stirred, but were not yet ready to relinquish sleep and dreams. He sighed; if only life were less complicated, he thought. If only I could give them all my attention and shut out the evil that is going on around us. Reluctantly, he left them to take a bath and prepare for the day's work.

It took a while for the shockwaves to settle after the shooting, but then Heather's first reaction was to go straight to Sekari Hospital to see Kovina. Of course, this she couldn't do unless Edward drove her there. She fumed – even if she had possessed a driving licence, they couldn't afford the luxury of a second car. She couldn't hop on to a bus or call a taxi and no expatriate neighbours lived close enough to beg a lift. The feelings of frustration which she had managed to keep in check since David's birth grew with each succeeding day; she felt hard done by, imprisoned in the small compound week after long hot week with little to break the monotony of her daily existence. The humidity didn't help – salty sweat gathered and trickled down her arms and legs even when she sat reading, or writing letters home. Any exertion left her exhausted and bad tempered and after a particularly gruelling day when David had been fractious and demanding, she tackled Edward, suggesting that it was high time he taught her to drive. He was hot and weary too after some disappointing meetings where nothing seemed to go right and little had been achieved, but he agreed, albeit reluctantly, to give Heather driving lessons.

From then on, most evenings were spent with Heather driving their battered little Austin A40 up and down the bush road while Edward patiently advised, admonished and bit his tongue. It was not the happiest of times. Heather was not one to accept criticism with an easy grace and as a result they had their first quarrels which graduated into flaming rows. The lessons were necessarily, and possibly mercifully, of short duration, as darkness fell early in Facriwa, but time and time again fraught and heated situations arose causing frayed tempers, tattered nerves and hasty words. Edward's patience was stretched to the limit and Heather's fuse grew short, mainly through exasperation at her own ineptitude, though she would never have confessed as much to him. The lessons ended with Heather elated at having managed an incident-free three point turn, or the usually quiet and unflappable Edward, having heaved the car out of a ditch with the aid of a few chortling African helpers, making straight for the drinks cabinet to pour a stiff drink, or two, or three.

What Edward found most annoying was the fact that Heather was learning to drive under what he considered to be ideal conditions. Admittedly the roads were atrocious with potholes, deep ruts and other hazards, but this far out from Sekari there were no road signs, no traffic lights, pedestrian crossings or roundabouts to contend with. There was little traffic apart from an occasional mammy lorry or perhaps a cyclist wobbling precariously along the dirt road on a dilapidated old bicycle which looked as if it had been salvaged from a scrap heap. Despite the lack of traffic, Heather soon discovered that driving on quiet bush roads was not always easy. A sudden tropical cloudburst could turn the deep powdery surface of choking dust into a thick syrupy quagmire in seconds. She was also quick to learn to cope with emergency stops after a few collisions, usually fatal, with chickens, dogs, pigs or goats that found sleeping in the middle of the road a pleasant enough way to pass an hour or two.

When Heather suspected she was expecting another baby, Edward was delighted and wasted little time in driving her to Sekari Hospital where the doctor confirmed her suspicions. Edward was like a dog with two tails and although she protested that they could not afford it, he whisked her off to the Bristol Hotel for a celebratory lunch. The power supply in the hotel was always erratic and on this day of all days, not only was there no electricity, the management had run out of gas cylinders so nothing could be cooked and they had to make do with a couple of corned beef sandwiches and a glass of the local beer. Despite this, Edward's spirits were barely dampened and Heather remarked as she surveyed the paving-slab-size sandwiches, 'At least we are being spoiled here, Edward.'

'In what way?' he asked, opening his mouth wide.

'The crusts have been cut off!'

For their pudding they were given half-set raspberry jelly with brown bits floating in it. They argued as to what the bits were. Heather thought they were bits of fluff from the cook's apron but Edward reckoned they could once have been live things that had fallen into the jelly and had been unable to swim to safety. The matter was not resolved, but their spirits were high and they didn't really care about the true identity of the floaty bits.

They returned to the hospital in the afternoon to visit Kovina, and found him fidgety and irritable, impatient to be discharged and eager to get back home again. The inactivity didn't suit him and he was not an ideal patient. He thanked Edward for his part in bringing him to the hospital with Safo and thereby saving his life, but offered no information as to what had taken place on the night he was shot. Edward knew he'd had visits from the District Commissioner and the police, but no intelligence had been forthcoming from either source. It was as if a vow of silence had been taken by all concerned, and true to Edward and the doctor's prediction, Safo had disappeared altogether, along with several other young men from his village.

Before they left the ward, Kovina's wife, Grace, arrived with their three children. Heather was surprised to see that she was dressed in a brightly coloured African mammy cloth. She would have expected her to have adopted European dress like her husband. Grace was taller than most women from tribes within the area and held herself proudly as if she thought herself a cut above the rest. Heather studied the woman closely. She hasn't been carrying calabashes of food from the market or debi-cans full of stream water on her head, she thought, and her bottom doesn't stick out like the other women's from the constant balancing act. She must have a young unmarried sister or some other relative to help with the running of her household. Kovina's two daughters took after their mother with the high cheekbones and wide forehead typical of the northern tribes, while the son, a tall young man, had his father's more rounded features and, dressed in khaki shorts and shirt, was a miniature version of his father. The boy stared unblinking and unsmiling at the two white visitors, looking them over with an arrogance surprising in one not long in his teens.

As they made their way to the car park, Edward commented, 'If appearances are anything to go by, that young man seems to have one hell of a chip on his shoulder. I wonder why?'

'I wouldn't have thought he'd got it from his father,' Heather said, and added somewhat brusquely, 'I'll drive home, Edward, I haven't had a chance to drive on a proper tarmac road yet.' But before he could reply, an African girl ran up to them and grabbed hold of Heather's arm.

'Help me! Please! You must help me!' she said, her voice barely above a whisper but her eyes full of entreaty. Heather recognised Comfort at once. She could see she was pregnant again, a fact made more obvious by the mammy cloth she was wearing. It was heavily patterned with large unlikely botanical specimens, their petals alternating between bright pink and blatant blue with long purple and white stamens protruding from the centre like rude tongues. One of these disasters from some apprentice designer's drawing board was positioned slap in the middle of Comfort's swollen belly. Edward was patently fascinated by the animated floral display this produced and only came to his more gentlemanly senses when Heather purposely trod on his foot.

'Don't stare, Edward!' she hissed.

Agonizing at the thought of another baby almost certain to be lost, thanks to the witch doctor who had such a strong hold on Comfort and her family, Heather invited the girl to get in the back of the car and held the door open for her.

'We'll take you back to Tegey,' she said, 'and on the way you can tell us what we can do to help you.'

Edward took the wheel, relieved that Heather would miss the chance of driving on a proper road, as she would be too busy talking to Comfort and discovering why she had come to them in such evident distress. His nerves were thankful for the reprieve.

Comfort had miscarried another child since the witch doctor had shown his displeasure after hearing that Heather had been trying to help the girl. She gabbled away in pidgin with barely a stop for breath in her rush to tell her story. She had had enough of Komfo and was past caring about his threats.

'You mus' help me, Missis. Dis time I mus' keep my piccin safe from dat man.'

'I don't see how I can help you, Comfort. We've been through all this before. You know as well as I do that if your husband finds out that you've been talking to me, he will beat you again.'

'No, Missis. Him done gone away.'

'Where's he gone?'

'Him no tell me. Him jus' 'fraid too much and him run away.'

'What's he afraid of?'

'Him be at dat place where Kovina done get shot. He 'fraid de District Commissioner tell police to lock him up.'

'Does your husband know who shot Kovina?' Heather asked urgently, hoping that at last she would hear something concrete about the events of that night.

'Him no tell me. Him plenty scared. Him scared too much and him run away.' Comfort shook her head as she repeated the words. She either could not, or would not tell any more.

Much to Edward's annoyance and dismay, Comfort visited their bungalow twice before her baby was born, always arriving very early in the morning before many people were up and about, and returning to the village by way of a back track through the bush which was seldom used except by hunters as dusk fell. Heather warned Sammy that he and Milah must not mention these visits to anyone, but they needed no cautioning, fearing to bring Komfo's wrath down upon them once again.

Heather bought tins of powdered baby milk and taught Comfort how to use the scoop provided to measure the correct amount, and how to mix it with boiled water to make up a feeding bottle. She showed the girl how to sterilise the bottle and keep it clean.

'You will have to boil water and keep it in a pan or calabash just for the baby's food. No one need know, but you must make sure it is covered with a clean cloth while it is cooling so that flies and dust don't get into it,' Heather told her. She was filled with a fierce determination to ensure that Comfort should rear this baby, but Edward was perturbed about the secret visits and Sammy made himself scarce whenever Comfort arrived.

Fortunately for all of them, Komfo had other problems to worry about at the time. The police and District Commissioner had called on him on more than one occasion asking too many awkward questions about his nocturnal visits to the burial ground. The witch doctor had discovered early on in the appointment of the present DC, James Heber-Scott, that he was impervious to all his blandishments and offers of his strongest spells to ensure that his tour of duty in the territory would be long and propitious. Komfo's veiled threats as to the evils that could befall the Commissioner if he failed to acknowledge that Komfo possessed magical powers far beyond those of any other witch doctor also fell on deaf ears. Wisely, the DC had listened attentively to all Komfo had to tell him, absorbing most of it with a pinch of salt. While quite prepared to believe that the man had a wide knowledge of the plants and roots which contained healing properties, the potency he claimed for the ground-up bones of his ancestors, dried snake skins, baboon hairs and suchlike failed to impress and certainly didn't have the intended effect of making the DC feel uneasy, or cause him to lose any sleep.

Either Comfort's clandestine visits to the Greenwoods' compound went unnoticed, or Komfo's other more pressing political matters kept him preoccupied and temporarily unconcerned, for neither the girl nor her family were cross-examined or challenged by the witch doctor. She gave birth to a girl and immediately set about putting Heather's instructions into practice, so the infant thrived, soon growing plump and content.

Heather was overjoyed when Comfort arrived on the compound early one morning, proud to show off her little daughter.

'What is her name?' Heather asked after admiring the sleeping infant and congratulating the girl on her progress.

'I git her name from de bible. Musah, dat man at de Mission tell me story 'bout Ruth. Her name be Ruth. You like dat name?'

'It's a lovely name,' Heather said. 'Has your husband come back? Has he seen the new piccin?'

'No. He no come back, but him know 'bout de piccin an' he sen' me money.'

When Heather told Edward about the visit of Comfort and her daughter he breathed a sigh of relief, hoping that the happy outcome would put an end to the clandestine visits.

'I hope our next baby is a girl,' he said.

And it was. Verity was born in England months later while they were on home leave, and Edward adored her from the moment he first saw her. David was lifted up to see his sister and contemplated the pink scrap lying by his mother's side. He crinkled his nose at the sweet warm baby-smell of her. He was a quiet, serious little boy, very gentle, like his father, and this small doll was to bring out an unusually strong protective instinct in one so young.

Heather was pleased for Edward's sake that the baby was a girl, but the pregnancy had been a difficult one. The exhausting heat and humidity of Facriwa had worn her down and she arrived home a few months before the birth sapped of energy and dispirited. She was ashamed of her short temper as her body thickened and her ankles swelled. She craved the English climate, the luxury of a proper bath with hot water straight from the tap. There were so many simple things to look forward to: switching on electric light, picking up a telephone, drinking a glass of water without first having had to boil and filter every drop. She had become over-sensitive to small irritations which had hitherto been accepted as part of the cost of living in a colony which still had a lot of catching up to do. The lack of such rudimentary things assumed the proportion of far greater annoyances and she found herself harbouring one resentment after another.

They had travelled home on one of the Elder Dempster mail boats and although she had never been seasick before, she excelled herself and was sick for almost the entire voyage. A long and painful labour added further strain to her raddled nerves and weary body so that when the baby was finally placed in her arms, she turned away and burst into a flood of tears. She was on the brink of rejecting the child but, as if sensing its denial, the baby gave vent to a loud cry of distress which brought Heather's maternal instinct to the surface at once. She looked down at the crumpled little face reddened seemingly by indignation, the blue eyes appearing to look back at her accusingly as the small mouth puckered ready to make a further aggrieved wail of protest. She held the child to her breast and as soon as she started to suck, Heather felt calm; the tension slipped away and from that moment a special affinity was born between them. Verity would always know how to twist her mother round her little finger.

Their time in England fled by all too quickly and although Heather was in no hurry to return to the hardships of colonial life, she accepted that it had many compensations. She would be glad to have Sammy there to take over the day-to-day housework, leaving her free to care for the children.

Sammy might have been scatter-brained and unreliable at times, but she knew she would be unable to cope for long without him or some other houseboy. It had been arranged before they left Tegey that Sammy's eldest daughter, Hawa, should help him with some of the laundry work. Sammy would show her how to heat the heavy flat irons on top of the monster stove, to spit on them to assess their heat, then wipe them clean with a pair of Edward's worn-out underpants. These were kept specifically for the purpose unless Sammy deemed them insufficiently past their prime, in which case, he would wear them himself until he judged them to be mature. Heather had become so used to the washing being dry within an hour of being hung out on the line in her African garden, she resented battling with a spiteful English teeth-chattering wind to hang out Verity's nappies on the garden clothes line, or having the house steamed-up when all the washing had to be draped around the kitchen fire where it quickly made the windows weep with condensation. The children were spoilt by their grandparents who gave them expensive toys and indulged their every whim, but she reckoned this would do no harm – they would soon be back in Africa and they may not see each other again for two or three years.

Her spirits lifted considerably when Edward returned from a visit to the Colonial Office in London with news that they would not be returning to Tegey. Edward had been posted to a new experimental farm near Mampi, a large town in the north where they would be allocated a bigger bungalow with – joy of joys – electricity and running water. To such luxury would be the added pleasure of expatriate neighbours and the social life that came with them. The thought of returning under such improved conditions cheered Heather and reassured her mother who had been worried about her daughter 'going back to that primitive and dangerous place with two small children.' She would also be distanced from Komfo, her bête noire. The sad part would be that she would be more than a full day's drive from the Mission and her wise friend, Musah. Her thoughts turned to Kovina and she wondered if he had left hospital. Would he be sorry to hear of this new posting and would he still visit them now that they would be living outside his district? Perhaps the door had closed on that part of their lives, but intuition told her they would surely meet again.

Had she been able to see into the future, to anticipate the circumstances under which their paths would cross once more, she may have chosen to stay in England.

CHAPTER 10

Heather and Edward were not the only ones pleased with the new posting; Sammy and his family also welcomed the move. They were now also the proud tenants of a brick-built house with two rooms, a proper shower and a corrugated iron roof, instead of the old thatched mud quarters. His children had never lived in a house with electric light before, and spent the first few days in their new quarters switching the lights on and off, jumping up and down and squealing with laughter until the novelty wore off.

Heather was disappointed to discover that the kitchen at their new location was separate from the main building as before, and that heating water for baths and preparing meals still had to be done on a log-eating stove, though she fancied this one had a friendlier demeanour. It didn't appear to scowl at her as had her old one in Tegey.

The electricity supply was such that in addition to the lights and the refrigerator, it could, on a good day, cope with the radio, a toaster, a kettle and an iron. Heather counted these small improvements as blessings, even though the power supply was erratic and Tilley lamps and candles were always at the ready to deal with frequent emergency blackouts. From his first sight of it, Sammy didn't trust the electric iron. He viewed it with suspicion and then with fear when he kept getting the flex tangled round his ankles. In the end he went back to using the heavy old flat irons, which Heather reckoned he preferred because he liked the sizzling sound they made when he spat on them to test their heat.

'Dat new iron be no good, Missis,' he told Heather. 'Him done bite me and him done bugger up Massa's shorts propah.' He showed her the angry burn on his hand where the iron had 'bitten' him and the brown scorch on Edward's white shorts. Heather agreed wholeheartedly that it would be far safer for him to return to the faithful old irons, welcoming the change for she had missed hearing the houseboy's happy out-of-tune singing as he pressed the clothes. In his brief battle with the electric iron the cheerful songs had ceased and were replaced by indignant mutterings and curses as the reptilian flex followed his every move like a blood-sucking leech.

They had been living in the new bungalow at Mampi for some time before Kovina put in an appearance. He was a good deal thinner after his lengthy stay in Sekari Hospital. He told them that an infection, followed by one complication after another, had prolonged his recovery from the surgery that removed the bullet from his abdomen. He still had two weeks' sick leave before he was due to return to work at the District Commissioner's Office, and thought he would take this opportunity to pay them a visit to see how they had enjoyed their home leave. He admired Verity, the new arrival, and renewed his acquaintance with David, who brought him a red fire engine for inspection. It was one of the new toys given to him by his grandparents and he watched Kovina as he wound it up and set it to run along the floor.

News had reached them soon after their arrival back in Africa that Komfo had been arrested and was serving a term in Sekari gaol for inciting a riot, about which Heather was vastly relieved, but when Kovina brought them up to date with all the latest news from Tegey and Sekari, she discovered her relief was short lived. Apparently Komfo had escaped when a fire broke out at the gaol, which it was suspected had been started by some of his supporters to secure his release.

Heather was also disturbed to learn from Kovina that Musah had been ill with malaria and had left the Mission quite suddenly. No one knew why, or where he had gone, but one of the older students at the school had taken his place for the time being.

However, Comfort and her baby daughter, Ruth, were thriving and her husband had returned to the village, though rumour had it that he was one of the gang who had been involved with starting the prison fire that enabled Komfo to escape.

Kovina still made no mention of the events leading up to his injury, provoking Heather to ask outright what had happened at the juju-plagued burial ground. He chose not to reply and, deliberately avoiding her questioning gaze, he turned to Edward with a barely perceptible shake of his head. Then, as if thinking better of it, he said dismissively: 'It seems that I interrupted some sort of sacrificial ritual being carried out by Komfo and members of his clique. I should never have seen or heard what was taking place and they felt the need to silence me.'

'And what exactly was going on?' Heather persevered, determined not to be put off once again. But Kovina preferred to give the impression that he hadn't heard, and quickly changed the subject.

Mampi boasted a British Council library and a small expatriate club house which occasionally had a film show or a dance so that there was more scope for social activities, but most of her spare time, when not busy with the children, Heather spent improving the large garden she had inherited from the previous owner. As Mampi was near a wide river which did not dry up during the dry season, there was an ample water supply and she now had the luxury of a garden hose. Sammy was relieved to know that he need no longer save the bathwater.

For a time life ran smoothly, if with a certain undercurrent of unease as small pockets of unrest erupted spasmodically and were promptly dealt with by the army or the police. Such disturbances usually flared following political gatherings when feelings ran high and tempers were frayed. Up until now friction had been mainly between tribes who took sides according to the leanings of their individual chiefs, but recently a new element had sprung into being. Some of the road blocks manned by Facriwan police were being attacked, the guards overpowered and killed. The attackers then donned the uniform of the dead policemen and took the place of their victims at the road block. As cards and mammy lorries drew up at the barricade, the drivers were dragged out of their vehicles and forced to hand over their money or any goods the bogus police thought worth snatching. Those imprudent enough to refuse to hand over their belongings were disposed of without ceremony. So far, none of the expatriates in the area had been involved in any of the incidents, but now the District Commissioner issued a warning advising expatriate wives not to travel beyond certain designated boundaries unaccompanied; there being no point in taking chances while such a volatile situation prevailed.

Heather was hardly affected by any of the unpleasant episodes; over the weeks she had become so used to hearing horror stories of what was taking place that a psychological barrier had sealed off part of her mind; as soon as talk of some new atrocity was aired in her presence, the shutters would come down. In the beginning, the suffering, cruelty and sheer futility of it all had distressed her, but after a long battle with her conscience, she finally gave up worrying and accepted the fact that there was nothing she could do about it. If the Facriwans felt the need to beat the living daylights out of their fellow men, that was up to them.

However, this state of affairs changed when a bomb was planted on the railway line into Mampi. As a result, the arrival of the Government specie box containing cash for Edward's labourers was delayed and he was unable to pay them. One of the headmen led a deputation to Edward's office at the experimental station some five miles out of town, but finding he was not present, he and his followers marched to the Greenwoods' bungalow to demand their wages. On the way they collected a number of inquisitive bystanders who had nothing better to do and joined in just for the fun of it and in the hope of witnessing a scrap.

Heather was busy putting shade mats over some young lettuce plants in her vegetable plot when she found herself surrounded by an excited mob of workers and hangers-on, shaking their fists, shouting, and waving pangas or sticks picked up along the way. The headman's call for silence was ignored as he told her they had come for their wages. Trying not to panic, she tried to explain above the racket going on around her why they had not been paid and told the headman that they would all get their money as soon as the railway line had been cleared and the train was able to get through.

David had been playing indoors when the noise from outside alarmed him and he ran out on to the verandah to see what was going on. As soon as he caught sight of his mother hemmed in by the menacing crowd, he picked up his small cricket bat, ran down the steps and waded in amongst the men, waving his bat and shouting:

'Leave my Mummy alone. Go away!'

The crowd fell silent and drew back a pace as the small boy launched himself at the first man in his path, whacking his knees with the bat. The steam was immediately taken out of the situation as the Africans laughed and hooted at their unfortunate brother who hopped about from one foot to another trying in vain to grapple with the package of furious indignation that now sank its teeth into his hand as he tried to keep the wriggling child at arm's length. But as soon as he saw his chance, he brought his hand down and dealt David a resounding slap across his head. His action had a dramatic effect on the onlookers. A low growl grew into a roar as the nearest men set about him in a flurry of flailing fists and sticks. The reason for their march on the bungalow was temporarily set aside; no matter what the provocation, they were not prepared to see one of their number hit a white man's piccin who had been trying to protect his mother.

Heather ran towards her son as he rubbed his head, trying to hold back tears of pain and frustration, but before she could reach him, a man broke through the crowd and scooped the boy up, cradling him in his arms as he walked away from the crowd and up the verandah steps. Heather followed, reaching them as the man gently set David on his feet, still keeping a protective arm round his shoulders, then he looked up and smiled. It was Musah.

'There's no need to worry now,' he said, patting David's head. 'They'll go away now that they've had a bit of excitement.'

'Oh, Musah! Thank God you came! I was so frightened and they wouldn't listen to me when I tried to explain,' Heather said, and sank on to one of the verandah chairs, her legs shaking after the shock of the encounter. She called to Sammy to bring them a drink while her nerves settled and she was able to pay more attention to her unexpected visitor.

'I didn't know you were here in Mampi,' she said. 'Kovina called on us a few weeks ago and he told us you'd been ill and had left the Mission, but he had no idea where you'd gone.'

'I only arrived this morning,' Musah explained. 'I was on the train that was delayed, so I left it and got a lift on a mammy lorry for the last stretch of the journey.'

'Was Kovina right, have you been ill?'

'Yes, but it was just a bout of malaria. When I recovered I decided it was time to move on. So I've been travelling all around the country to see what is happening in different areas.' He shook his head. 'It's not good. It is relatively quiet here, but in other parts there is much trouble, and I fear it will get a great deal worse before it's over.'

'I don't think it will be over until Facriwa has its own government, do you?' Heather asked.

'No. I'm afraid you're right and even then the squabbling between tribes will still go on. Self-government won't bring the overnight transformation that a lot of people expect. It will take time for all the improvements to be made and the young men are impatient, they want everything to happen at once.' He smiled ruefully.

'Was it chance that brought you here to Mampi, or did you know about Edward's new posting?'

'I knew you were here within hours of your arrival.' Musah gave her a sideways look and smiled.

'Oh yes, of course! How silly of me.' The Facriwan grapevine was still beating out minor events as well as drumming headline news the length and breadth of the Colony. Heather found the drums were not as vocal here as they had been in Tegey. Perhaps Mampi had too many buildings and the throbbing couldn't penetrate the concrete jungle of offices and shops, or perhaps she had grown so used to them, their impact had lessened. Nevertheless, their voice was still more reliable than the telephone which broke down every time there was a storm, or as was now frequently the case, the lines were cut deliberately.

'You realise that Komfo also knows where you are?'

Heather was taken aback by the sudden question.

'I hadn't really thought about it, Musah, but of course if you know, so will he and every other Tom, Dick and Harry, I shouldn't wonder.'

'You mustn't forget that he still nurses a grudge. Not only against you, but also your husband.'

'But why? What's he got against Edward?'

'Don't you see? He intended that Kovina should die up there at the burial ground but Edward arrived in time to get him to hospital and save his life,' Musah said, squatting on the floor with David and playing with a wooden garage and his Dinky toy cars. 'And it was partly because of the information Kovina gave the District Commissioner when he was in hospital that the witch doctor ended up in prison.'

'But Edward couldn't have left Kovina there to die.'

'Some men would have done so, and it might have been better for Edward had he not become involved.'

'Oh, I think that's going a bit too far,' Heather said, but despite herself she felt a mounting dread at the thought of the vindictive little witch doctor. She realised suddenly that she had never seen Komfo and had no idea what he looked like, though she always pictured him as being a small, evil-faced, ferrety looking man.

'What does Komfo actually look like?' she asked Musah.

'He's small, thin and wiry but extremely strong. He has been known to crush stones in his hands. He was born deformed,' Musah said, closing his eyes to conjure up a clearer picture. 'One of his legs is shorter than the other which makes him walk with a limp. Two fingers are missing from his left hand.' He thought a minute, then continued: 'His voice is strong, very deep, unexpectedly so in one of such small stature, and this alone seems to put fear into some men.'

'Perhaps his deformity should take some of the blame for his vicious nature,' Heather thought aloud, grudgingly giving Komfo the benefit of the doubt. 'There must surely be some reason for his spiteful character.'

Musah shook his head. 'When he was sixteen or thereabouts he poisoned the midwife who had tended his mother when he was born. He told the village elders that the midwife had laid a curse on his mother to make sure all her male offspring would be born incomplete.'

'And was that so? Did Komfo have any brothers?'

'He had two brothers. One was stillborn and the other lived for only two days. He had three sisters and they are all alive and were born with no abnormality.'

'Oh, it's all beyond me!' Heather said with some vehemence. She pondered over this latest piece of the puzzle, fitting it into the picture being built in her mind.

Musah's voice broke into her thoughts. 'I see David is not wearing the amulet I gave you for his protection.'

Heather was still brooding over Komfo's strange power; how much of it was fact and how much the product of overactive imaginations force-fed with stories of spells, spirits, evil curses and black magic? She didn't give Musah's observation the attention it warranted and waved her hand vaguely in the direction of David's bedroom.

'It's quite safe. It's in his drawer.' Then as she perceived the hurt in his eyes. 'It's not safe for David to wear it, Musah. He would be sure to lose it, you know what kids are.' She could have added that the other children would have made fun of him if he had worn the leather charm, and as his mother, she herself would have been thought superstitious and eccentric for allowing him to do so.

Later in the day, Edward was extremely angry when Heather recounted the day's events. He would sack the headman, he said, and any other of the labourers who were in the thick of the fracas.

'The cheek of it – in my own garden! What the hell did they think they were playing at?'

'I think they just wanted their money. They were afraid they weren't going to be paid. They weren't really malevolent towards me.'

'You don't understand the temperament of these people – their tempers can flare up in a minute. You could have been dealing with a ticking bomb, and goodness knows what would have happened if Musah hadn't arrived when he did. What did he come here for anyway? Is he looking for work?'

'He didn't say as much, and I didn't think to ask.'

'Well, if he's looking for work, you could offer him a job as gardener. He might like a change after looking after the Mission gardens for so long.'

'Can we really afford it?' Heather asked.

'This garden is twice the size of the one we had in Tegey. You can't manage it on your own and there are plenty of other ways he could be useful.'

'He didn't say whether he'd be coming back. Perhaps he spoke to Sammy before he left. He may have told him if he's on the way back to the Mission. It would certainly be a help to have him around, and David thinks the world of him. Musah played with him and told him stories this afternoon while I was busy with Verity.'

'If any more trouble arose, Sammy wouldn't be much help – you know he's a firm believer in spells and evil curses and is scared stiff of Komfo. On the other hand, I should think Musah is just the sort of chap to take anybody on,' Edward said.

'I don't know how much they paid him at the Mission; he may want more than we can afford.'

'We can only ask him, and we can offer him much better quarters than he had at the Mission.'

'Sammy won't think much of that. His family has spilled over into the spare quarters,' Heather told him.

'That's his own lookout – he knows he's not entitled to them.'

Heather laughed. 'He's saving up for more cows to buy another wife,'

'He can have as many wives as he likes but they can't all stay on this compound,' Edward said. 'We're not going to end up like that new young bachelor...what's his name?'

'You mean Robin Moorfield, the Cable and Wireless engineer?'

'Yes. His houseboy's got three wives with three or four kids apiece. It's absolute bedlam over there. God knows how he puts up with it.'

'So Sammy has a bit of catching up to do!' Heather said.

'I wouldn't encourage him, although chances are that Milah would wipe the floor with Sammy if he introduced some nubile young wench into his household.'

'Don't you believe it. Milah would be delighted to be the queen bee and have someone she could boss around and make do most of the housework, not to mention digging the vegetable patch.'

'Well, what about it? Shall I get a new young bride to help you around the house?'

He ducked to avoid the book Heather threw at him.

A yelp from the doorway drew their attention to where Sammy stood, mouth agape and eyes popping to see Missis throwing things at Massa.

'It's all right, Sammy. We aren't fighting,' Heather told him.

'Don't you believe it. Missis done beat me up propah.' Edward said, cowering away from her and rubbing imaginary bruises. Sammy looked from one to the other for several seconds while it sank in, then he fell against the wall in paroxysms of laughter, tears pouring down his cheeks. Sammy never did things by halves.

CHAPTER 11

Much to Heather's delight, Musah started work as their gardener and her 'right hand man,' an arrangement which suited them all very well. Edward was particularly pleased as it relieved him of some of the worry when he had to leave Heather and the children alone in the bungalow at night. Along with most expatriates in the district, he had been conscripted to help the police to patrol areas where there were pockets of unrest. They usually got wind of political meetings, which were now banned unless they had prior authority from the District Commissioner or a senior police officer, and then precautions could be set in place. Illegal meetings invariably led to bloodshed, so now jeeps fitted with searchlights toured the Mampi streets after nightfall to seek them out and disperse them, if possible without the use of force.

An element of risk was naturally attached to these patrols and although Edward would normally opt for a quiet life, he admitted the forays were exciting, adding a hint of danger and a pinch of spice to his day-to-day routine. On a recent patrol his jeep had been pelted with bottles and stones when one of the police in his group had leapt off the vehicle to investigate a body at the side of the road. Without warning, the 'body' had sprung up and attacked the policeman with a knife, so later that night when Edward had to probe a pile of ragged clothing in a storm drain to see if it contained anything sinister, he approached it with more than his usual caution. Taking no chances, he prodded the dark mound with his foot, only to discover the body of a man who was well and truly dead, having had a six inch wooden spike driven into his skull. He was the victim of a group of vigilantes who had set themselves the task of clearing Mampi streets of prowlers and vagrants, following a spate of night-time burglaries and arson attacks for which members of their tribe had been accused. The method used for despatching anyone they caught followed the customary punishment used by their ancestors on anyone bringing their tribe into disrepute. It was remarkably effective.

Heather had noticed a change in Edward. To all outward appearances, he seemed to have become hard, almost callous, and immune to the atrocities which daily grew in number. She wondered if he were growing insensitive or simply maturing and becoming more able to cope with repugnant situations. Was he beginning to accept the harsh realities over which he had no control? There was no way she could tell, but she knew he had become more loving, more attentive towards her; and her own feelings for Edward were far deeper and stronger than when they were first married. Perhaps the children had brought them closer, or was it the new dangers that faced them? She was always on tenterhooks when he was away on night patrol and sleep was fitful until he returned at dawn.

Tonight she had felt more uneasy than usual as he kissed her goodbye and walked towards the police jeep. A cloud of premonition settled round her as she bathed David and Verity, and later, as she read their bedtime story, she did so automatically without taking in the meaning of the words and giving them little expression. The children were quick to sense her preoccupation and took advantage, refusing to snuggle down to sleep, and making every excuse their ingenuity could muster: they were too hot, they were thirsty, they weren't tired, they wanted the toilet yet again, until she finally lost patience and spanked the pair of them. She went to bed late, feeling guilty at her lack of patience, and drifted in and out of a troubled dream-filled sleep until Edward returned just before dawn. She clung to him in sheer relief, at last able to dispel the foreboding that had plagued her.

'You mustn't worry so, my love,' he said, smoothing the hair back from her damp forehead. 'I'm never on my own – there are usually five or six of us, and we can always summon extra help if we need to.' He tipped her chin and kissed the tip of her nose. 'Now promise me you won't worry any more, and just remember, the Facriwans have no real quarrel with us.'

'I know that, Edward, but as you've told me, when there's a crowd of them they're so unpredictable.'

On that point he was unable to argue.

At daybreak her premonition and fears were realised when she discovered David's empty bed.

David was nowhere to be found. The tell-tale grease smears on the boy's bedroom door were a sure and frightening sign that he had been abducted. Heather was convinced that Komfo was responsible and raged at the young native policeman who was unfortunate enough to be the first to arrive on the scene following Edward's call to Mampi Central Police Station and the District Commissioner's Office. By the time a more senior police officer appeared with the DC, she was outwardly more calm, but inside she was seething with the need to hit out at somebody or something. Musah and Edward had already left the bungalow to try to gather information from people known to be close to Komfo and who might, if a suitable reward were offered, be prepared to disclose his whereabouts or give some clue as to where David had been taken.

Heather was unable to cry. She was numb, gripped by an ice-cold fear for her son. She returned to his room again and again to stare dry-eyed at the empty bed, at the trough in his pillow where his head had rested, willing herself to wake up and find it was a nightmare, willing the anguish to go away. She picked up one of his favourite toys, a stuffed giraffe, smoothing it, patting it, holding it against her cheek as if it too must have feelings and was missing him. She fumed at her inability to do anything; the waiting would destroy her. She forced herself to keep busy, finding unnecessary jobs to do around the bungalow, pushing Sammy away from the ironing board, banging the iron down on the clothes, venting her spleen as best she could and trying to lessen the pain gnawing at her insides. She tried to find something, anything to blot out the terrifying kaleidoscope of images that constantly flashed through her mind. Her brain played tricks on her; she thought she heard David crying and rushed back into his bedroom and sat on the edge of the bed, his pillow clasped tight against her chest, her face buried in its softness as she rocked back and forth.

Although still very young, Verity sensed the tension and alarm of the adults around her and clung to her mother, nuzzling into her skirt for comfort. As a rule she went to David when she was bothered and upset and now she couldn't understand why he wasn't there. She crawled under the table and sucked her thumb, missing him. Heather found her there and picked her up, cuddling her, rubbing her soft warm cheek. Verity put her chubby little arms around her mother's neck and gave her a fervent, sticky kiss to make things better. Together they collected up the piles of freshly ironed laundry to put them away and as she lay David's shirts and shorts in his bedroom drawer, Heather caught sight of the amulet Musah had given the boy. She picked it up and sat on the bed to take a closer look at the pattern of the fish worked into the leather. The red stone of its eye caught the light from the window and shone clear and bright as a raindrop on a rose petal. Her hand burned and she had a sudden sensation of being lifted up and dropped into a vortex – a whirlpool of wind and water closed round her. She shut her eyes to ward off the dizzy spell, for she told herself that is what it must be, but then she was caught in a net; it was closing round her tighter and tighter as she struggled to get free, gasping for breath and opening her eyes trying to see up to the surface, but she saw the face of the old man once again. He looked directly into her eyes, his face stern, forbidding, until he smiled. His smile was warm and reassuring; it lit up his eyes and seemed to release every pent-up nerve in her body, like the sudden loosening of a puppet's strings, and she felt as if a great weight had been lifted from her.

Then, just as before, the vision disappeared, leaving in its place a stillness, a quiet calm in which she lay on cool grass with a pale uncluttered sky above and only the mesmeric sound of water rippling over smooth pebbles. She came round as from a trance, and as the calming perception faded, she recalled another time, years ago, when she had experienced just such tranquillity. She had been twelve years old and her father had taken her into an old church in the West Country. The memory returned clear and fresh and she could see her father pointing up to the sun slanting through the stained glass windows. Her eyes were drawn to a portrayal of the disciples. One of these 'fishers of men' held in his hands a fish with a gleaming red eye. She sat on a pew at the back of the ancient building with her father, staring at the blinding light of that eye, and experienced the sensation of being held firmly, warmly, completely safe. It seemed to have lasted for a long time, but must have been only seconds.

Heather closed her fingers around the talisman and asked herself if David would have been safe if only she had let him wear it. Was that why the old man had looked at her so sternly? What power could such a primitive piece of native leatherwork hold? Could it have protected him, and from where did its strange psychic influence come that it could affect her so strongly?

The questions had to be swept aside as Sammy kept knocking on the door to draw her attention. She shook free from the thoughts spinning round in her head and went into the sitting room with him to find Kovina standing in the middle of the room. She would never understand what made her react in such a way to this tall African who had such a curious effect on her, but without hesitation she ran to him and rested her head on his chest. As simply as if he had been doing so all his life, Kovina folded his arms around her and kissed the top of her head as if he were comforting a crying child. At that moment Edward walked into the room with Musah. The two men stood in the doorway, as motionless as statues, taking in the extraordinary tableau, until Heather broke away from Kovina's embrace and rushed to Edward.

'Is there any news? Did you find out anything? Does anyone know where Komfo has taken David?' Eager for news, the questions poured from her. She was but a hair's breadth from hysteria. Her son's disappearance, the strange influence the amulet had upon her and now Kovina's unexpected show of affection all conspired to throw her mind off balance. She was shaking, her legs were unsteady and she started to sway. Edward caught her in his arms and carried her to a chair. He held her hands and spoke softly.

'I'm sorry, love, I'm afraid there's little to tell. No one knows – or no one wants to tell us – where Komfo might be, though there have been several reports of people seeing him here in Mampi. Musah knows several of the elders of the local tribes and has set up a line of enquiry and with a bit of luck that should produce some information. But it will take time.'

Musah interrupted sharply, speaking urgently to Kovina in their own tongue, then he nodded briefly to Heather and Edward before both men left the room. Heather tugged at Edward's arm, needing further assurance, but he looked down at her hand blankly, and hesitated before covering it with his own. She noticed that his hand was shaking.

'What is it, Edward? Is there something you're not telling me?' Fear sharpened the pitch of her question.

'As far as the police are concerned there is nothing to link Komfo to David's disappearance.'

'But don't they know about his threats, his antagonism towards us when we were in Tegey? Don't they know he tried to kill Kovina and that you saved his life?'

'Yes, I expect so. I just don't know.' There was a weariness in Edward's voice. He sighed and rubbed his hand across his forehead. He had aged in the last few hours and he looked weighed down, drained. 'Musah spent a long time speaking to the Police Inspector and I dare say he put him wise as to what has been going on. They seemed to know each other. It's odd, but I got the impression that they have worked together before,' he sat down heavily and closed his eyes. 'Anyway, I don't think there's anything more we can do now. We just have to be patient and wait.'

'You look tired out,' Heather said. Edward didn't move or acknowledge her concern. His stillness frightened her. She thought it looked as if he were experiencing some inner turmoil and was battling to hold himself in check to contain the violence it spawned. Guilt caught up with her as she realised she had only thought of herself and her own fears. It must be as bad or even worse for Edward; he had done a full day's work followed by a night's duty scouring Mampi in a police jeep, and had come home to find his son had been snatched away from them. She knelt beside him and lay her head on his knee.

'I'm sorry, dear. I didn't stop to think…' she swallowed, wanting to cry. But knew she mustn't cry now. Edward had had enough without her tears adding to his worries. She braced her shoulders and attempted to be practical. 'You've had nothing to eat. Shall I get Sammy to make you a snack?'

Edward shook his head. 'The thought of food makes me feel sick, but I could do with a drink.'

She took his hand, rubbing it between her own, trying to bring comfort, trying to make amends for her lack of understanding. 'Tea or coffee?'

'Whisky.'

'Whisky? Are you sure?' she asked in surprise. ' Isn't it a bit early?'

'Not the way I'm feeling at the moment,' Edward replied, looking at her, his eyes full of meaning.

For a moment she was perplexed. Why was Edward looking at her like that… almost accusingly? Then it came to her, and she understood.

'Oh, Edward, please don't read anything into what you saw just now, or what you think you saw.'

'Why not? It looked pretty obvious to me.'

'Oh, no! You've got it all wrong. I can explain. Truly I can explain. Kovina turned up unexpectedly just at the time when I needed someone to lean on, someone to cling on to. I don't know how or why it happened. It just did, but it meant absolutely nothing. I was frightened and needed to be assured that everything was going to be all right.'

'Couldn't you have waited until I got home?'

'It wasn't like that, Edward. It was a spur-of-the-moment thing.'

'I'll have to take your word for that.'

'If you don't believe me there's nothing more I can say. If you can't accept that it meant nothing then I'm sorry. I thought you knew me better than that.' Her shoulders slumped. She felt defeated. Punished for something she hadn't done. Suddenly she felt cold and rubbed her hands together as if it were the middle of winter. How could she make him understand when she didn't understand herself? What was happening to them; why did these things have to happen all at once? She knew she had to make another effort, she couldn't bear to risk losing Edward's trust.

'It's hard to explain,' she said, 'just before Kovina came I'd been looking at that amulet Musah gave me for David. I was wondering if David would have been safe if he'd been wearing it. I thought it was my fault he'd been taken. It had a strange effect on me. It was like being lost in a mist and I felt dizzy and disorientated. I saw an old man…I…he…oh, it's so difficult to explain and I don't suppose you could understand unless you felt it too.'

'Are you all right now?'

'Yes. It was a passing thing but it frightened me – it was like being unable to escape from a dream, not being able to wake up, until the old man smiled at me and I felt calm. Then as my fear lifted I heard Sammy banging on the door and I came back to reality to see Kovina standing there and I just ran to him. I don't know why. I honestly don't know why.'

'I'm sorry,' Edward shrugged. 'We'll say no more about it.'

She could have told him about the extraordinary hypnotic power Kovina had over her, ever since she first saw him standing beside Edward on the dockside the day she first set foot in Facriwa. But she couldn't bring herself to talk about it. Now was not the right time; she couldn't even begin to think how to explain it, or what caused the strange phenomenon. If it was a mystery to her, what would Edward make of it, especially under the present fraught circumstances when their nerves were already in tatters with worry over David's disappearance? No – now was not the right time.

Lunch was a pretence, a miserable affair; wrapped up in their own thoughts, they had little to say to each other and they toyed with the meal Sammy had brought to the table, pushing the food from one side of the plate to the other. Sammy shuffled round the table in a new pair of thonged sandals made from old car tyres which flapped and squeaked on the polished floor. Under different conditions it would have provoked some teasing but the houseboy's hunched shoulders and downcast expression portrayed his own misery, and his mood of hopelessness did nothing to lighten their mental burden.

Sammy harboured his own fearful suspicions as to what David's fate might be, and they scared him. He had heard furtive whispers in the market that Komfo was hiding out in an area across the river a few miles north of Mampi, and this prompted him to pack his eldest son off to do a little spying to find out more.

There was little Heather could do but pace up and down bemoaning the enforced inactivity as Edward prepared to return to the police headquarters. He tried to telephone their office for news, but as was often the case, the phone was out of order.

'Can't I come with you?' she asked. 'I feel so helpless, stuck here doing nothing. I can't just sit around here at home all day waiting for scraps of information. I must do something or I'll go mad.'

David patted her shoulder and kissed her cheek.

'I know, waiting around is soul-destroying, but I shan't be gone for long. I'll get straight back as soon as I've found out if there's anything new. Hugh was going to try to get through to Sekari to see if they've got any fresh information as to Komfo's whereabouts, just in case he's involved.' Hugh Greatridge, the Chief Police Officer, was a friend of theirs and would be doing all he could to get David back safely.

'Of course he's involved!' Heather cried. 'Who else would take David? You must make them see that, Edward. Tell them what happened when we were in Tegey.'

Edward put his arms round her and hugged her close. 'It's better that you stay here, love. Remember, Verity needs you too, and Sheila Greatridge and some of the other wives will be calling round to see if they can be of any help. You shouldn't be on your own at a time like this.'

'I don't want any bloody wives! I don't want anyone! I just want to be left alone. I just want David back. That's all I want, just our son back here with us.' She gripped hold of his arm until he felt the bite of her fingernails.

'Of course you do. That's what we all want, and everyone's doing their best to find him. Just hold on and try to be patient. I know it's hard, but remember, he's only been missing a few hours.'

'And what's been happening to him in those few hours? He'll be so frightened. He's only a little boy. What's that evil wretch doing to our son?' Heather's voice rose in her agitation and distress.

'No one knows for certain if Komfo is involved yet. It may be someone else holding on to him in the hope of getting ransom money from us.'

'You don't believe that. You know damn well you don't, so don't try to make me believe it. You know as well as I do who's behind this.'

'We can't know for sure,' Edward repeated quietly, unable to look her in the eye.

Heather turned away, biting on the tight ball of the handkerchief she had been twisting round and round in her hands.

'I'm sorry, but I do know.'

There seemed little point in continuing the argument and Edward kissed her again, squeezing her hand briefly before he left.

By the time Sheila and two other friends arrived, although pale-faced, and to all outward appearances perfectly calm and composed, Heather was inwardly flaming with an anger and dread she found almost impossible to keep in check. Her visitors did their best with comforting words and reassurances, but they were at a loss as to what to say to alleviate her suffering. Such a thing had never happened before in the Colony, so there were no comparisons to be made, no experience to draw from. It was beyond comprehension and so unthinkable that neither expatriates nor Facriwans could take it in. A pall of brooding unease hung over Mampi. This new event had damped down even the present political squabbles.

CHAPTER 12

It was not long before Sammy's son returned from his mission to discover if there was any truth in the rumour that Komfo was holed up across the river, and in the airless pent-up atmosphere of the servant's quarters, he told his father and Musah what he had learned from the tribesmen on the riverbank. Komfo's reputation had not filtered through to them, which explained why they were not intimidated by the witch doctor and spoke without fear of reprisal. To what extent the information they had given the boy could be relied upon was questionable, as all tribes were prone to exaggeration and embellished any story they had to tell as a matter of course.

As soon as every scrap of intelligence had been wrung from the boy, Musah left the compound to borrow a canoe from one of the fishermen living in the huddle of thatched huts that grew like mushrooms along the riverbank. Sammy maintained that he must stay at the bungalow to look after Massa and Missis. Musah agreed, knowing that Heather and Edward would be even further concerned if their houseboy suddenly went missing, and that Sammy was already scared to death of the witch doctor and would be of little use in the search for him and David. It was best that he travelled alone – the frightened servant would only hamper his progress. He gathered a sack full of ebony and ivory animals on loan from a wood carver, intending to pass himself off as an itinerant trader making his way to the coast, if anyone should stop and question him.

He rowed across the river to a small village on the far side where he arranged with one of the elders to have a palaver with their Chief. The Chief was old, bent and gnarled as an old tree and, with his hooked nose and dark watchful eyes, had the appearance of a vulture. After the customary preliminary talk of local and tribal affairs and the pouring of a libation to the Chief's ancestors, the two men retired into the dim smoky interior of the Chief's hut with the gin bottle where a sum of money changed hands and Musah made known the reason for his visit. The Chief hitched his coarse brown robe over his shoulder, screwed up his eyes and picked his teeth with a chewing stick for some seconds before he spoke.

Yes, a stranger had indeed arrived in the area not many nights ago, bringing with him an entourage of men. The Chief did not know their number but they were living in a large cave halfway up the rocky escarpment some distance behind the village settlement. In the early hours of that morning there had been much coming and going to and from the cave. The Chief explained that the young men of the village took turns to sit in a tree growing on a high point on the hill above the cluster of thatched huts, keeping watch during the hours of darkness. For as long as anyone could remember, marauding outcasts from tribes living in adjoining territories had slipped across the borders to carry out night raids on villages along the river, stealing their women, cattle, food from the storage huts and anything else that took their fancy. The man sitting on guard last night on the lookout platform hidden amongst the branches of the tallest tree, had watched all the activity round the cave, but now, when questioned by the Chief, he couldn't say whether a white child had been amongst the people going in and out of the cave; he had been too far away and as the moon had often been streaked by clouds, it had been too dark.

The Chief summoned his elders and when Musah told them of David's abduction there was a rumbling sound of anger from the gathering and a palaver was held at once to devise a plan to enable them to gain entry to the cave and search for the missing child.

A small bush fire would be started and some of the farmers from the village would go to the cave and ask the men there to come and help them beat out the flames before their crops were destroyed. A thin, wiry little man was given the task of entering the cave with Musah if their plan succeeded. Musah looked doubtfully at the dwarfish man who was to accompany him. The Chief smiled knowingly, reading his mind.

'It is all right, my friend; Lima may be of small stature, but he is quick and agile, and is stronger than many men of twice his girth.'

Musah nodded and thanked him for his help.

The plan worked well, though the cave-dwellers were initially reluctant to assist in halting the spread of the bush fire. The promise of chickens for their cooking pot helped them to make up their minds. But a shining black tower of a man stood guard at the entrance to the cave, his great muscular arms folded across his chest as if he meant business. Wearing only a ragged pair of shorts, a necklace of animal teeth and a vicious-looking dagger tied to his leg with a leather strap, he stood motionless in the sunlight like a polished statue in a gallery. He came alive only when asked to help the villagers put out the fire, then he spat in the dust, gave a deep growl and resolutely shook his head. He was not leaving his post.

Lima looked at Musah and slowly shut one eye, then crept away and stationed himself behind some scrubby thorn bushes a few yards to the right of the yawning mouth in the rock face. Musah remained in his hiding place, crouched behind a large red termite hill away to the left, waiting for the next move in the strategy. The firefighters moved off in a chattering pack towards the billowing smoke way down below, and were soon out of sight. All was quiet except for the hum of busy insects and an occasional call from a purple glossy starling. As he lay in wait, Musah's eyes felt heavy in the soporific heat of the day until the peace was shattered as Lima let out a blood-curdling yell, swiftly followed by an agonised scream of absolute terror. Every nerve in Musah's body was on the alert as he steeled himself, ready for action if all went according to plan. The guardian of the cave stood rigid for a split second, then his jaw dropped as if he too were about to scream. He looked quickly to his left and right before making a dash towards the bushes from where the hair-raising racket had come. He never knew what hit him. There was a sudden blurred flurry of movement and Lima was on him, proving the truth of the Chief's assurance as to his agility and strength. The giant fell to the ground as if pole-axed and lay still. Lima quickly bound his ankles and wrists and rolled the inert body out of sight under a prickly thorn bush.

Musah ran to the cave, stopping once inside to give his eyes a chance to get used to the dim interior. Some distance ahead he could see the flickering light of a candle; he approached it slowly, making as little sound as possible. The candle was standing in an old baked bean tin, part of the label still adhering to the rusting metal, and balanced on a narrow ledge jutting out from the rock-face. The wall was adorned here and there near the entrance with pale tufts of fern growing from narrow crevices and hanging down like wet feathers. The atmosphere was damp and cool after the heat outside, with the smell of wood smoke and the strong pungent scent of rancid fat.

When Lima caught up with him they went forward, Musah leading the way and holding the candle aloft. The passage gradually narrowed, sloping upwards and curving round to the left. Small rustling, twitching sounds came from above their heads and when Musah raised the candle they saw the roof of the cave was covered with hundreds of bats, huddled together and hanging down like bunches of strangely shaped black fruit. The ground rose sharply as they penetrated further into the escarpment and suddenly, without warning, they came into a large cavern. The smooth walls were decorated with signs and symbols crudely painted with pigment the colour of dried blood. Light filtered down from a small opening in the roof high above them, and a mound of smouldering embers lay on the ground directly below the natural chimney.

Smoke-blackened cooking pots were scattered around the fireplace and a large shallow bowl lay on its side, spilling out a collection of bones. The two men gazed about them, taking everything in: kerosene tins, a pile of logs, candles, yams, rice dribbling from a gash in a sack propped against the wall, and several empty beer bottles scattered on the ground near two large packing cases.

Musah lighted a fresh candle and handed it to Lima. Their shadows cast distorted shapes around the cavern as they made a swift but methodical tour of inspection. Musah prised open two wooden slats on one of the packing cases and Lima stood on tiptoes to peer inside, his eyes widening at the dull metallic shine of the guns crammed together like sardines and roughly padded round the sides with coir matting.

Tucked away in the darkest part of the underground lair they found a mound of old clothes lying on a heap of straw and coarse sacking. Musah prodded it with his finger. It moved slightly and he poked it again, holding the candle closer. The cloth parted and David's face peered out at them. The boy rubbed sleep from his eyes with the back of his bound wrists and squinted up at them. Musah lifted him up from the bed of straw and removed the rag tied round his mouth while Lima quickly pulled at the thongs binding his ankles and wrists. He was not much bigger than the child and smiled reassuringly at him as he rubbed the limbs where the fetters had bitten into the young captive's tender skin.

The boy watched, his face worried and tear-stained.

'I was frightened,' he said, 'but I knew you would come. Can we go home now, before those men come back? I want Mummy.'

Musah examined him carefully, brushing away bits of straw from his face and hair.

'Don't talk now, David,' Musah warned quietly as he patted the boy's head. 'You can tell us all about it later. We must be quick and get you away from here as fast as we can.' He took a small jar from his pocket and went to rub some brown muddy cream on to David's face.

'Stop it! What are you doing?' the child cried, backing away.

'We have to make you look like one of us,' Musah laughed as he unfolded a piece of dark cloth which had been tied round his waist and wrapped it round the boy. 'Now,' he said looking him over critically, surveying the disguise, 'I think we could almost pass you off as my son.'

They made their way back through the long narrow passage as swiftly as they dare, forever on the watch, and prepared to flatten themselves against the wall should the cave dwellers return and try to prevent their escape. Once out into the open, they didn't return to Lima's village but circled round through the bush in the opposite direction, Lima leading the way until they reached a point higher up on the river. There they found Musah's canoe moored to a tree stump, having been brought upstream by one of the village elders in readiness for the journey home. Lima left Musah and David as they scrambled down the steep bank to the river's edge. The boy shook hands solemnly with his rescuer, much to Lima's embarrassment. He had never had his hand shaken by a white person before, leave alone a small boy, and didn't quite know what to make of it. But it felt good and he would report the fact to the Chief when he got back to his village to let him know that the mission had been safely accomplished.

Although subdued, and inclined to be tearful, David appeared none the worse for his adventure though he was ravenously hungry. He told his ecstatic mother and greatly relieved father that the food he had been offered in the cave smelled rotten and he hadn't been able to eat any of it. He had been covered in rough sacking which prickled his skin when he was snatched from his bed, and still half asleep, he had caught only a vague glimpse of his captors. He had been forced to drink a sweet liquid which made him feel sick and sleepy; his memory of being roughly bundled into a boat and rowed across the river was patchy and blurred.

Heather held the boy in her arms, rocking him as if he were still a baby, her relief all but choking her so that she could barely speak. She crooned softly and gave vent to her emotions by kissing the top of his head over and over again until, put out by such indignity, he managed to wriggle free and run off to hug Verity who was bewildered by all that was going on around her.

Edward took Musah aside and learned how he had followed the lead brought by Sammy's son, and of the help given by Lima, some farmers and the chief of a village tribe across the river. Edward wept inwardly, finding it difficult to sufficiently express his gratitude for the unknown Africans who had risked their lives to help recover his son.

A police guard was put on patrol to keep watch on the bungalow until the kidnappers had been apprehended, but Heather was taking no chances and as soon as David had been bathed to wash away Musah's brown pigment, was freshly clothed and smelled a bit sweeter, she brought the amulet from his room. She made no comment as she placed it round her son's neck, neither did the gardener, though he smiled and nodded his approval before returning to his own quarters where Sammy, Milah and their piccins had prepared a feast, all agog with excitement to hear the story of how he had rescued Massa's boy-piccin.

Attempts to apprehend Komfo and the men who had abducted David continued over the following months, made even more urgent by the discovery of the packing cases full of guns. Despite this, the witch doctor always managed to keep one step ahead of the police and he slipped through their fingers time and time again. Apart from a few nights when he was scared of sleeping alone in his own bedroom, David didn't seem too badly affected by his experience and was inclined to boast about it to his young friends, but the event had a deep and lasting effect on his mother. She suffered harrowing nightmares from which she awoke soaked in perspiration and shaking with a fear that held her in so fierce a grip that it stayed with her, shadowing her throughout the following day. Edward understood the repercussions going on in her mind caused by the trauma of those few hours in which David had been lost to them, and tried to cushion her distress, but to little avail. Her eyes were big and dark, sunk into hollowed cheeks and no amount of gentling could ease her from the depression that wrapped itself around her, taking her away from everyone into a bedevilled world of her own. She would no longer leave the bungalow unless the children were with her, and they were no longer allowed to play in the garden alone; Musah or one of Sammy's sons had to stand guard over them every minute they were out of her sight.

Edward tried many wiles to coax her out of her dejected state, suggesting that the children should stay overnight with friends so that he and Heather could go to a dance or to see a film at the Mampi gymkhana club.

'You've got to get out, you're making this place a prison for yourself and the children,' he reasoned, 'and it's not good for any of us.'

'I'm all right. Just leave me alone. How can I ever feel that David and Verity are safe as long as that evil man is somewhere out there?' Heather said quietly. She sensed Edward's disquiet about her state of mind but there was nothing she could do; she too was bewildered by it, disturbed by her own private belief that she could no longer think rationally.

'The police will catch up with him sooner or later, I'm sure of that,' Edward said confidently. 'After all, we aren't the only ones after Komfo's blood, and there must be plenty of others with old scores to settle.'

'But too many people are scared of him; everyone who comes in contact with that tyrant seems to be hypnotised by his power. Even those who work for him only stay with him because they're too frightened to disobey him. It's as if he's got everyone in a trap, a maze from which there's no escape and they don't know where to turn.'

'All the more reason to believe that one of these days he'll go too far with his demands on their allegiance and sooner or later, someone's going to snap and inform on him. He'll get his comeuppance before long, just you wait and see.'

But Heather wasn't listening – she had heard it all so many times before. Edward tried another tack: 'Let's forget about the wretched man, even if it's only for a few hours. Let's throw a party. Come on, we should be thankful that Musah found David safe and sound. We should be celebrating, not shutting ourselves away and brooding about what could have happened to him. It's time to draw a line under the whole thing and have a party.'

At first, Heather showed no enthusiasm, but gradually Edward persuaded her, backed up by a little coercion from the children, especially David, who thought the party should include balloons, crackers and a big iced cake with candles. Sammy was also very much in favour, knowing very well that any such occasion would require large quantities of food and drink, and in all probability some of this would come his way. Missis always gave him any food that was left over. Another thing which he took into account was the extra standing it would give him among the other houseboys and cooks when he went to market. A party could be relied upon to engender the interest and curiosity of all the expatriate servants, for it entailed extra help in the kitchen and extra money in the pockets of whoever Sammy chose to assist him with the preparations.

Lists were made and preparations were set in motion; crates of beer, tonic and soda water were stacked in the bathroom ready to be put in the bath on the day of the party and covered with blocks of ice ordered from Mampi Cold Store; their own refrigerator was not big enough to cope and even if it were, the electricity supply was far too unreliable.

Kovina visited the compound the day before the party. Heather caught a glimpse of him as he went into Musah's quarters and wondered why he had come to see the gardener. No doubt he would call on her presently to tell her about it.

But he didn't, which made her wonder if he might be feeling embarrassed over Edward walking in just as he had embraced her on the day David went missing. Perhaps Musah would tell her the reason for Kovina's call when they made their customary inspection of the garden later in the day. Again she was disappointed as Musah made no mention of the visit and she couldn't ask – it would look as if she were prying into their affairs. And, she thought, wasn't that exactly what she would like to do? She was intrigued as to what the two men were up to. They seemed to have a rapport and this she attributed to the time they spent together as boys years ago at the Catholic Mission, but she felt there must be more to it than that. She figured that Musah must be a little older than Kovina; perhaps he had once entranced him with his stories just as her own son now listened to the absorbing tales the engaging gardener had to tell.

The party was in full swing. Heather felt relaxed for the first time in weeks and thought this was because of what had happened earlier in the evening when she had given David his bath. She had held his amulet in her hand for a moment, carefully avoiding looking at the ruby eye of the fish as she had placed it on the bathroom medicine cabinet. From the corner of her eye she had caught sight of what appeared to be a rainbow on the bathroom wall. Rain dripped from the highest point of its arch and fell on to her sandals. When she had taken a towel from the rail to wipe away the raindrops, only to find that her feet were completely dry, a skein of sensation she could only describe as an echo worked its way up from her toes to the top of her head. It was as if she had put down a burden, or had been released from an inner prison. On reflection, she told herself, it was probably the stiff gin Edward had prepared for her earlier that had something to do with the loosening of the tension that had built within her over the last few months. And perhaps the light shining into the ruby eye of the fish had caused the rainbow to appear on the wall. She would never know.

Their guests were seated at tables on the wide verandah or stood in groups round the makeshift bar Edward had set up in the dining room next to the buffet supper table. Conversation was diplomatically steered away from personal matters, and concentrated instead on the latest reports of riots and strikes in other parts of the Colony. Everyone had a different bit of gossip or another unconfirmed rumour gleaned mainly from their Facriwan servants or workmates. Even allowing for exaggeration, when pieced together, the finished jigsaw showed a distinct worsening of the situation throughout the country.

Someone wound the gramophone, putting a Victor Sylvester record on the turntable, and couples started dancing, welcoming the chance to take their minds off more serious matters if only for a brief spell. The first distraction came when David's cat, Cooper, walked up the verandah steps and on to the 'dance floor', proudly bearing a small snake in his jaws. He was a good hunter and brought dead snakes into the house as regularly as any of his counterparts in England would deposit a moribund mouse on to the Axminster and wait for its owner's pat of approval. Unfortunately however, Cooper had failed on this occasion to complete the coup-de-grace, for when he lay the snake at Heather's feet and sat bank on his haunches to receive due accolade, the snake promptly made a dash for freedom and slithered off to find sanctuary under the sideboard, causing everyone to leap on to chairs or rush from the room. Edward soon hooked the reptile out from its cover with a walking stick and recognising it as a harmless type, let it go into one of the flowerbeds in the garden. Nevertheless, the incident was considered a valid reason for a round of doubles.

The party resumed noisily and with marked enthusiasm when a distraction of a very different calibre hit them just after midnight.

CHAPTER 13

A police jeep came hurtling up the drive scattering gravel like a bow-wave from beneath its tyres as it skidded to a halt at the foot of the verandah steps. Danny Winters, one of the men who worked at the wireless station, jumped from the vehicle, raced up the stairs and ran into the bungalow. He was a newcomer to Facriwa and had only been in the Colony a few weeks, and it was soon apparent to everyone at the party that the young man was distraught. He was gasping for breath and his voice was pitched unnaturally high as he blurted out his news in stuttering fits and starts.

'The train from the north – it arrived about ten minutes ago. Very late. Nearly all the passengers dead or dying.' The words were panted from him, his eyes re-living the horror of what he had seen. He paused for breath as Edward put a glass into his trembling hand and led him to a chair.

'Take your time, Danny, just steady up a minute until you've got your breath back. No need to rush.' He put a hand on the man's shoulder.

Danny gulped down some of the drink and crumpled back into the chair, exhausted by the event he had just witnessed. No one had warned him of anything like this when he was interviewed for the job in London; he was raw, unprepared.

'It's just awful. God knows how the driver made it as far as this. There are bodies all over the place. I don't think any of them have been shot,' he brushed his forehead with the back of his sleeve and took another mouthful from the glass. 'They've all been mutilated, hacked about. Cut to pieces, stabbed with spears.' His hand started to shake uncontrollably and the drink slopped over the edge of the glass, leaving darks stains on his trousers. His face was putty-coloured, his eyes wide and staring as he tried to describe the scene. He slumped forward, his shoulders shaking as great rending sobs overtook him.

'Does anyone know who did it?' Edward asked gently.

It was some minutes before Danny could reply.

'The driver was incoherent with fright, and in a great deal of pain. He's been badly hurt, but from what we could make of his rambling, it seems that the train was flagged down at the Beji Junction. You know the place… where it has to slow down because of the sharp bend. Then a mob just swarmed all over the carriages attacking everyone with machetes, killing haphazardly, even the children. No one was spared.'

'Do you know if the train was full?'

'No. It's hard to tell; some of the passengers may have been able to run away into the bush when the attack started. Dr Maclean was on the scene almost at once, but he needs help to move the survivors to the hospital. It looks as if the attack had been planned because all the ambulances at the hospital have had their tyres slashed or the rotor arms removed.'

As Danny was giving them the news, the guests were quietly preparing to leave, anxious to get to the scene to see what help they could give. The full impact of the event would take time to sink in.

'I don't think any of the ladies should go,' Danny said, 'there's little you can do unless you have any nursing experience. It's too late…too late… and the sight will just sicken you.' He leaned forward and held his head in his hands, trying to obliterate the obscenity from his mind.

The scene of carnage would remain forever in the minds of those who saw it. The acrid stench of death, the screams of those with arms and legs barely still joined to their bodies and the keening cries of those who had discovered relatives amongst the dead would remain engraved on their minds with cruel clarity. The sight of heads with empty eye sockets, ears cut off, bellies slashed open and blood and entrails staining the dusty floor of the carriages turned even the strongest stomach. Helpers did their best, injecting morphine, bandaging, comforting, or just covering bodies that were beyond help; most of them leaving the track at intervals to vomit their revulsion into the bushes, eyes bruised with the cruelty of what they saw, ears trying to blot out the crying, the wailing.

Those onlookers who came just to stare held bush lamps high above their heads, surrounded by moths and flying termites drawn by the flickering light as it played a sombre game between the shadows. His sleeves rolled up, and his face drawn, Reggie Maclean worked his way down the stricken train, issuing quiet instructions to his team of aides as to which of the injured should be taken to the hospital and which would soon have no part to play in this life.

Edward went from carriage to carriage with a police officer searching for someone among the ill-fated passengers who might yet be conscious and lucid enough to give coherent details of what had happened – and perhaps be able to recognise and name some of the perpetrators of this lust to kill and maim. As he entered one carriage he saw a woman lying on the floor. Her breasts had been severed but she was still alive. She was moaning softly but as she heard Edward's movements in the carriage her eyes opened; dulled with pain, they signalled to him and he looked around the blood-spattered compartment but could see nothing in the poor light. He knelt beside the woman and as he took her hand a faint sound came from under one of the seats. He bent low to peer beneath and saw a baby lying bundled up in a cotton blanket. He guessed it had been hastily hidden away to save its life as the attackers struck. He lifted the infant from its place of safety, cradling it to his chest, overwhelmed with relief and thanks at finding something alive and unharmed. He rocked it, humming tunelessly to cover the pent-up anger that welled inside him. The baby's mother watched with dimming eyes and tried to lift her arms to the child but they fell to her side. For a brief moment her eyes sought Edward's and he held the baby close to her cheek, but already her eyes had glazed, her head rolled to one side and lay still.

There was one white man among the dead; a catholic priest who had been visiting friends while on local leave from his missionary school in the Gold Coast. His genitals had been cut off and his throat cut with such force that he was almost decapitated.

For several days following what came to be known in the press and on radio as 'the train of death' incident, an uneasy quiet lay over Mampi township while people tried to come to terms with the massacre, still hard put to believe what had actually happened. This was so much more than the tribal squabbles which occurred regularly, ending in a skirmish of one sort or another, the poaching of cattle or tit-for-tat burning of crops. It was beyond the comprehension of most of the population and was stark proof that whoever was behind the atrocity meant business. It was a fearful warning to all that the person behind the carnage was a force to be reckoned with and one prepared to use his power to kill anyone, be they white or black, who stood in his way.

Musah asked Heather if he might go back to the Mission for a few days.

She agreed at once, but he gave no reason for the visit, only reassuring her that David, the 'small master', would be quite safe during his absence provided he wore the amulet at all times. The gardener was very protective and watchful in his care of David, and the boy, sensitive as most children are to that kind of affection, had a special regard amounting almost to hero-worship for the man who had found him in the cave and brought him safely home.

'Of course you can go, Musah,' Heather said, 'and while you're down in Tegey, see if you can find Comfort. I would like to know how she and Ruth are getting on.' She would have liked to asked him to enquire after Kovina also; she had neither seen nor heard anything of him since that brief glimpse as he went into Musah's quarters the day before the party. It seemed odd that he had not been in touch with them since David's safe return or the massacre on the train. There were so many questions she wanted to ask him. She was still puzzled by his visit to Musah and wondered if he knew of Komfo's whereabouts, or if the witch doctor had anything to do with the train of death. Would he go that far? Edward could offer no answers when she tried to sound him out, though he admitted he was pretty sure Kovina and Musah had some sort of covert alliance, be it political or something to do with Kovina's work. One thing seemed certain; both men had reason to want the witch doctor brought to justice.

The last day of the month was pay day for Sammy, when Edward gave him ten pounds. This was supplemented by Heather with bags of sugar and rice, and sometimes tins of sardines or corned beef. Heather knew that the houseboy took some of the tins of cat food she gave him for David's cat, Cooper. She had seen him in the kitchen spreading it on his bread.

'I think Sammy prefers the tins of cat food to the corned beef,' Heather told Edward one morning as they sat at breakfast with the children.

'Then why don't you give him two tins of cat food instead of one tin of corned beef? It would work out a darn sight cheaper,' Edward suggested with a grin.

'Sammy eats lizards and bats,' David broke in enthusiastically. 'Can we have lizards and bats too?'

'No, I don't think so. I don't think you'd like them. They're full of small bones,' Heather pointed out reasonably enough. But Verity banged her Mickey Mouse spoon on the table with vigour.

'Lizard, lizard, lizard,' she shouted, flicking her cornflakes about the table and on to the floor. Her vocabulary grew day by day and she always tried to copy her brother.

'Oh, do shut up!' David scolded, and prodded her with his fork.

Verity's face puckered, ready to let everyone know she'd been spiked.

'That's quite enough, you two,' Edward warned.

Sammy asked for two pounds extra when Edward paid him his money that day.

'What's up? What's it for this time, Sammy? Is Milah begging you for another new dress?' It was customary for the houseboy to haggle for more money each month, and sometimes Edward would part with some extra shillings, always on the understanding that it would be deducted from the coming month's pay, though it seldom worked out that way.

'No, Massa. Some big man from de town come see me. He say I must ask you for more money.'

'Who is this man?'

'He say he be officer from de gov-ment. He say if you no give me more money I must stop work. He say I must give him de extra money.'

'And what is this man from the government going to give you for the money?'

'Him no tell me dat. He say if I no give him money he go beat me propah.'

'Next time he comes to ask for money, you tell him to come and see me,' Edward said, angered by the attempted extortion.

'No, Massa, I no fit do dat. If him find out I tell Massa, him done go beat me.'

Edward soon learned from other expatriates in the area that their servants were also being coerced into going on strike for more money, most of which was intended to line the pockets of the mystery men organising the strike. The majority of them refused on principle to hand over the extra cash which, rumour had it, was to boost the funds of Komfo's political party. There was even talk of the money being spirited across the border to buy arms and ammunition. A few of the older and more loyal servants who refused to go on strike were badly beaten up on their way home from the market. After three or four weeks, the servants who had gone on strike realised they were going to get no pay at all, would have to vacate their living quarters, and could even end up with no job to return to. Eventually, most of them started to trickle back to work, morose and disgruntled to discover that things had gone on very well without them. Finally, the strike fizzled out, and the shadowy instigators were thwarted for the time being, but it left behind an unpleasant atmosphere and the distinct impression that further trouble was brewing.

Sammy had reluctantly joined the strike along with the other servants and Heather breathed a sigh of relief when he returned. Although she was perfectly capable of doing the housework and cooking, the extreme heat and humidity rendered her exhausted by midday. On the other hand, there were points in its favour; the children thoroughly enjoyed the experience for it introduced them to some new games. Heather put great piles of laundry into the bath with soap and warm water and David and Verity removed their shoes and socks and had the time of their lives jumping up and down on the sheets and clothes to stamp out the stains and dirt. Edward watched this carry-on with a wry smile and said it was giving them good training for treading the grapes when they retired to some glorious vineyard in sunny Spain or Portugal to make their fortune.

However, the laundry activities often ended in tears as Verity accused her brother of splashing soap into her eyes and took a swipe at him with a wet pillow case. He quickly responded to the attack by ramming a pair of his father's underpants over her head. The lively episodes always ended with more water on the floor than in the bath and in the end had to be suspended.

Anxious to help his mother and to show that he was grown up, David tried his hand at chopping wood to feed the ever-hungry stove, until Heather caught sight of him from the window, wielding the heavy axe and missing his fingers by a hair's breadth. Much to the boy's chagrin, all wood-chopping was forbidden just as he reckoned he was beginning to get the hang of it.

The children also helped in the kitchen; Verity stood on an upturned box to reach the table as they rolled out pastry with great enthusiasm, while Heather kneaded dough for bread. By the time they had finished moulding the pastry into animal shapes or had rolled it into balls, it had acquired a strange grey colour. Nevertheless, they were not in the least put off when the unidentifiable lumps of cooked pastry were taken from the oven – and they ate their own products with far greater enjoyment than anything Sammy had ever produced.

Sammy turned up in the kitchen early one morning ready to light the stove and make the bread for the day as if he had never been away. He sang happily to himself and the small matter of the strike was never mentioned by any of the adults, though David soon let his friend and houseboy know in no uncertain terms that he had done the washing, wood-chopping and cooking more or less single-handed in Sammy's absence.

'Dis small Massa, him be plenty clebber houseboy,' Sammy said, patting David's head affectionately as Heather came into the kitchen.

There was no word from Musah. He had been gone for more than a month and none of the travellers from Tegey and Sekari had any news of him.

'He told me he would only be away for a few days,' Heather told Edward. 'I'm worried about him. I don't like this silence.'

'Musah can look after himself. There's no need to worry about him. He'll turn up soon, you'll see.'

'It's all very well to say that, but I can't help feeling anxious. It's not like him. and I'm afraid he could have got mixed up with some of Komfo's bully boys down there. I'm sure he's done nothing but brood about getting even with the wretched man ever since he kidnapped David.'

'You've just got to accept the fact that we have absolutely no proof that Komfo had anything to do with it. Although the police believe he was involved, there's never been any concrete evidence that he was, either with that or the train massacre.' Edward said, but he could see the anger and disbelief in Heather's eyes and closed the subject quickly before the impending outburst.

'I have to go down to Sekari myself in a few days, and if he's not back by then, I'll make some enquiries.'

'Can't we all go?' Heather asked eagerly. 'Can't we come with you? It would be

a break for the children.'

'I don't think that's a good idea. It's a long way and the roads are almost impassable in places after that recent lot of heavy rain. We'd be stopped at all the road-blocks and the kids would be bored stiff and crotchety long before we'd got halfway there.'

'Oh, go on. Don't be such a spoilsport. I could fill the wicker hamper with food and we can stop on the way a couple of times and have a picnic. It could be an adventure for the children. They'd love it.' Heather was watching Edward's face for his reaction, and pressed home her idea. 'We can call at the Rest House for tea and perhaps get news of Musah from old Adei, the houseboy there. He's a good friend of Musah's and is sure to have the latest information.'

Edward saw the look of determination on Heather's face – and the pleading eyes of the children, and unwillingly gave in.

He was all too aware of the hazards they faced on the journey, but David and Verity had listened attentively to the conversation, so the opposition was formidable. He soon realised that he didn't stand an earthly against the united front.

CHAPTER 14

The car was loaded up with the picnic hamper, toys, drawing books and the cases needed for an overnight stay at the Park Hotel in Sekari. They set off very early in the morning, when it was comparatively cool and the dawn mist still hugged the ground, drifting in patches here and there like lace around the topmost branches of trees while it waited for the sun to wipe the slate clean on another new day.

Few travellers were about at such an hour and after a brief stop at a road block on the outskirts of Mampi, manned by a handful of sleepy native policemen, they made good headway on the three hundred mile journey. The red earth road wound its way through high forest, the car wagging a swirling tail of dust behind it. They came across troops of colobus monkeys, the mothers carrying their young on their back or with them hanging precariously to soft underbelly fur, calling raucous warnings to each other as they ran across the road. They passed through small villages with thatched roof mud huts clustered at the side of the track, the scantily clad children running out to wave and shout, scattering squawking chickens, scrawny hunting dogs and bleating goats in all directions. There was little sign of trouble, though each cluster of huts, no matter how small or isolated, had one hut with a pole standing outside bearing a red, green and purple striped flag with a black sword emblazoned in the centre.

'What flag is that? I haven't seen any like it before.' Heather asked.

'I should think one of the new political groups must have adopted it,' Edward said.

He frowned – there seemed to be a great many of them; whichever political party had the flag as its emblem appeared to have all the villages in this part of the country firmly in its grasp.

Much to Edward's annoyance they had a puncture and everything had to be removed from the back of the car to get at the spare tyre. It was already hot and they looked like red Indians, their faces covered with the insidious laterite dust which found its way into the car and then became streaked with sweat as the temperature rose. They had cold drinks from a flask and the children disappeared behind bushes at the side of the track to answer the call of nature while Edward changed the punctured tyre. They re-loaded the car and had travelled only a mile or two down the road before Heather discovered Verity had not put her knickers back on so they had to turn round and go back to retrieve them from the bushes where she had hung them.

Hot, weary and grubby, they arrived at Igabe Government Rest House where the houseboy-cum-watchman quickly appeared from nowhere, made tea and gave them all the local news. When questioned, he told them he had seen Musah, but he could not remember when – two, three or four days ago? One day was much about the same as any other to the Rest House keeper – however, he did remember that Musah was visiting all the villages in the district checking which of them flew the flag with the black sword of freedom. There was another man with him. He was tall, and seemed to have some authority. The houseboy said he thought his name was Kovina, and that he was from the District Commissioner's office.

'I knew those two were up to something. I just knew it!' Heather said.

'And what makes you say that?' Edward asked, though it had been pretty obvious for quite a while that there was some sort of link between the two men.

'Don't you remember? I saw Kovina going into Musah's quarters weeks ago on the day of the party. He didn't call in to see us and Musah didn't mention the visit. I thought it was a bit fishy that he had come all the way from Sekari and didn't call in. Don't you think it's odd?'

'No. Not really. I don't see why they have to tell us about their private lives. Musah is just our garden boy after all; and what is Kovina?' He gave Heather a look full of meaning, 'Just a friend, would you say? Just a chap who helped me when I needed an interpreter? A man who warned you right from the start to steer clear of Komfo: a prudent warning which you chose to ignore.'

'And the man whose life you saved, Edward. Don't forget that!'

Edward nodded; he wasn't likely to forget the incident.

'I wonder what it is about Kovina that has bound us to him?' he said thoughtfully. 'It's almost as if he has some hold over our lives – a signpost telling us where to go.'

It was Heather's chance to bring things out in the open and she grasped it.

'I wish I knew. Ever since I first saw him on the day I arrived, when you spoke to him on the dockside and he looked up to where I was standing on the ship, I've had this strange feeling as if I've been caught in a cobweb. It's hard to explain, because I simply can't explain it.' Heather stopped, searching for the right words. 'There's something weird, something almost supernatural about him, but then there's something deep and unfathomable about the whole country with its strange superstitions, beliefs and customs. Nothing is simple and straightforward and no matter how many times I begin to believe and hope that things are getting on an even keel and everything is going to be normal, something happens to upset the balance. Every time I've handled the amulet Musah gave David I've had the strangest sensations. I even saw a rainbow on the bathroom wall with rain dripping from it. I dare not look at the talisman closely any more. It frightens me, yet I know there can be no harm in it – and it doesn't appear to have any uncanny effect on David; he wears it all the time now.' She wiped away beads of perspiration that had formed a salty moustache on her lip before continuing: 'If Musah is to be believed, it has some sort of protective aura, but I wonder if I'm getting caught up in all this African sorcery. There are times when I think I must be going mad.'

Heather was glad to admit to the phenomena that had been bothering her for so many months. Things she had wanted to talk about but felt unable to put into words. What was the matter with her? Had she gone so far down the road, sucked into the African world of fetish, black magic and supernatural witchcraft, that she could credit that the image of a rainbow on the wall of her own bungalow could have the power to listen, watch and report back to some other being? It was all so impossible…and yet so disturbing.

'There's a great deal we don't understand about African beliefs and superstitions and I doubt if we ever will,' Edward said. 'Over the years tribes have intermixed and overlapped and each of them have their own customs and rites that have been handed down through the generations so that the rhyme or reason for them has been lost or diluted, yet they are still practiced like a religion because it is what their fathers and grandfathers did before them.' He hesitated before adding: 'As to the peculiar reaction you say you have to Kovina…well, only he can give a reason for that.'

Heather didn't reply. She felt Edward was still suspicious of the friendship between them, so there was nothing more she could say.

As he had been speaking, Edward had drawn a pattern in the dust on the table with his finger. Heather saw it was just like the fish on the leather amulet.

The bank of bulky grey rain clouds that had been gathering when they arrived at the Rest House were now darkening the sky and bathing the compound in an unearthly haze, as if waiting for something to happen. The atmosphere in the small wooden building seemed to close in on them, and there being no electric ceiling fan to shift it round the room, the air felt thick and suffocating. Edward leaned out of the window and stared up at the sky.

'That storm is catching up with us – we'd better get a move on. If it lasts long parts of the road are going to be washed out, and if that happens we'll be in real trouble.'

Heather collected the children from their game of snakes and ladders and they started off on the journey once again. They had only covered a few miles when the storm broke. The sagging clouds were no longer able to contain themselves and let loose such a downpour that the windscreen wipers gave up the unequal struggle. Lightning split the sky apart and all the boulders of heaven crashed and growled above them so that they couldn't hear themselves speak for the din. Edward pulled over to the side of the road and waited until the storm had got over its initial angry outburst and had settled down to a more gentle pattern. The grumbling thunder was left behind as they drove further south and the windows could be wound down, letting the damp earthy smell surround them as they sang 'Ten Green Bottles Hanging on the Wall' at the top of their voices.

The treacherous coating of thick squelchy mud on the road's surface slowed them down, but despite this, the car nearly hit a wooden barrier stretched across the road as they rounded a bend. Several men stood on the verge at either side of the road and as soon as the car slithered to a halt, they surged forward, swarming round and banging on the roof with their fists, wrenching open the doors and shouting, 'Out! Out. Get out!' They were not wearing army uniform or the smart dark blue shorts and shirts worn by the Facriwan police force; they looked like a motley collection of vagabonds, scruffily dressed and their manner uncouth. The man who appeared to be their leader was of no great stature, but his stern face was deeply scarred with tribal marks. His round features and wide mouth might have looked benign in repose, but hostility sparked from him and his eyes shone with black intensity. He held a rifle awkwardly but still managed to give the impression that he knew how to use it and would take little prompting to do so.

'Get out!' he spat the words at them, denting the side of the car with the butt of his rifle.

Frightened, they left the car, their limbs taking exception to the sudden movement, needing time to unravel after sitting in the same cramped position.

'Quick now. No waste my time,' he screamed at them.

'What a rude man,' David said, staring at the African with obvious displeasure. 'Why don't you hit him, Dad?'

'Be quiet, son,' Edward said, his face white and expressionless. 'Do exactly as he says and do it at once.' The boy showed no fear and Edward grabbed hold of him, knowing David was just as likely to run up and sink his teeth into the man's leg, but the boy pulled away, annoyed with his father for not putting up a fight.

Heather moved closer to Edward and David, putting a protective arm round Verity, who plucked a handful of her mother's skirt and stuffed it into her mouth, her eyes growing wide and dark with concern.

The leader waved his arm at them, signalling to some of the rabble to herd them on to the strip of wet grass at the roadside.

'Come here. Quick!' he shouted again, his apparent pleasure at giving them orders very much in evidence.

The car was systematically searched, everything was taken from it and piled into a heap on the road. Their cases were opened and the contents strewn into the mud. Heather winced as they pawed into her lipstick and face cream; toothpaste was squirted from the tube and rubbed over the faces of a few of the men who laughed with mischievous delight until it went into the eyes of one man who leaped about bellowing and rubbing his stinging eyes with one hand and shaking his fist at them with the other. A skinny black youth picked Heather's nightdress from her case and held it against his body, miming, thrusting his pelvis forward suggestively while the onlookers clapped their hands at the show.

'You got no gun, no money?' their leader shouted, then he saw Heather's handbag tucked under her arm. 'Give that to me,' he demanded.

'Certainly not,' she said, trying to make her wavering voice sound defiant, though her eyes belied her fear.

'Give it to him, Heather,' Edward hissed a warning. The tense situation could turn into something far more deadly in a matter of seconds if this man didn't get his own way. For a moment Heather faltered, then gripped her bag more tightly. The men standing around moved in closer, raising their weapons threateningly, waiting for the leader to give the signal to strike. She looked directly into the eyes of the man nearest her – and recognised him; he had brought his mother to her long ago, an old blind woman needing treatment for an ulcer on her shoulder. She stared at him and he lowered his panga. Edward took a step towards her but one of the men pushed him roughly to one side.

Gripping her handbag more tightly, Heather spoke out with a bravado she was far from feeling.

'No! I'm damned if I'll be bullied by these ruffians!'

'Then I will kill your son,' the man said, and made a grab for David. Edward leapt forward, and as he did so a shot rang out and the gang leader dropped his gun and fell to the ground, grasping his leg with both hands. Another shot rang out, quickly followed by another. Most of the Facriwans threw themselves to the ground, while those nearest the trees bordering the road scarpered into the bush as fast as their legs would carry them. Edward and Heather looked towards the tall trees affording cover further along the track from where the shots seemed to have come. Kovina appeared from the shadow of the trees with several men in army uniform who quickly surrounded the bandit group, relieving them of their pangas and herding them, surly, muddy and dishevelled into the back of a lorry which had driven up as if by some pre-arranged signal.

Déjà vu, Edward thought. It seemed like the repeat of a film he'd watched in a different life. Smiling, Kovina walked up to him and put a hand on his shoulder.

'Just repaying a debt, my friend,' he said.

Heather's relief was such that her shaking legs gave up the struggle to hold her upright and she sank down on to the wet grass, still holding her children close to her. Edward ran and clutched them to him, trying to embrace them all at once, burying his face in Heather's hair.

'You crazy idiot, why did you put us at such risk?' he said, his arms still encompassing his family as the tension that had been building in his stomach like a time bomb gradually subsided. Tears joined the streaks of dust and sweat on Heather's cheeks.

'I couldn't let them get away with it. And anyway, I had my hand inside David's shirt, hanging on to his amulet. I was just hoping and praying that its magic might work for all of us.'

'That's a bit rich, coming from one who doesn't hold with African mumbo-jumbo and witchcraft,' Edward reminded her with a grin.

'Your face is dirty,' David observed, looking critically at his mother while still tightly holding on to her hand. The incident had frightened the boy, and although too young to understand the reasoning and wisdom behind his father's reluctance to fight the man who had been so aggressive, he was a wholehearted champion of his mother's defiance.

Edward turned to Kovina. 'Who were those men?' he asked, though he had a pretty good idea.

'They belong to this new political group formed by our friend Komfo. They call themselves The Black Sword Party.'

'Typical,' Heather broke in, 'that's just typical of that horrible little man. "Black Sword Party" indeed – yes, it just fits his mentality: something with which to hack his way to power.'

'Ah well, you can say that, but it all depends which way you look at it – it's not power but freedom, according to the witch doctor,' Kovina said, amused by her reaction.

'We saw their flag in nearly every village we passed through on our way down from Mampi,' Edward said. 'They seem to have won over everyone in the area.'

'Don't you believe it. Most of the villagers are quiet people, happy in their ignorance of outside affairs. They have enough to eat and enough to drink and they're content to jog along as they and their ancestors have done for years; but when they are offered money to stick up a pole with a brightly coloured flag outside a hut and to allow one of the Black Sword Party officers to install himself there as a little God Almighty, they are only too willing to agree. And that's the safest thing to do; those village chiefs who became suspicious and started asking questions have had their entire village burned to the ground, often cremating babies and the elderly who have been unable to run away into the bush.'

'We didn't see any signs of that on the way down here,' Heather said, thankful to have missed such a sight.

'You won't find much evidence of it until you get closer to the big towns where the chiefs have more knowledge of what is going on. They are the ones who have realised that in choosing to walk the road to freedom, they must also accept that there will be explosions along the way. They are the ones more likely to distrust the self-appointed politicians and put up a fight, especially if they belong to one of the bigger and more dominant tribes which already hold considerable power of their own.'

'And what about Sekari? Is everything quiet there?' Heather asked, the safety of her children foremost in her mind.

'Yes, on the surface everything is pretty calm at the moment. If Komfo should be caught, then things might change and there could be a few fireworks, but at the moment no one seems to know where he is or what he's up to. He seems to have the ability to pop up anywhere, cause a vast amount of disruption and then disappear again.'

'Vanishing in a cloud of dust like the genie in a panto,' was Heather's bitter reply.

'Panto?' Kovina asked.

'Short for pantomime – it's a sort of play put on especially for children at Christmas,' Heather explained.

'There's little that is fit for children where Komfo's performances are concerned, either at Christmas or at any other time,' Kovina said, shaking his head. He turned to Edward. 'If you want to make a move now, I'll follow you in a police jeep just to make sure you don't get held up by any more rogue road blocks.'

'How come you managed to turn up just in time to save our skins? Were we being followed?'

'The District Commissioners are supposed to be kept informed of the movements of all expatriates within their area to ensure their safety, but in this case, the police had been tipped off about the mob at this illegal road block and they've been under surveillance for the last twenty four hours. We know they have been stopping cars and relieving the driver and passengers of their money or anything else that takes their fancy, but we have been waiting until we could catch them red-handed.' He grinned. 'And we seem to have done that pretty well!'

Heather and the children started collecting their belongings from the wet grass and mud and packing them into the suitcases. David was put out to find his books were mud-spattered and torn.

'Never mind, we can replace them when we get to Sekari,' Heather promised.

'Can I have a new doll?' Verity asked plaintively, not wishing to be left out.

'Why? Did the men spoil Daisy?' her mother asked. Daisy was Verity's favourite; a blue-eyed baby doll with a pink rosebud mouth and flaxen curls.

'She's gone,' Verity said, her mouth turned down, preparing to cry at her loss.

'Those men took her away.'

'I don't think so – I expect she'll be about here somewhere,' Heather soothed the child. But a quick search proved fruitless. Daisy was nowhere to be seen.

'I expect one of the men who ran away into the bush kidnapped her,' David said as he squeezed his sister's hand to comfort her. 'Dad will buy you a much nicer doll,' he promised.

But Verity was bereft. 'I only want Daisy,' she said, and sucked her thumb to help dilute the sadness of her loss.

A power cut was in progress when they arrived at Sekari, and the toilets on their floor of the hotel were blocked. The plug was missing from the wash basin and David discovered a dead lizard beneath his bed.

'Everything is much the same as usual,' Heather observed drily when Kovina called later to see if they were comfortably settled and fully recovered from their unpleasant experience at the road block.

'Wait until we have self-government,' he laughed, 'there won't be any power cuts or blocked drains then!'

'Want to put a bet on that?' Edward asked.

They arranged to meet in the bar after the children had gone to bed. 'I may have a surprise for you,' Kovina said as he left.

They were certainly surprised later on when he walked into the hotel lounge bar with Musah, but a Musah they never knew existed. Heather looked twice before she recognised her friend and garden boy dressed in long grey trousers, white shirt and a grey silk tie. While Edward ordered their drinks, she quizzed this new-style Musah.

'My word, you look quite a toff. Should I call you "sir" now?' She joked to put him at ease.

'No, Madam, that will not be necessary,' he laughed. Her concern was superfluous for it soon became apparent that he was quite relaxed.

'Does this metamorphosis mean I have lost my garden boy?'

Musah chuckled. 'I can only guess at the meaning of that word, but no, I will be returning to Mampi to work in your garden. It is an excellent cover for my present assignment, but perhaps it would be best if Kovina explained.'

'I've been seconded from the District Commissioner's office to the police for a while, mainly to assist in tracking down Komfo,' Kovina told them. 'I asked the DC if I could recruit Musah to help, as he knows the more remote areas and the local chiefs better than most and has a good understanding of some of the lesser-known dialects. We have also managed to persuade some of Musah's old mission friends to infiltrate Komfo's bunch of followers.'

'That's good news,' Edward said cheerfully, handing round glasses of Sekari's home brew. 'Have you managed to find out if Komfo was definitely behind David's abduction?'

'We have two men in custody at the moment who are willing to give evidence that Komfo planned it, though it's unlikely that he was directly involved. He's far too clever for that.'

'So it will just be his word against theirs?'

'I'm afraid so. But there are many other crimes stacking up against him. It's now almost certain that he was behind the massacre on the train and is also responsible for the burning of the villages. We know he plans to be one of the new rulers of Facriwa as soon as the British leave. He's promised to promote extra business opportunities for many of the present Lebanese, Greek and other overseas traders as well as guaranteeing road and bridge building contracts to overseas companies, although he has no authority for this. He must be getting funds from somewhere, though some of the money is doubtless coming from a spate of bank robberies in the south. Of course, if we had not been able to get David back from the kidnappers, he would have demanded a large ransom, relying on the British Government to pay for the release of one of their own nationals without a murmur.'

'Does he expect all the expats to leave Facriwa the minute the Colony gets self-government?' Edward asked. 'Surely he must realise that months, if not years, of handing over will be needed to fill posts requiring highly qualified personnel. I know there are many more Facriwans going overseas for training than there used to be, but there aren't yet enough to fill all the vacancies that are bound to occur.'

'And whose fault is that?' Kovina said quietly, making it more of a statement than a question to which he expected an answer.

Heather interrupted, impatient to get to the bottom of the more immediate problem.

'Never mind about all that. What about the witch doctor? Do you have any idea of his whereabouts? Do you know where he is at this very minute? What on earth is the point of having self-government if you end up with people like him running your country?'

'The latest police informer's report seems to indicate that he's slipped across the border again to fix up some arms deal, but I still believe he is not far away,' Kovina replied.

'There's little doubt that he's been in and out of the Colony many times recently,' Musah joined in. 'He's almost certainly getting financial backing from neighbouring countries who are all waiting to join the queue for independence, and you can bet they'll expect help from the new Facriwan government when their time comes.'

There was a lull in the conversation while they digested the possibilities of what lay in store for Facriwa.

'So, Musah,' Heather said at length, 'do you know when you're likely to finish your work here with Kovina? When will you be coming back to Mampi?'

'There's not a great deal left for me to do down here. Tomorrow I'll be returning to the Mission at Tegey for a day or two to make a few enquiries, then I hope to go on to Mampi to see if someone has been watering the plants while I've been away,' he replied with a smile.

'We wanted to pop into Tegey on the way here but the bother palaver at the road block put paid to that. It would have meant arriving here at the hotel long after dark. I was hoping to find out how Comfort and her daughter are doing, but perhaps you would have time to do that? I hope Komfo has been too preoccupied with his nefarious schemes to have bothered her family any more. Comfort told me that her husband had been up at the burial ground with him on the night Kovina was shot – so he may still be mixed up with him.'

'I expect so – once you've been caught in that man's net it's not easy to wriggle free,' Musah, said, adding, 'I'll make a point of seeing Comfort for you.'

Later, as they prepared for bed, Heather and Edward discussed the 'new' Musah.

'I don't see how he can possibly come back to work as our garden boy, do you?' Heather asked.

'I don't know. I think Musah's a bit of a dark horse. I get the impression that he's been working as some sort of undercover agent for the District Commissioner and the police for some time. Even when he was still working at the Mission gardens, I often saw him when I was trekking round to outlying cocoa farms or poultry breeding stations; he seemed to pop up all over the place.'

'Huh! And you never told me? Didn't you ever ask him what he was doing when you saw him?'

'No. I knew little about him then, and anyway, it was none of my business. It wasn't until much later, when I saw him with Kovina a couple of times, that I began to put two and two together and wondered what was going on.'

'I suppose he was never dressed like a European then?'

'No, of course not. I'll be seeing the DC tomorrow and I'll probe him about it if I get half a chance.'

'D'you think Musah will want to come back to work for us?'

'I've no idea, but he seems to enjoy gardening and he's really fond of the kids. It's probably just what he needs, an ideal cover during the day, but God knows what he gets up to after dark.'

'And I suppose we mustn't ask?' Heather said.

Edward didn't reply, but the look he gave her was answer enough.

CHAPTER 15

Edward finished the work he had to do at Sekari and the family prepared for the return trip to Mampi. They had spent a whole afternoon on a shopping spree to replace some of the things damaged at the road block. David had his new books and Verity now owned a replacement for Daisy, which although acceptable and already the survivor of much dressing and undressing, did not have the same niche in Verity's affections that Daisy had once filled. Heather had bought material to make new dresses for herself and Verity and several packets of seeds for her garden; finally, Edward shocked them all by buying himself a hand gun and was immediately bombarded with questions.

'What are you going to shoot with that?' Heather wanted to know.

'Any goddamn thing that gets in my way!' Edward replied, his voice full of American gangster type bravado. 'But it's really to make sure I'm equipped, if need be, to defend myself and protect my family,' he said more seriously.

'Can I have a go with it, Dad?' David asked, eyes bright with excitement.

'The kick from this would knock you back into the middle of last week, Davey,' his father told him. 'It's not a toy.'

Verity, a down-to-earth child, asked, 'Are you going to shoot the man who took Daisy away?' Solemn faced, she looked up at her father, genuinely interested in the demise of the doll-thief.

'I may not go quite as far as that,' Edward said, tweaking her auburn curls, 'but when I see him I'll certainly knock his block off.'

'Can we watch?' David said perking up at the thought.

'Don't encourage them,' Heather warned, trying to keep a straight face. She and Edward had agreed that it would be best to avoid any reference to the trouble at the road block; the sooner it faded from the children's memories, the better, or they could be left with a legacy of childish nightmares.

They came across a few barriers manned by genuine police or army patrols on their journey home, and as soon as they drew up at each one, the tension could be felt. Edward's gun was covered by road maps and hidden under his car seat. He was glad it was there, though he dreaded the prospect of having to use it. As it happened, they didn't even have to leave the car at any of the wooden barricades; the guards were content to have their papers handed out of the window for inspection before waving them on. Edward learned later that Kovina had circulated instructions to all security posts along the route to allow their car to pass with as little hindrance as possible.

They had no time to stop at Tegey village and Heather craned out of the window in the hope of catching sight of any of their old friends. Pius, the owner of the Paradise Store, waved to them from his perch on the top step of the rickety verandah round his shop as they drove by. Their old bungalow looked forlorn and neglected as if it had its eyes shut, waiting for the arrival of a newly appointed agricultural officer. Heather would like to have stopped for a look at the garden she had begun to create, to see which plants had survived, but they had many miles to cover before darkness fell and it was no longer considered safe to travel on bush roads at night. Several incidents had been reported of trees felled across the road to halt traffic and to strip travellers of their possessions. The cars were then driven off into the bush, repainted, and given false number plates before being used in robberies in other parts of the colony.

When they arrived by the bush track leading off the road and up to the old burial ground, Heather's mind went back to the day she had sat on the rock with David on her lap and Edward's sudden arrival, slipping and slithering down the slope and covered with driver ants. Edward's thoughts were of the last time he was here with the little pygmy, Safo, and their race to get Kovina to the hospital. At times it seemed to have happened a hundred years ago, but now it was as if it was a memory of yesterday. Neither of them aired their thoughts, though they both had a secret desire to visit the plateau at the top of the hill where Kovina had witnessed something which had provoked an attempt to remove him permanently.

It was good to get back home again and to be greeted by a happy, smiling Sammy. He was all prepared for their arrival, which was unusual, but

Heather was too tired to ask how this came about. Hot water was bubbling away in kerosene debbi cans on the stove ready for a bath, supper smelled delicious, fresh bread had been baked and ice cold beer was waiting in the fridge.

'All's well with the world,' Heather said as she took David and Verity off for a bath while Sammy and Edward unloaded the car. She held David's amulet in her hand as David wriggled into his pyjamas, and wondered if it would have been taken from them had it been seen by the men at the road block, or whether they would have understood its significance and the power it held. Would they have been too frightened to act as they did? She would ask Musah about it when he came back.

But suppose he didn't come back? Suppose his new status made him feel differently about working as a handyman and garden boy? Wouldn't he find it demeaning? Musah's special qualities had been apparent to her from their first meeting. And then, as she put the leather thong of the amulet over David's head, she asked herself if it were possible that some of its strange power had passed into Musah before he gave it to David. Her mind held a clutch of impossible-to-answer questions as she tucked David into bed and looked at Verity, already fast asleep with her new doll, Belinda, held in the crook of her arm.

Musah returned sooner than expected, attired once more in his long drab brown cloth and brown sandals and looking again as if he had stepped from the pages of an illustrated Old Testament Bible. Heather didn't know he was back until she saw him from the verandah as he walked round the flower beds, a watering can in one hand and a trowel in the other. She felt warmed, made safer by his presence. Musah is my amulet, she thought, our meeting must have been pre-ordained. She dismissed the idea before it could take hold, telling herself sternly, I'm getting as whimsical and superstitious as the rest of them.

She walked down the verandah steps into the garden to join Musah on his tour of inspection, and then was at a loss as to what to say. He looked up when he heard her approach.

'The small Massa, is he well?' As always, his first concern was for David.

'Yes, Musah. He is very well, thank you. He doesn't know you're here, otherwise he would have been plaguing you long since to tell him a story.'

'Before he comes, I must tell you that I saw Comfort and Ruth in Tegey.

They are both well and Comfort is expecting another baby.'

'Oh, that is good news. And what of her husband, is he with her or is he still off somewhere with Komfo?'

'He's in prison awaiting trial. He was amongst the men Kovina and the police rounded up at the road block when you were stopped. They are hoping to squeeze some information out of him about the men who escaped into the bush.'

Heather wondered what squeeze meant in this context, and abruptly dismissed the thought. It was probably better that she didn't know.

'He must also know where Komfo is. His men must know where he goes to ground.' Heather's voice was animated – excited by the thought that they might be near to catching the slippery witch doctor.

'It seems that he has many places to hide. The police are aware of several of his bolt-holes and these are being carefully watched, but he's recruited contacts all over the Colony who are prepared to offer him a hiding place for an hour – or a month. That is one of the reasons he's always one step ahead,' Musah leaned forward, and pushing the trowel under a weed in the flower bed, he flicked it out in one deft movement. 'One day he'll be too clever. One day he'll walk into a trap. There will come a day when someone he has bribed or blackmailed into helping him will strike back, and I wouldn't choose to be in his shoes on that day.' Musah picked up the weed and threw it into a nearby bucket. He looked up at Heather, head on one side and quoted; '"To every man who sins comes nemesis."'

'You never cease to amaze me, Musah!' Heather laughed. 'Who would expect you to come out with the words of the Greek goddess of retribution?'

Musah smiled. 'Only those who know of the good people who befriended me at the Mission School when I was a boy and thought I was worth teaching such things.'

'You must have been very special to them.'

'It was the other way round. They were very special to me.'

'And what of the amulet you gave David? How could you bear to part with it if it was given to you by your father – and couldn't you still gain protection from it yourself?'

Musah nodded. 'Yes, but my ancestor, whose spirit lives within the amulet, commanded me to pass it on to your son, and through him, you have a rainbow path to my great grandfather.'

Yes, Heather thought, I've seen both the rainbow and your great grandfather, and I want to believe what I saw. But surely it has to be an illusion, such things are not possible. But to her friend she said: 'Oh, Musah! This is the twentieth century! It's too hard to believe. It's beyond all credibility.'

Musah bent to break off some dead flower heads. Then he straightened and, looking directly into her eyes, said: 'Can you honestly tell me that you haven't felt some of the power that comes from the amulet?'

Heather hung her head, unable to return his gaze, remembering the times the leather pouch had manifested its strange force. Eventually she said quietly, 'Yes, I have felt something.'

She was saved further analysis of the amulet's strange power by David, who ran down the verandah steps, still in his pyjamas, and raced across the grass to throw himself into Musah's embrace, boiling over with questions.

'Where have you been? Has Mummy told you what happened to us at the road block? Did you know Daddy has a new gun?'

'Hey, hey, young Massa! Give me a chance. One question at a time if you please.'

Glad of the reprieve, Heather left them to it and walked back to the bungalow, her mind deep in tangled skeins of thought.

Just before dusk she saw Musah leaving the compound. He walked briskly, transformed once more into the African man-about-town in his long grey trousers, white shirt and grey silk tie. I wonder what he's up to now? she asked herself.

She was to see him again later on that evening when he turned up at the bungalow with Kovina. Sammy showed the two men into the sitting room where Edward sat reading an air mail copy of the Telegraph and Heather was busy putting smocking stitches into a party dress for Verity.

'This is an unexpected visit,' Edward said, 'Come and sit down and give us the latest gossip.' Heather put her sewing to one side and asked Sammy to bring their guests a drink, eager to hear what they had to say.

Musah looked disturbed, and Kovina was also unhappy as he placed a brown paper package on the table by his side.

'Verity's doll has been found,' he said without preamble.

'Where? Who had it? Was it one of the men at the road block?' Heather asked.

'Yes, and one of the men we rounded up told us where we could find some of those who ran away. We think we've caught just about all of them now.'

'That's good – can any of them tell you where Komfo is?' Edward asked.

'Not so far, though we think they have a pretty good idea.'

'I'd feel like beating it out of them,' Heather said, her voice bristling with anger.

'Heather! Just stop it! Think what you're saying. D'you want us to sink to Komfo's level?' Edward reproached her, upset by her outburst.

Musah had listened quietly to the exchange, but now he rose from his seat and unwrapped the package Kovina had brought with him.

'I don't think Madam means what she said. It is frustrating, this delay in bringing the man to justice and it is a natural reaction after all that has happened.' He held Daisy out to Edward, bypassing Heather's outstretched hand. He looked apologetic and said gently. 'I think Massa should see the doll first.'

Edward took the doll, gasping at what he saw. Daisy's hair had been crudely chopped off, leaving a coarse stubble like an unshaven beard. The doll's clothing had been removed and her blue eyes had been gouged out, leaving shallow, vacant black holes. The doll's torso resembled a porcupine. Small sticks had been sharpened and thrust into it. Nauseated by what he saw, Edward threw it from him in disgust. It rolled across the floor and came to rest at Heather's feet. She stooped to pick it up, but her hand never reached the doll. Musah snatched it up and covered it once more with the brown paper, but Heather was stricken by the brief glimpse afforded her.

'It's grotesque! Who could do such a thing? Tell me, what sort of warped mind could bring someone to do that to a child's plaything?' she cried, shaking with a white rage.

Edward went to the cabinet, poured a drink and handed it to her, but she swept it aside. The sound of splintering glass brought Sammy rushing into the room to see what was going on. The houseboy gave one startled look at the spilled drink, the stark faces, and quickly backed out again.

'I don't want to be placated with a drink,' Heather said quietly, her face a mask, the skin taut across her cheekbones. 'Something's got to be done about that man. He must be mad…completely mad. He should be locked up.'

'It was probably not Komfo who did this,' Kovina said.

'That makes no difference. You can be sure he was behind it. He had something to do with it.'

'We'll soon find out.' Kovina said, putting his empty glass down and getting up to go. Musah picked up the package and also made a move to leave. Heather was too upset to give the men more than a curt goodnight before she went in search of Sammy and a dustpan and brush. Edward walked out to the car with the two visitors. He could see that something was still bothering them about the discovery of the doll. Kovina explained as he got in the car. 'There is an underlying significance, Edward. We suspect that the doll may have been used as a model for your daughter or your wife.'

'You mean…oh God, no!' Edward kicked viciously at the gravel on the drive. 'Thank you…thank you for warning me. I take it that it is a warning?'

The men nodded in silent affirmation. Musah put his hand on Edward's shoulder.

'Do not fear. It will not be long now before we catch up with him, but you must watch your family closely,' he said, and Edward turned and retraced his steps back to the bungalow.

Heather was rigid with the same iron bar of fear she had felt in the hours following David's kidnap. The sight of the doll had an almost paralysing effect on her nerves. White-faced, she took the fresh glass of brandy Edward handed her, hoping it would blunt the distress that would surely keep her tossing and turning all night.

'This won't solve the problem,' she said, looking at him above the rim of her glass.

'I know that, but it might help you to sleep.' He put his arm round her shoulders and kissed her cheek. 'I think we'll move the children's beds into our room for the time being. It'll give us more peace of mind,' he said. From now on, until Komfo was found and dealt with, he would be afraid to leave his family to go to work. 'Why don't you ask Mary Forwood to come and stay for a week or two? It would be good for you to have company just now.'

'Safety in numbers, you think?'

It wasn't that, Edward thought, so much as the feeling that the utter frustration of being unable to do anything to relieve their present anxieties would make his wife curl up inside herself again and cut herself off from the world around her; but she brought his thoughts to a halt.

'Why don't we go after Komfo ourselves?' she asked out of the blue.

'Where, in God's name, would we start?'

'Can't we try some witchcraft of our own?' Her voice quickened as an idea took shape in her mind. 'Why don't we find another witch doctor, one who is as powerful as Komfo, and get him to advise us? The police don't seem to be getting anywhere.'

'I thought you didn't believe in witchcraft. Aren't you just clutching at straws?'

'Perhaps. But surely that's a darn sight better than sitting around waiting for that man to strike again. You're in touch with the chiefs of all the villages round here, some of them must belong to other tribes with different customs. They can't all be scared stiff of Komfo. Can't you ask them for some strong juju, something really potent?' The idea gained greater viability the more she thought about it. She clasped her hands between her knees and leaned towards Edward, excited, urgent to be doing something.

Edward welcomed this fighting spirit and wanted to encourage it, though he had little faith that it would get them anywhere. If the police hadn't already gone up that avenue, then surely Kovina or Musah would have done so. Was it even ethical to pit one witch doctor's spells against another? Despite his doubts, he felt he must support this line of hope for Heather's sake.

'It's worth a go,' he said at last. 'I have to make a trip round some of the villages tomorrow. I'll see what I can find out.'

With a positive plan of action, Heather slept soundly that night, but Edward had little sleep until just before dawn when he dreamed of coming home from work to find Heather and Verity with their hair shorn, their eyes sightless.

Heather had a surprise visit from the District Commissioner the following morning after Edward, reluctant and worried, had left for work. The DC informed her that a police guard would be keeping a discreet watch on the Greenwood house and garden until the witch doctor had been apprehended. She didn't tell James Heber-Scott of their plan to solicit the aid of another witch doctor to outwit their bête noire, and listened attentively to his assurance of Komfo's imminent arrest. She nodded, but kept her thoughts to herself; she had heard that story so many times before.

Instead she asked James what he knew of the juju spells and witchcraft practised in the Colony, not realising she had inadvertently let the cork out of his bottle.

'Oh my goodness! I could talk all day and long into the night about such things, and still tell you less than half of what I've seen and heard,' he said. 'Facriwan people are by nature inordinately superstitious, as you must have discovered for yourself. Some of their customs and beliefs have been handed down through many generations, while others have been imported and adopted from all parts of Africa. Most tribes have a profound belief in witchcraft, which still kills more people than those lost in the days of slave trading. It's not so long ago that if a witch doctor decreed someone was guilty of causing the death of a relative, who had in all probability died of malaria, the accused person would have been condemned to a terrible death. Roasting alive was one of the favourite methods, closely followed by mutilation by degrees.' James looked thoughtful, bringing to mind a case in which he had been called upon to give judgement some years before. 'That means chopping pieces off the accused bit by bit until he succumbs, you 'understand?' The question was asked in all seriousness. Heather winced and nodded. Most of them believe they can gain power over their adversaries by means of obtaining some of their hair or blood. That's why you see the villagers burning their hair when it has been cut off, and some tribes even bury their nail clippings, lest they fall into the hands of someone evilly disposed towards them.' He tented his fingers and looked at Heather over the top of his glasses as he continued: 'If they cut themselves and blood drips, or if they have a nose bleed, the blood must be covered with earth without delay and stamped on during the course of a ritual dance. It is all quite fascinating really.' The DC munched the biscuits and drank the coffee Sammy had brought.

In her mind's eye, Heather saw Daisy again; poor naked doll Daisy, sightless, and shorn of her golden locks.

'Of course,' James continued, getting into his stride on one of the topics which he found most interesting, 'human eyeballs, especially those of white men, were some of the most powerful charms used by witch doctors. Not so long ago, graves were rifled for them, so great was the belief in their power. When I retire in a couple of years, I shall write a book about it. Yes…engrossing subject, don't you think?' He dug into his pocket for his pipe and slowly filled it with tobacco from a leather pouch. He struck a match and looked across at Heather. 'Are you all right m'dear? You look a bit peaky.'

Heather dismissed the image of Daisy's empty eye sockets – windows on to an impossibly cruel world; cruelty she must try to come to terms with, attempt to understand, or confront madness. She pulled herself together.

'Yes, I'm all right. It's this sticky heat, it makes me feel washed out some days.'

'You want to get that man of yours to take a couple of weeks' local leave. Get off down to the coast for a spell. It's still just as hot there of course, but at least you get a bit of breeze off the sea, and the change of scenery would do you good. You should visit some of the old castles built along the coast by the Dutch and Portuguese in the fifteenth century. Worth a visit, interesting stuff.'

'Yes, I've read about them Are any of them still used, or are they just crumbling remains?'

'Oh, goodness gracious me, no! In those days they built to last. They changed hands frequently during the sixteenth and seventeenth centuries and no doubt bits were repaired and added to. They have tremendous granite walls and battlements which have withstood the test of time. Some were used as barracks during the slave-trading days. And a few still have cannons pointing out to sea to ward off invaders. You can still see the iron rings in the walls where the slaves were shackled before being shipped off. Nowadays they're used for all sorts of things: Government offices, Post Offices, clinics, training centres and the like.'

Heather wasn't all that keen to see where slaves had been shackled before being shipped off to other parts of the world to pick cotton or work on sugar plantations, but she was diplomatic.

'I would like to see them one day, and learn more of Facriwa's history, but first I would like to know that Komfo is back behind bars. I shan't feel my family is safe until then.'

CHAPTER 16

A long period of calm lulled everyone into a soporific sense of security. Several months passed without any strikes or threats of strikes, and political meetings were now being held with some semblance of order. At last it seemed that progress was being made towards the self-governing status that the Colony craved. Progressive and highly educated African officials, still young in the art of diplomacy, were preparing for the day when the life and government of the country would be held in their hands. As confidence grew, plans were drawn up by fledgling politicians for the building of more schools, the laying of more tarmac roads and better water and electricity supplies. Proposals were mooted for clinics to be made available for remote villages, and more African doctors, teachers, lawyers, engineers and civil servants would be trained to replace expatriates who would soon be due for retirement or would be posted elsewhere. Financial backing for the new schemes would be hard to come by unless investors in other parts of the world were more certain of the stability of the new state emerging under a different flag.

Heather, Edward and the children went home to England for two months' leave and bought a small bungalow at a little seaside town in Somerset. It was within easy distance of the homes of both their parents so that the children were able to make frequent visits to their grandparents. They drove into Bristol to shop for things to take back to Africa, took picnic baskets to the zoological gardens and walked across Clifton Suspension Bridge with Heather's father, Grandpa West. They looked down on the rocks either side of the gorge and watched the River Avon flowing below. He told them that when he was a small boy he had seen a man throw his two little girls over the bridge, but they had been wearing long umbrella-like skirts and petticoats which lessened the speed of their fall and they landed safely in the mud. Their father leapt over the bridge after them but fell on the rocks and was killed. David wanted to experiment with Verity's new doll, Belinda, and throw her over the bridge, but Verity hung on tightly to the doll and wouldn't part with it. She woke that night screaming in terror as a swarm of black men encroached upon her dreams and tried to wrest the new doll away from her.

'D'you think Verity's been scarred by the experience at the road block?' Heather asked Edward after she had finally settled the child and snuggled up beside him again.

'It's hard to say. I wouldn't have thought so,' Edward replied. She's never referred to it until now. I think David sparked off this nightmare when he suggested throwing her doll over the bridge.'

The considerate English climate was welcome to Heather after the unremitting heat of the tropics, and she said as much to Edward as they lay on the lawn after their Sunday lunch of roast beef and Yorkshire pudding.

'You say that now, but we're having the best of it being here in June. You wouldn't think so much of it if it was the middle of winter with cutting winds and snow. Don't tell me you've forgotten what it can be like!'

Heather pulled at a tuft of grass. 'No, I haven't forgotten. Well not really.' She looked up at the tall beech trees at the top of the garden. 'It just seems hard to imagine those trees standing in the nude without a leaf on them and this grass covered in snow.'

'Do you realise,' Edward said thoughtfully, 'David and Verity have never seen snow, except in their picture books. They're missing out on such a lot of things, being stuck in the back of beyond in Africa, and having to be guarded every time they go out in the garden to play.'

'Yes, I know, but they're seeing a different part of the world, learning about other people and their way of life. That must count for something. And surely things will be different once Komfo has been put out of action? Life should be more settled when Facriwa gets its own government, shouldn't it?'

'Who's to say? It all depends how the individual tribes accept being ruled by men of the same colour as themselves, but who probably have different beliefs and customs. There's sure to be a jostling for position, each tribe wanting its own representatives to have the biggest say as to what's going on. I think it will all take time.'

'I wonder what Kovina and Musah are doing now?' Heather said, dodging the balding tennis ball David and Verity were using to play their own highly complicated version of French cricket. She called across to them. 'Watch what you're doing, keep clear of next door's greenhouse. Keep the ball low. If you break the glass you'll have to pay for it out of your pocket money.'

'I've no doubt Musah's keeping one eye on your garden and the other on the goings-on in the political world around Mampi and Sekari,' Edward said. 'And most likely the pair of them are still on the lookout for your friend the witch doctor.'

'It's really odd, the way that man can disappear into thin air.'

'It's not odd at all. He has all those friends in the spirit world to magic him away, to say nothing of his ancestors, who were all probably just as evil as him. Come to think of it, his collection of human bones, snake skins and monkey's teeth must be pretty powerful juju for helping him to vanish in a cloud of dust.' Edward ducked as Heather aimed a clod of earth at him.

'Stop making fun. It's easy to laugh at the wretched man while we're here far away from it all and can sleep soundly in our beds. When we're actually there in the middle of it and surrounded by miles and miles of bloody Africa with the sound of drums pulsing through the night and the sun making leather of our skin during the day, we can't help but see things in a different light.' Heather shook her head. 'Africa can be a scary place.'

Musah was indeed keeping an eye on Heather's garden, in as much as he was paying Eko, one of Sammy's children, a few pence a week to help keep it watered and weeded. Apart from that, he split his time between working closely with Kovina at the government office in Sekari and doing a little detective work of his own in the area round the escarpment where he and Lima had found David in the cave. He had told the District Commissioner and Kovina about the cache of guns they had discovered, and the army had sent a patrol to pick them up. Despite intensive questioning of the villagers who had kept such a vigilant watch on the comings and goings to and from the cave, there had been no sightings of the gun-filled crates. They were later found to have been smuggled across the border, just as Musah had suspected. It did not take him long to discover their source, and this led him to further news of Komfo's whereabouts. He made a return visit to the cave, this time hoping to carry out a proper inspection without the need for haste and the fear of discovery. This time he went well prepared and had no need for flickering candles to guide him as he put a match to a bush lamp as soon as he entered the cave. He stopped several times to examine the crude drawings scratched or painted on the walls. There were strange lines and squares set out like a game of noughts and crosses, pictures of men with spears, antelope, monkeys, and a snake with its jaws stretched wide as it devoured a small animal. Here and there thin fissures in the rock-face allowed tears of water to trickle down, staining the surface rusty red, like blood drying on a wound. A rat scuttled over his foot, disturbed by the trespasser in its domain.

Holding the lamp aloft, searching all the time for something which might have been missed on his previous visit, Musah followed the narrow passage as it sloped upwards. He had forgotten how it branched to the left with the ground rising sharply before opening out into the large cavern like some underground stage. There were fewer dark shadowy patches, with the lamp showing up things which had escaped him when he had last been here with only a candle to light his way. Even so, he nearly missed a small opening cut into the rock-face. At first it looked like a ledge about a foot off the ground, but when he held the lamp closer he could see that it was the entrance to another passage. He stepped into it and followed a narrow tunnel, ducking his head where the ceiling was low and uneven with old stalactites jutting down from it. The passage grew narrower so that he was forced to keep his elbows tight against his body and hold the lamp awkwardly in front of him. He had only walked a few yards when he found himself in another cave – a cave within a cave. But this was different – this was unexpected. Now he was able to stand erect without fear of hitting his head. The ceiling was high, domed, and perfectly shaped. Light came into the cave through four small slits cut into the dome and directly beneath it stood a large stone slab like a sacrificial altar. A light winked from its flat surface and Musah found himself being drawn towards it, caught within a magnetic field. For a moment he was afraid to look, not knowing what he might see. Placing the lamp on the ground beside him, he was surprised to see it was clean and looked as if it had been recently swept. Finally, he gazed upon the surface of the stone which was engraved with the outline of a fish, scales finely chipped, and the fin and tail perfect in design. It was the shining ruby of its eye that completed the work of delicate beauty and made him catch his breath. It was exactly like the fish on his grandfather's amulet. His vision became blurred as he fell forward on his knees as if in prayer.

Musah had no idea how long he knelt there, but guessed by the stiffness in his joints when he sat back on his heels waiting for the numbness to recede, that it must have been some time. He remained seated on the floor, his head in his hands, trying to fathom the coincidence of the fish emblem, when he was addressed in a low voice with an accent strange to his ears.

'Does something bother you, son?'

Musah turned and saw a man dressed in the robes of a monk. He looked just like one of the men he had seen in picture books at the Mission when he was a boy. Those men had been walking in sandaled feet along the cloisters of an old English abbey, their arms folded across their chest and their hands thrust deep within the sleeves of their dark brown robes.

'Yes – I have never been to this place before, but I feel I know it. It is strange, Father. It is as if I belong here.' As soon as he had spoken the words, Musah realised how odd they must sound. Why had he called this stranger Father? Was it because the robed figure had addressed him as son? Or was it out of an instinctive politeness for someone who appeared to be a holy man? He felt awkward, embarrassed. These were new emotions for him, a man who was always forthright in his dealings with others and expected the same in return.

'Perhaps you have come home,' the man smiled. 'I mean – of course – that this might be your spiritual home.' He bowed his head and was silent for a while, letting his words sink in. Then he asked, 'Tell me, what brings you to our little place of devotion?'

Musah wondered at the title given to this beautiful underground sanctuary, and then wondered still further at what he had just called it. This 'sanctuary' was like a small church, despite its lack of a cross or statue of the Virgin. It was so different from the Mission, where crucifixes and statues were on displayed on every wall, window-edge and bookcase. Wherever space offered, it had been filled with an icon of some description so that there was scant chance of forgetting you were in a Catholic Mission. Here, there was simply the fish etched so delicately and with such a high regard for accuracy, into the stone of what appeared to be an altar. Added to this was the quietness, although it was not a place of complete silence; there was a soft whispering sound as of busy water trickling over rocks, which he found disconcerting. It forced him to question whether this place and its aura had the power to dull his senses, or was he allowing his imagination to dance ahead of him?

At length he addressed the robed man.

'I am searching for someone, a witch doctor, whom I believe to be evil,' he hesitated, probing for the right description. Perhaps it was wrong to call Komfo evil while in this sacred place. Again he puzzled over his choice of words. What had prompted him to call it a sacred place? Had he been influenced by the altar-like stone, the man dressed like a monk? Questions and still more questions.

'You are quiet – lost for words perhaps?' the robed man suggested. 'Or are you having an argument with your conscience?' he asked kindly. The question broke into Musah's thoughts.

'I was trying to be fair in my description of the man I wish to bring to justice.'

'Oh, so he's broken the law?'

'I believe he is responsible for the death of many people.'

'For what reason? Were they victims of a tribal dispute, some religious conflict, or had it something to do with the present political situation?' The old man rested his hand on the stone, slowly running his finger along the outline of the fish.

'I think it has its roots in politics. Komfo, that is his name, is the witch doctor of Tegey. He has great knowledge of medicine, inherited from his father and grandfather, but he doesn't always put it to good use. He has used this knowledge to serve his own ends and not for the good of his tribe or the people of Tegey.' Musah rubbed his hand across his forehead, wanting to be scrupulously honest, plagued by his upbringing into making allowances, yet still facing the probability that Komfo was responsible for the massacre on the train, and the abduction of his young friend, David. He could hear the voice of the man he considered to be his adoptive father, saying: 'Always look at any dispute from both points of view. Listen carefully to what everyone has to say and do not come to any hasty decision.' But he needed no more time; he had weighed all the evidence with care and his voice was stronger as he continued: 'He manipulates people in such a way that they do things they know to be wrong, but once they've become involved, he has a hold over them. They are trapped. They are too frightened to go against his orders and even more scared of going to the police or the District Commissioner. Many of their friends who have attempted to question his authority have died in circumstances which can't be accounted for, and are hard to explain away.'

'I have already heard of this man. I will do what I can to help you find him,' the robed man said, nodding his head, though with no suggestion of complicity.

'There is another part of this underground labyrinth which has a room much larger than this, where a young white boy was held captive after being abducted. Do you know of it?' Musah asked.

'Yes, and as far as I know it's been used recently as some sort of armoury where guns and ammunition were stored. I'm told it has been reported to the District Commissioner who has dealt with the matter.'

'Have you any idea how the guns arrived there?'

'Yes. There is an opening in the roof. It's difficult to find and almost impossible to see unless you know what you're looking for. I'll take you there if you wish.'

Musah nodded. 'So is this a chapel? Does it belong to a Holy Order?'

'As far as I know, it belongs to no one. The choirmaster of my church discovered it quite by accident some time ago when he brought a party of visiting anthropologists and geologists here to investigate the caves. This was long before the main cave was used by the smugglers. Apparently it has outstanding acoustic qualities and he sometimes brings his choristers here to practice. I come here occasionally to meditate. This little shrine, temple – call it what you will – has a soothing quality, a tranquility all of its own, which is not present in many finer places of worship.'

'Did your church have this stone brought here?' Musah looked at the outline of the fish as he asked the question. The ruby eye glowed red and he suddenly felt off-balance and leaned heavily against the stone for fear of falling.

'No, and little is known of its origin, but a visiting priest from North Africa told me he has seen others like it in many North African territories, which is hardly surprising; the fish has been used as a Christian symbol since the second century and is credited with great mystical power.'

'I can vouch for that,' Musah replied. 'I was given a leather amulet by my father that had been handed down to him by his father. I've no way of telling how far it went back, but it certainly has strange powers. It also has the outline of a fish scored into the leather and a red stone for its eye.'

'Have you got this amulet with you?'

'No. I'll never have a son of my own to pass it on to,' Musah told him, regret apparent in his voice, 'so I gave it to a young white boy who was in need of protection.' He sensed that this man would require no further explanation. 'But the amulet will be taken care of. It is in good hands.'

'Perhaps that also explains why you feel you belong here. There is a link between the fish on the amulet and the fish on this stone. Who knows? They may even have come from the same place,' the man said with a smile.

Musah shook his head, sceptical. 'Unlikely, I think. It would be too much of a coincidence.' But he touched the red eye of the fish with his forefinger and felt the strange warm current of power course along the veins of his arm. The sensation was not unpleasant and it didn't alarm him. He accepted this injection of power as being perfectly natural.

The two men left the chamber together, their heads bowed, not only to conform to the low ceiling, but deep in thought. As they emerged into the daylight, the sharp breath of hot air made their eyes sting while invisible strands of humidity enveloped them. The sun, a fiery red ball, beat down upon their heads as they trudged slowly up a long steep stone-strewn track to the top of the escarpment. Sweat made salty trails through the dust on their faces, stinging as it trickled into their eyes, and dripped from their chins, patterning the dust on the parched ground and rolling into marbles of red laterite.

They came out on to a small flat plateau, covered almost waist-high in thorny scrub bushes and shrivelled misshapen trees struggling for existence in the parched soil. Way off in the distance, Musah could just make out the blurred outlines of a small settlement rising like a mirage from the shimmering heat haze. His companion seemed to know the way, though there was no discernible path through the scrub. Stopping abruptly, the priest reached forward and pulled at a large clump of withered gorse-like bushes which appeared to be woven into some sort of camouflage frame and came away cleanly after a second heave, uncovering a large hole in the ground. Musah leaned forward and peered down into the chasm, recognising at once the dim cavern where he and Lima had discovered the wooden crate full of guns and the pile of rags under which David had been hidden. It appeared to be much the same as when he last saw it; a few candle stubs stuck in rusting tins, a bush lamp lying on its side with the glass smashed, and still the same pervading stench of rancid fat that made him want to retch.

He stood back, trying to gauge the size of the gaping pit. Once the crates of arms and ammunition had been smuggled in from neighbouring territories, it would have been a simple operation for Komfo's followers to lower them down through the hidden rooftop entrance unseen by those watching from their look-out post down below the escarpment, obscured as they would have been by the vast double chin of overhanging rock. Smuggling operations could have been going on for months and a lucrative business set up, selling arms to the highest bidder. If Komfo was involved on a grand scale he would have needed many tight-lipped helpers – and must have made enemies along the way, Musah reckoned. He turned, shielding his eyes from the sun, and nodded towards the village in the distance.

'Surely the people living over there must have seen what was going on, Father?' he asked.

'They would only see what they were intended to see,' the priest said knowingly. 'Movement round this plateau would only have taken place at night, and mostly, I would guess, while some tribal festival was going on. A lot of ritual dances are performed here. In fact the chiefs and headmen might have unwittingly assisted in the smuggling activities.' He considered for a moment. 'I'll take you to my house. It's just beside the church. You must stay with me tonight and I'll arrange for you to have palaver with the village chief, though I should warn you there is no love lost between this tribe and the one at the bottom of the escarpment.'

'Do many of these people worship at your church?' Musah asked.

'Most of the women and children come,' the priest chuckled, 'but I would not be too sure that they do much worshipping. I believe they come more out of gratitude to the Sisters who teach them and hold the morning clinic. I am a doctor of medicine as well as a doctor of divinity and it is mainly the men who come to see me, often to adjudicate over some tribal dispute, or,' he laughed ruefully, 'to remove a spear if they have already decided to settle the matter in the usual way. I'm close at hand, you see – if they want an official ruling on some problem they should go to the District Commissioner but a lot of them can't be bothered to travel that far.'

'Doctor Livingstone, I presume!' Musah said, and giving a mock bow, he shook hands with the man he already regarded as a new friend.

'I'm afraid not, just Doctor Flemballe. Julian Flemballe. I am half-Belgian, half-French. I came here some years ago from a leper colony in the Congo.'

They replaced the cover screening access to the cave and the priest led the way through a patch of tall rustling dry grass to a small clearing where a bicycle was propped against the stump of a rotted tree trunk. He gathered up his robes in a bundle over one arm and throwing his leg over the crossbar, perched himself on the saddle.

'Hop on!' he said, indicating the small wooden seat fixed above the rear wheel. Laughing, Musah did as he was told, and suddenly felt sixteen again. They made precarious progress, rattling and clattering along a pitted narrow path strewn with gravelly stones at a remarkable speed until they came to the village. As they neared the huddle of thatched mud huts, they were greeted by groups of children who waved and shouted greetings to their pastoral friend. Dr Flemballe's bungalow was adequately furnished, and reasonably comfortable, but with no fripperies whatsoever; much the same as the Mission house at Tegey, Musah thought, looking about him. Everywhere, though, were books. They bulged from overfed bookcases and glass-fronted cupboards, towered like high-rise blocks of flats in the corners of the room, were stacked on small tables and some lay open on a big dark mahogany desk.

'You do a great deal of reading, Doctor,' Musah observed.

'Studying, mainly – I'm doing some research into river blindness with a friend of mine, a professor at the London School of Tropical Medicine,' Julian said, busying himself with glasses and a bottle opener. 'Local beer all right for you?' he asked.

Musah nodded, glancing at the neatly written lines on the page of a red exercise book on the desk.

The two men ate a frugal but sustaining meal served by the doctor's houseboy, Benin, who glided in and out quietly on bare feet; a shadowy figure, never speaking or being spoken to, attending his master's needs as if by some private telepathy. He allowed himself one searching glance at Musah from hooded hawklike eyes, and seemed satisfied with what he saw. Musah knew that Benin would report his arrival to a member of his tribe who would pass the information on to one of the elders. News didn't drag its feet in this part of the world. His mind reverted to thoughts of Komfo and his involvement in the gun-smuggling racket.

The drums started soon after dusk and to Musah, their rhythm seemed to beat with a stronger pulse, a greater urgency. He remarked on this to

Julian Flemballe, and told him he had difficulty translating the message.

'It is an announcement by the elders of the tribe. There is to be an initiation ceremony tomorrow; some of the young men of the village have passed the tests set by the elders and they are to be officially accepted onto the tribal council.'

'May we go to this ceremony?' Musah asked.

'I can go. I'm accepted. They know I'm harmless and won't interfere, but you come from a different place, a different tribe. They may accept you – or they may decide to kill you,' Father Flemballe said with a disarming smile.

It was apparent to Musah that although his host treated his wish to attend the ceremony seriously, he was reluctant to condone his attendance, believing the risk might be too great.

'I don't think you need worry on my account,' he said, 'I know many tribes in this region and have stayed with some of the elders in the past. I've no doubt they'll have wasted no time in checking me out, and arriving on the scene with their pastor will surely add to my credence!'

There was an air of excitement about the village the following morning. Benin served the two men their breakfast with a briskness that had not been there the night before. Sounds of crashing crockery came from the kitchen as he hurried to finish his chores and be off with his family to join the snakelike line of villagers making their way towards the meeting place.

Musah and Flemballe left early before the sun would limit any energetic exercise. They made an odd picture as the bicycle wobbled unsteadily along the rutted track. They came across rough images made of grass, mud and small twigs propped against termite nests or lying on mounds of pebbles forming makeshift altars. Some were of animals and birds, others were human in shape.

'They are determined to invoke the good will of the spirits for today's festivities,' the doctor chuckled, puffing out his cheeks as he pedalled, the exertion lining his tanned face with channels of sweat. They caught up with a group of girls, naked apart from narrow strips of woven grass or leather, their only bow to vanity being the necklaces and bracelets made with seeds, dried berries and shells. The girls stood aside to let them pass, giggling and hiding their eyes behind flapping hands. As the men left them a few yards behind, the girls fell against each other shrieking with laughter at some private joke and the doctor and his passenger found themselves chortling in return.

'That is so good to hear, Musah,' Flemballe said, 'there is little outright laughter in this part of the world.'

'Hardly surprising,' Musah replied, 'most of them have little to laugh about.'

Quite a crowd had gathered by the time they arrived on the scene. Most of the onlookers sat on the ground in a semi-circle, facing a makeshift stage of well-pounded earth strewn with coarse dry grass. A ramshackle wooden table stood to one side with two blue and white enamel bowls placed upon it containing gin for the pouring of the libation, and specially treated water in preparation for the ceremonial cleansing that must follow the initiation ritual.

The young men chosen for the initiation ceremony were all dressed in white shorts and singlets and sat in a circle set apart from the other onlookers. They looked nervous and spoke quietly to each other.

The newcomers found a slightly raised patch of stubbly yellow grass from which to watch the proceedings. It was party time, and was obviously expected to last for a number of hours as several of the onlookers had brought chairs of a sort, while others sat comfortably on their haunches surrounded by cooking pots, calabashes brimming with fermented palm wine, baskets of bananas, dried fish and stodgy rice wrapped in cones of leaves. The doctor unstrapped a large black umbrella from the crossbar of his bike and they were thankful for its shade as they sat listening to the pleasant drone of voices all around them, interspersed from time to time with the whimpering cry of a child or the barking of a dog.

A hush fell as the Chief swayed into view, carried on a large raffia hammock by four tribal warriors. Another man held a big fringed durbar parasol above the Chief while an albino African with pink staring eyes and skin mottled like a map with shades of pink, white and brown fanned him with a fistful of palm fronds. The impressive entourage came to an unsteady halt, almost tipping the Chief from the hammock into the dust: an unrehearsed hiccup which caused a deal of altercation and fist-waving. A blue-turbaned boy came forward and placed the throne ready for the great man. This was a rough wooden stool covered with stained red velvet material from which the pile had long since been eaten or worn away. The sides were liberally studded with beer-bottle caps which shone impressively, giving the throne a brittle veneer of regality.

The Chief finally disembarked awkwardly from the unstable palanquin, trying to maintain his dignity by standing to attention, straight and tall, for a few moments, his colourful woven robe thrown over his shoulder like a Roman toga. He raised his right hand in greeting, then in a solemn clear voice called upon the spirits of past chiefs to bless the proceedings. He took his place on the throne and the turbaned youth handed him a stick ornately carved from its brass ferrule up to the curved handle where the decoration was further enhanced by the skull of a monkey and a spray of vivid green feathers. He tapped the stick on the ground three times then clapped his hands three times. Proceedings were then allowed to commence.

Elders of the tribe and members of the council came forward one by one to speak of tribal matters, to report on disputes with neighbouring tribes and to tell of pressure being brought on the Chief to join a political party to ensure a place in the new Facriwan Parliament once self-government had been achieved.

At this point Musah allowed his attention to waver as he searched the sea of faces gathered round the meeting place. Some he recognised from gatherings he had visited all around the country; they were no doubt here to report the general feeling of this area back to their seniors in the wider political battlefield. Then he caught sight of two men he recognised as members of Komfo's pack of troublemakers back in Tegey. Slowly he scanned the faces in the crowd and his throat went dry as he saw Komfo with two burly bodyguards either side of him. They were standing in a group some distance away on the far side of the arena and Musah would have to circle his way round the crowd to reach him. Not wishing to draw attention, he turned to Dr Flemballe and spoke to him in a whisper. It was imperative that Komfo should not suspect that he'd been spotted.

'I've seen Komfo!' he mouthed. 'he's over there,' and he nodded in the direction where he had seen his quarry. It would not be wise to point a finger with so many eyes watching all that was going on. Swiftly, but as unobtrusively as possible, Musah left the doctor and made his way between the onlookers, stepping over sleeping children, avoiding a woman suckling a baby at her breast, while trying to keep one eye on the witch doctor. His excitement mounted as he came nearer to his target, his mind running ahead as to his plan of action were he able to get close enough to follow him after the initiation ceremony. He could do nothing to apprehend him in this crowd, with his two bodyguards beside him. He made slow progress, stopping now and then to give the appearance of listening attentively to what was being said by those taking part in the ritual. The sun was high, the cloth of his brown robe stuck to his body in dark patches on his back and under his arms, his stomach muscles were taut with anticipation and frustration. If only Kovina were here with a few police officers or soldiers, Komfo could be caught at last.

As Musah grew near to the little group he now edged along crab-wise to avoid showing his face to the men he wanted to follow; if they recognised him they would be off. But as had happened to so many stalkers before him, as soon as he arrived at the best vantage point there was no sign of his quarry; once again he had vanished, to be gobbled up within the colourful crowd. It was as if he had existed only in Musah's imagination. Once again Komfo was at liberty to wreak havoc on his countrymen whenever and wherever opportunity arose.

CHAPTER 17

Kovina listened attentively to Musah's account of the events of the last few days, nodding his head from time to time and making notes on the pad on his desk. Musah thought his friend was going up in the world with his office now moved next door to that of the District Commissioner.

'So,' Kovina said eventually, 'Komfo got away from us once again. Don't worry, one of these days he'll be just too clever for his own good. We've been close to catching him several times recently. He must sense the net is closing round him and fear will make him careless.'

'Maybe, but I'd like to have him safely locked up before Edward Greenwood and his family return from home leave.'

'It would indeed be good to welcome them with such news, and there's still a chance we may do so. We're keeping an eye on his gun-smuggling enterprise, and that could give us a lead if we discover his contacts over the border. He must have got wind of your visit to the cave and you can be sure he'll have had informers in Father Flemballe's parish.'

'There's little doubt about that,' Musah agreed, 'but sooner or later someone is going to be brave enough or mad enough to come forward and inform on him.'

'That sums it up – but you could add "angry enough" to the list.'

Kovina smiled and tapped his desk with an ivory paper knife.

'If we could persuade someone that they have an even stronger juju than Komfo, or a witch doctor with greater power than him…that might work,' he said.

'I know of no such man,' Musah said thoughtfully, 'unless…'

'Unless what?'

'I was wondering whether Doctor Flemballe could help us. He seems to be greatly respected. Perhaps he could be persuaded to pass the word to the village elders who come to see him that a traveller from the North, with many ancestral spirits guiding him, has arrived in the district. He could say that this stranger has incredible powers.'

'That wouldn't work unless you can produce someone who is entirely unknown.' Kovina pointed out.

'The doctor used to work at a leper colony in the Belgian Congo. He might be persuaded to invite one of the African ministers he used to work with to pay him a visit.'

'But do you think this new friend of yours would be willing to go to such lengths? After all, he's a man of the cloth!'

'Julian Flemballe would be on the side of law and order and, I think, not averse to a little subterfuge to help us catch our prey,' Musah said remembering the spark of amusement in the minister's eyes.

Rubbing his hands, Kovina rose from his seat. 'Well, what're you waiting for? Go back and see if you can set something up – anything's worth a try.'

'No, I should give it more thought, and anyway I must see what's going on at the Greenwoods' bungalow and make sure the garden's in good order for their return next week.'

'Just don't leave it too long. Your plan could work. Let me know when you've decided.'

A great fuss was made of Musah when he arrived at the bungalow. Sammy, Milah and the brood of children surrounded him, clapping their hands and asking for news. Musah had brought a strip of brightly coloured cloth for Milah, a straw hat for Sammy and sweets for the children. He made a tour of inspection of the garden, satisfying himself that Heather would find everything to her liking. Several of the new young shrubs they had planted only a few months ago had already doubled in size and all the hibiscus and bougainvillaea cuttings he had set in pots under a matting shelter had taken root. He knew Heather would be pleased to see that the bananas and paw paws were now bearing fruit by the fenced off vegetable garden, if Sammy's children didn't 'lift' them first. Musah nodded his approval and patted Sammy's eldest son on his fuzzy head.

'You've done well, Eko, you fix um propah. Missis be pleased wid you pass all,' he said, dropping into pidgin for the boy's benefit. Eko beamed; such praise was seldom given but in this case was well-deserved, and Musah knew the boy would double his efforts as a result of those few words.

Sammy assured him that all was ready for the return of Massah and Missis. He patted the refrigerator.

'Him done work propah. Plenty beer in dere, an I boil plenty water for drink.'

'Did you filter the water propah?' Musah asked. Sammy rolled his eyes, spat in the dust, shuffled his feet.

'Ob course,' he said disdainful that Musah should think otherwise.

'You don't want Massa and Missis and the piccins to get belly palaver as soon as they get back.'

'Dey get plenty strong medsin to fix um if dey done get belly palaver,' Sammy assured him airily.

On the day of their arrival, David and Verity couldn't wait to investigate their old haunts and hiding places, and shot from the car like a couple of torpedoes as soon as it came to rest on the drive.

Sammy and Musah were waiting at the foot of the verandah steps to greet the family. Determined to impress, Sammy was uncomfortably resplendent in over-starched almost-white trousers and shirt, while Musah wore a long white Hausa style robe. The children threw themselves at Musah, chatterboxing noisily and with such rapidity that they could barely be understood. There followed the business of standing against the kitchen door to compare the marks Musah had made recording their height before they left, and gratification when he told them they had grown like giants while away in England.

Heather and Edward took time to unravel their stiff, cramped bodies after the long drive from the airport. Now that air travel was beginning to take over, they missed the slow sea voyage back to Africa. The boat trip had given them a chance to get used to the tropical heat gradually; coming down the steps from the air-conditioned plane straight on to the shimmering runway was like walking into an unventilated greenhouse in midsummer. The heat rose in a stifling embrace so that for a few minutes it was difficult to breathe and clothes stuck to perspiring bodies long before they reached the airport terminal.

'I'd almost forgotten what it's like to be this hot,' Heather said, brushing wisps of damp hair from her forehead and easing her skirt away from where it stuck to her legs. She hadn't expected Musah to be there to greet them and looked directly at her friend and ally, a question in her glance.

Musah shook his head. That was the only communication necessary regarding Komfo. Heather heaved a sigh and shook her shoulders. I won't let that venomous little beast get me down this time, she promised herself.

There was much excitement after the travellers had been revived by the inevitable cups of tea, for then it was time to distribute the presents brought from England for Sammy and his family. Dinky toys for the boys, dolls for the girls, a glass necklace and a colourful scarf for Milah to wear round her head like a turban when she went to market, and by special request, bright red socks, sunglasses and a mouth-organ for Sammy. There had been an argument when Heather bought the mouth-organ.

'You must be mad, buying that for Sammy!' Edward had said. Unkind memories remained of being woken one Christmas morning when David found a drum and trumpet at the foot of his bed, and the ensuing cacophony had continued well into the New Year.

'Don't worry,' Heather had assured him. 'Sammy will soon tire of it after showing off and boasting in the local bar for a few nights. Someone will offer him money for it and it will soon change hands.'

When the children were in bed and Sammy had cleared away the supper things, still dimly feeling his way around wearing the treasured sunglasses which he refused to relinquish, Musah returned and told Heather and Edward about the gun-smuggling, his visit to the cave, his meeting with Doctor Flemballe and the brief sighting of Komfo.

'We're hoping to set a trap for Komfo,' Musah explained, 'so I'll be away for a few days while I find out if Doctor Flemballe is willing to provide an accomplice – a sort of pseudo witch doctor.'

'It sounds very involved. How do you intend to go about it?' Edward asked.

'I'm not sure, and nothing can be arranged until I've seen Kovina again.'

'I suggested to Edward some time ago that we try to rope in a witch doctor with superior powers than Komfo,' Heather said, 'but none of the Chiefs he spoke to were prepared to help us find such a man.'

'No. That would be a useless quest. We would have to go much further afield, even into a neighbouring country, to find someone who wouldn't be intimidated.'

As Musah prepared to leave, Heather gave him a small package.

'My father asked me to give you this,' she said. 'I told him you had given David your amulet for protection and that it had been passed down from your father and grandfather.'

Musah unwrapped the package to reveal a small leather-bound box. Inside, a gold Hunter lay on the dark blue velvet lining.

'It belonged to my grandfather,' Heather explained, 'so it's a fitting exchange. It still keeps good time, though I doubt if it has the same powers of guardianship,' she added with a smile.

Musah's face worked with emotion as he held the watch, unable to speak. He brushed his eyes with the back of his hand and held Heather's hands between his own for a few seconds before leaving the room without a word.

'I think he was quite overcome,' Edward said, putting his hand round Heather's waist and drawing her close to him. She lay her head on his shoulder, needing comfort from the fears beginning to gather like a swarm of angry bees.

Edward sensed the return of her old anxieties and kissed the top of her head. 'Come on now, it's been a long day and you're tired out. A good night's sleep will set you up ready to get your hands in the soil again – the garden's calling, you know.'

'You're right, as usual,' she said, grateful for his understanding, thankful for his love.

But it took her a long time to get to sleep on that first night back in Africa. Her mind refused to rest, fidgeting over her worries and fears. She had only the description of others to go on for Komfo, but she had formed her own grey picture of him which stayed, etched in her mind like a fading negative of an old photograph. He stood at the bottom of her bed, grinning at her malevolently, and when she went for a glass of water, he was leaning against the refrigerator, the short spear in his hand pointing directly towards her heart. She ran back to bed without the water and clung to Edward, shaking with fright, her teeth chattering. He gathered her up in his arms until the shaking stopped, then he hummed the tune of a lullaby he'd heard her singing to the children when they were small, kissing her temple until she slept. Beyond the compound the talking drums went on long into the night, sending their messages from village to village, pebbles of gossip being tossed into a lake of listeners who would take up the story and spread it ever wider.

By morning Heather's fears were soon covered with a blanket of domesticity as she fitted herself and the children back into a routine. Some of her expatriate neighbours called to give her news of happenings in Mampi while she had been away: a new birth, a love affair, the size of a snake found hiding under someone's fridge and all other such trivia. And in return they wanted to know if she had heard any of the rumours while she was in the UK that the demands of Facriwa's increasingly vociferous politicians for self- government were being listened to by the British Government. Had a date yet been set for the handover? Such an event would affect all their lives.

The children rampaged around the house and garden, pleased to be back with their old friends. They ran in and out of the kitchen tormenting Sammy, holding their hands over their ears and pulling faces at the appalling racket he made while puffing and sucking at his mouth organ.

Heather was surprised by the way the shrubs and trees had grown during her absence; she had forgotten how the tropical humidity urged quick growth, with seeds germinating and springing up like mushrooms almost overnight. She praised Eko for his work under Musah's guidance and the boy himself seemed to grow a couple of inches, his shiny black face exuding pride and happiness. He had always appeared to be the most dim-witted of Sammy's offspring, and Heather had observed how he had often been exploited by his parents, always being given the most menial of household chores. Although no malice was intended, he was also constantly the brunt of teasing by his brothers and sisters, who didn't quite know how to cope with Eko, the brother they called the quiet one, who was always seeking the reason for things. Small in stature and slow in speech, amiable, and willing to do whatever job was asked of him, to them, he was an oddity. Heather's praise, so soon after Musah's encouragement, made an immediate impact on the slim youth. He attacked the new site, which Missis said was to form a rockery, with vigour; someone believed in him and he was about to show that such belief was justified. He had no idea what a rockery was, and the notion of piling a lot of rocks together seemed strange to him, but now he had been given the incentive to learn, it wouldn't take him long to find out.

Heather was amused and touched by Eko's reaction and made a mental note to give the boy some of the picture books David and Verity had outgrown. The children were happy to co-operate when she suggested they should give the young garden boy some of their books, though David was puzzled.

'But Mum, Eko's not all there. He won't know what to do with them,' he said, stacking brightly coloured story books in a pile on the floor.

'How d'you know that? Heather asked. 'Perhaps it's only because he's never had the opportunity.'

'Sammy's other children go to school, but Eko never goes with them,' David pointed out.

'Would you like going to school if the bigger boys made fun of you?'

'I'd hit them,' David said matter-of-factly, and Heather could well believe that he would. Her son was growing into a stocky boy, well able – and willing – to stick up for himself. Verity knelt on the floor pulling painting books and crayoning books from the shelves of the bookcase in her bedroom, listening to the conversation. She didn't join in the discussion, but sat back on her heels, a frown of concentration pleating her forehead, and sucked her thumb, a childish habit she found difficult to discard.

Early the following morning, Kovina arrived to tell the Greenwoods the plan that had been set in motion to trap Komfo. Dr Flemballe had invited a friend of his from the Cameroons to be the prime mover; a minister said to be blessed with necromantic powers far in excess of those possessed by Komfo, and passed on to him by the spirits of his ancestors. Father Ogbara, the African priest who was to be involved in the conspiracy, viewed it as a vastly amusing escapade and was raring to get started. A man of Friar Tuck proportions, with a belly laugh deep and fruity enough to grace any music hall, he gave Musah grave doubts about whether he would be able to play the part they had in mind for him. He was to spend a short holiday with Dr Flemballe, who would let his powers be known to the men of his village. Word would soon get around in the market place and no doubt the drums would also play their part in the advertising campaign. There had been a marked increase in petty crime and cattle theft in the district and the doctor was to prepare a fiery sermon on the importance of bringing evil men to book. It was hoped that this would filter through to many of Komfo's enemies. With luck one of them would approach the doctor's guest for a strong juju to protect him from Komfo's retaliation once details of his whereabouts had been given to the police.

'It seems a pretty long shot to me,' Edward said, 'an awful lot is being taken for granted in this scheme you and Musah have cooked up.'

'That's as may be,' Kovina replied, smiling at Edward's pessimism. 'You can't even begin to understand the depth of African superstition as we do.'

'Anything's worth a try, even if the chances are slim,' Heather said. Like Edward, she thought the plot was weak and held out little hope that it would be the means of catching up with the clever witch doctor; but someone knew where he was hiding, and if this was the only means of flushing him out, so be it. After all, she had once been fired with a similar idea.

'There's another rumour that Komfo is holed up somewhere near Tegey village again,' Kovina told them.

'If that's the case, I'm surprised Comfort or some other people who've been cruelly treated by him haven't informed on him long before now,' Heather remarked, feeling the anger bubbling up inside her once again. Despite her fear, she added 'I'd like to go back and see what's happened to my old garden in Tegey, and see if Comfort's had any more babies, and if Ruth has survived.'

'You may get a chance to find out soon,' Edward told her. 'I was going to keep it as a surprise, but I may have to go to Sekari for a meeting with the Cocoa Marketing Board in a week or two, and I thought we could all go, and stop at the Government Rest House for a night to break the journey.'

'Oh, Edward! That would be wonderful. When are we going? How long can we stay in Sekari? Can we go to the Botanic Gardens?'

'Hey! Hold on a minute. I only said I may have to go – nothing's been decided, one of the other officers might go instead. It all depends who the Director of Agriculture chooses. You never know, he could say I'm far too important to be spared!' Edward grinned.

'Of course, darling, without you the whole of the territory would fall apart round our ears. How stupid of me to even consider you leaving your post. The crops would fail, the cattle would die, the irrigation channels would get bunged up and—' She wasn't allowed to finish the sentence as Edward picked her up and threw her across his knees as if to give her a spanking. Kovina smiled and got up to leave – these expatriates never ceased to baffle him.

'It's time I got back to work. I'll let you know if I hear any further news,' he said. His departure was interrupted when a tornado in the shape of David hurtled into the room, his face red and angry.

'You've got to tell her, Mum! You've got to make her come and help me finish my bridge.'

'Steady on. What's up?' Edward grabbed hold of his son.

'It's Verity, Dad. She promised to help me build my bridge. She promised, and now she says she's too busy.'

'Well if she's too busy, can't you do it some other time? What's the rush?' Edward asked.

David looked up at him, exasperated by grown-up's lack of understanding.

'No, of course not. We start back at school tomorrow and I want to finish it today. I told Musah I'd have it finished before he got back, and now Verity won't hold the end up for me.'

It was obviously a matter of some importance so they all trooped out of the bungalow to the shaded area Musah had made for the children to build a model village. It was a mixture of Meccano structures, Dinky toys, Verity's doll's house and a set of wooden farm buildings and animals. Now, the latest acquisition from England, the train set, was to be included in the hodge podge of differing proportions that made up the children's village of Yatton, a name adopted from a village at home in Somerset.

Heather left the men to sort out the architectural problem and went in search of Verity. She discovered her daughter seated with Eko on a large flat rock under the shade of a poinciana tree. A book lay open on Eko's knees and both children were so deep in concentration they didn't hear Heather's approach. She listened to her daughter, who had barely mastered the art herself, giving Eko a reading lesson. As Verity's none-too-clean finger pointed to each letter, she gave it a sound.

'That round one is an O and it says OH. Now you say it.'

'OH OH OH ,' Eko repeated after her, his eyes wide.

Heather crept away and never referred to the 'lesson', thinking Verity might be shy about her project. She was more sensitive than her elder brother, and any teasing could put her off. It was obviously giving her pleasure, and one day could be of some advantage to the African boy.

As progress continued on the new rockery, Eko himself kept quiet about the private tuition, but Heather was amazed at the difference in her young apprentice gardener and wondered if Musah would also notice the change. In a remarkably short time, Eko dropped the use of most of his pidgin English and Heather saw him rescuing a discarded Daily Telegraph from the dustbin and folding it carefully before stuffing it inside his tattered shirt. The small black and white print must have taken the boy's fancy, Heather thought, but goodness only knew what he would make of the difficult words.

Verity also kept the clandestine lessons to herself, but there was a distinct improvement in her own reading, and several more books left the shelves in her bedroom to find their way into Eko's hut.

Musah returned to Mampi with news of his experiment in skulduggery with Dr Flemballe, recounting events which had caused some amusement for the participants. Following the rumours dropped as to the incredible powers of Father Ogbara, the doctor's visitor, a queue had formed outside the priest's bungalow each morning. The line of Africans, not only from surrounding villages but from much further afield, waited patiently to have palaver with the plump stranger from the Cameroons, and by now he was credited with inconceivable powers the like of which had never before been witnessed in Facriwa.

While tending the spiritual needs of his flock back in the Cameroons, Father Ogbara had been impressed by the success of a visiting German osteopath, from whom he had learned a great deal. He now used his skills with excellent result on a number of Dr Flemballe's congregation who refused to go to the hospital for fear that white doctors would ensure they only left the building in wooden boxes.

It took only a few successful manipulations of dislodged collar bones and twisted knees by Father Ogbara for the news of his 'miracle' cures to spread. Before long he had ministered to many men and women asking for protection, not only against evil spirits, which suddenly appeared to be rampant in that part of Facriwa, but also equally evil relatives and neighbours. To each of them he gave assurance that God alone could shield them, but they were not convinced, not fooled for one minute. Their superstitious minds would only believe in the power which they were certain came direct from Father Ogbara's ancestors, and armed with this knowledge, they were content to rely on this for all manner of protection. Should this not come up to expectations, blame would automatically be laid on a wife whose laziness must have interfered with the spell, or a child whose constant crying had disturbed Father Ogbara's revered ancestors. In one case, the shadow of a dead tree, cast by bright moonlight and falling across someone's path, was given as the cause of the juju not having the desired effect.

Time alone would tell if the people it had been intended to influence had taken the bait and been brave enough to put it to the test.

CHAPTER 18

Heather arranged to leave the children with friends for the few days they would be away at Tegey and Sekari, to avoid them missing any further time away from school after their long leave in the UK. It would also be safer to be without the children in case there should be a repetition of the experience they'd had at the road block. Since the politicians were now assured that progress was being made in Whitehall to hand over power to the Facriwans, things had been comparatively calm, though sporadic flare-ups between groups jockeying for position in the hierarchy of the emerging African government still occurred from time to time.

Although Edward anticipated no unpleasant incidents, he decided to take his gun; there was no point tempting fate or underestimating the power still held by Komfo and his Black Sword Party, even though the police claimed to have most of the troublemakers under lock and key. There would always be a few who had managed to escape; those were usually the ones with zeal and belief in the cause, be it for their own advancement or for what they considered the good of their people.

The journey was uneventful until they were ten miles north of Tegey, when the weather took a hand. Skittish white clouds with puffed-out cheeks had shown off in spectacular formation across the horizon until now, when they suddenly transformed into heavily laden grey bolsters and the sky took on a menacing purple frown. The atmosphere was electric, the air stifling and Heather and Edward felt as if they were breathing through damp flannel.

'I think this must be what a fish feels like when it's just been landed,' Heather remarked, wiping her forehead with the back of her hand for the umpteenth time and leaving behind a smear of red laterite dust. Their clothes were soon sodden with sweat and stuck to their bodies until there was no room for it to be further absorbed and it trickled down to find a home in their shoes.

An undercurrent of unease ran through them as they approached the village where Komfo had first begun spinning his devilish cobweb, ensnaring all those who didn't do exactly as he wished. Those daring to question his authority were doomed – either to death or to a life of fear and anxiety.

The air was tense with expectancy as the first fork of lightning stabbed the earth, followed by a deafening clap of thunder, and then a balloon burst above them as if some heavenly dam had cracked open. The rain tore into the earth with tenacity, turning the surface of the track into a sea of red mud within seconds.

Conversation was impossible, and for a few minutes they sat in the car listening as the thunder reverberated and the world shook beneath the onslaught. Heather undid the buttons of her blouse, unzipped her skirt, slipped off her sandals and opened the car door. She stepped out into the deluge in her underwear and held her arms up to the sky. Opening her mouth to the elements, she danced in the mud, laughing, exhilarated by the pummelling of the rain, revelling in its blessed coolness. Edward watched from the shelter of the car, enjoying the sight of his cavorting wood-nymph of a wife, then, discarding his bush shirt and shorts, he joined her in the rain dance. They sang and danced together like children, their voices obliterated by the din made by nature at its most boisterous. A mammy lorry passed them laden with a crowd of rain-soaked, bedraggled, cheerful African road-workers who shrieked and waved at them, falling against each as they laughed at the spectacle of half-dressed white people capering about like piccins in the rain.

The storm ended as suddenly as it had begun, the rain ceasing abruptly, as if the clouds had been wrung dry. The air was soft, sweet and pungent with the scent of bruised growing things, and only the gentle hiss of water dripping from leaves and branches replaced the furore of what had gone before.

Heather and Edward rubbed themselves dry with towels from the case in the boot of the car, replaced their clothes and cautiously drove through the thick slippery laterite that coated the surface of the road like melted chocolate. The sun soon got to work and the track ahead began to steam as they approached the turn off leading up to the juju grove. Edward slowed the car and pulled in to the side of the road.

'It was up there where it all started,' Heather put her thoughts into words. 'Remember that day when you defied the juju spell and walked into a trail of driver ants?

'I'll say I remember it! There was I being bitten half to death and you thought it was hilarious!'

'Sometimes it seems as if it happened a lifetime ago, but now it feels as if it were only yesterday,' Heather said. 'You know – you, Kovina and Musah have all been up there; you've all seen it, felt its atmosphere, but I've only heard about it and its dark secrets.'

'Want to take a look now? We can go up there if you think it will dispel some of your old fears,' Edward offered.

'No! Certainly not! ' Heather shivered. 'It's more likely to bring back my nightmares and it would spoil our visit to Sekari. We've got better things to do than dwell on the souls of buried ancestors and whatever else has taken place up there. If we get a move on we'll have time to stop in Tegey for a few minutes.'

Paradise Store had changed little over the last few years, though it now sported a newly painted sign above the door: paradise emporium, and the counter had a bright yellow formica top. Heather preferred the old, much stained, wooden slab with its ingrained character of cigarette burns, deep scars and dents, the relics of countless palavers and village brawls. She recalled the hurt and bewilderment she had felt the day that Comfort had turned her back and walked out, ignoring her after she had tried to befriend the unhappy girl.

'Does Comfort still live here in Tegey?' she asked Pius. The store-keeper had grown fat and looked more grizzled than ever. He sat on a sack of flour, his back resting against a fly-blown poster extolling the virtues of the local Sekari brewed beer. He scratched his head with a long thumbnail, cleared his throat noisily and spat expertly into a small mound of dust heaped between a couple of sacks of sugar before he replied.

'Yes Missis. She get four piccins now.'

'Four!'

'Yeah, but she no catch no more piccin now,' he chuckled knowingly.

'Oh, and why is that?'

'Her husband done get caught with plenty other men who done help Komfo. The police done catch 'um. Now dey be inside Sekari Prison.'

His delight at this outcome was plain to see. After they had brought themselves up to date with more news, Heather and Edward left the store and returned to the car with the happy thought that Komfo would have a few less supporters to help him and less allies to shield and hide him in his gun-running and power-grabbing plans.

'That's the first time any of the locals have spoken to us so openly and with such obvious pleasure at the incarceration of any of the witch doctor's followers.' Edward remarked as they drove away.

'Yes. It's not so long ago that Pius would not have dared speak such words aloud in case he was overheard and punished.'

'For all we know, word has already reached as far as this about Musah's doctor friend. Perhaps the locals already know about this stranger with a juju much stronger than that of Komfo.'

Their time in Sekari passed quickly, with Heather shopping and meeting old friends to exchange gossip while Edward attended meetings at the agricultural and veterinary offices. Their evenings were mostly spent at the expatriates' club seeing a film, going to a dance or playing a game of darts, apart from the last night which they spent quietly in the bar of their hotel. Kovina joined them there in high spirits; the plan set in motion by Musah and Dr Flemballe seemed to be working well. Several people had come forward to report details of Komfo's dealings with the gun-smugglers across the border and with the political factions in neighbouring West African colonies. It was now apparent that he had formed a much wider network of people prepared to back him in his quest for power than had been supposed. Naturally they would expect monetary recompense once he was established and this would rarely be subscribed to the budgets of their countries, but he was far more likely to line their own pockets along with other favours: there would no doubt be some lucrative building and supply contracts in the offing.

Their discussion with Kovina was interrupted abruptly by a young Facriwan who strode into the bar and walked up to Kovina, claimed his attention imperiously, pointedly ignoring Heather and Edward after throwing one stabbing glance in their direction.

'Excuse me for a minute,' Kovina said apologetically and left the bar with the young man.

'Odd,' Heather said, lifting her glass, 'I wonder who he is and what that was all about. He seemed put out about something.'

'I've a feeling we've met him before,' Edward said, fiddling with a beer mat, tapping it on his thumbnail. 'His face looks familiar.'

Heather shook her head.

'Can't say I remember him…unless…' she frowned in concentration. 'Yes, I think I know who he is. Remember that day when we went to the hospital ages ago when I was expecting Verity? After I'd seen the doctor we went to the ward to see Kovina. It was not long after he'd been shot for snooping around up at the burial ground. His wife was visiting him at the same time and she had the children with her.'

Edward nodded, wondering where this was leading.

'I think that chap who just interrupted our conversation was Kovina's son. Don't you remember that "spit in your eye" look he gave us then? Well, that was the way he looked at us just now. You remarked at the time that he seemed to have a chip on his shoulder.'

'Yeah, I think you're right. So I wonder what he's got against us? What have we done to deserve such hostility?' Edward beckoned the barman to refill their glasses.

'Maybe he just hates anyone who's white,' Heather guessed.

'If you're right, there must be a reason for it,' Edward replied, as always wanting to believe only the best of anyone.

'Maybe,' but Heather was not convinced.

Kovina was alone when he returned about ten minutes later, so they were unable to get a second look at the young man. Determined to find out if her guess was correct, Heather asked, 'Was that your son who just came in?'

Kovina looked surprised.

'Yes, but how on earth do you know that? Surely we aren't that much alike?'

'We saw him a few years ago when you were in hospital.' Heather reminded him.

'Oh,' Kovina picked up his drink and didn't pursue the matter, seemingly caught up in a more pressing concern of his own. He fidgeted with his glass, turning it round and round in his hands before saying brusquely: 'I'm sorry, something has cropped up and I'll have to go, but I'll be coming up to Mampi later this month and I'll see you then if there's any news to pass on.' He looked distracted and left in something of a hurry.

Edward raised his eyebrows as they watched the tall African walk quickly down the hotel steps and out into the night.

As always, they had stocked up on books and magazines while shopping in Sekari and read in bed for a while before putting the light out. Sleep was a long time coming, for some reason they were both restless and on edge.

'I'll be glad to get back to my own bed,' Heather grumbled, turning over for the umpteenth time and making a futile attempt to box her feather pillow into a more accommodating shape.

'We aren't used to this luxury,' Edward laughed, 'we're more used to the rock-hard government-issue lumps of bedding we get at home.'

'It's not only that,' Heather told him, 'it's the din of that blasted air conditioner. Can't we turn it off? It's not working properly, it's only shifting hot air from one side of the room to the other.'

Edward stood on the bed and reached up to switch off the offending machine. Straightaway they could hear the drums throbbing in the night air. They lay side by side listening to the sound. It was louder, but pleasantly familiar after the persistent clanking of the noisy air conditioner.

'Is it my imagination, dear, or do the drums sound particularly portentous tonight?' Edward asked.

'No,' Heather muttered above a yawn, 'it's not my birthday for weeks yet.'

They made an early start on the long journey back to Mampi as Heather was anxious to get back home to see how the children had fared being left with friends for the first time. But they had to stop at the hospital to pick up some rabies vaccine. The hospital at Mampi had exhausted its supply after a rabid dog had run amok through several villages, fighting with other dogs and biting several villagers before being shot by a hunter.

'It won't take us long, someone at the pathology department has been told to expect us,' Edward said, noting Heather's impatience to be on their way. And he was right, they were indeed expected, but the keys to the vaccine refrigerator couldn't be found.

'One of the doctors has probably popped them in his pocket, it won't take us long to track them down,' a sister assured them. Like a ship in full sail, her starched uniform and flowing white head-dress billowing out behind her, she led them down a long buff-coloured corridor to her office and insisted they had a cup of coffee while they waited. She smiled sympathetically as she busied herself with cups and saucers. 'It's Facriwa, my dears, you can't rush things. You know the saying here: "Wait until tomorrow"' she said, adding under her breath 'or the day after, or the day after that!'

It took longer than expected to trace the keys, and then the vaccine had to be signed for and the batch number logged in a record book before it was carefully packed in a thermos flask of crushed ice and tightly wedged between luggage in the boot of the car. The sun was already high before they finally headed out of the hospital gates and on to the main road back towards Tegey.

'There won't be any time to stop now,' Edward said. 'It'll be best to head straight for home.'

'It's a shame, I wanted to see Comfort and her piccins.' The disappointment showed in Heather's voice.

'Yes, if it hadn't been for you, I doubt if they would have survived.' Edward took his hand from the steering wheel and patted her knee, then he leaned across and kissed her cheek. 'Never mind, there'll be other times.'

'Look where you're going!' Heather said in pretend alarm. But the affectionate gesture lifted her spirits and she put her arm round his neck, nuzzling into him. 'I quite like you,' she said.

'That's good. You know, you're not so bad yourself, come to think of it.' He gave her a cheeky sideways look and continued: 'Seeing as we quite like each other, shall we stop at the Rest House for a quickie?'

'Not a hope. Remember the bedroom has no curtain and it's broad daylight!'

'Aw shucks! Foiled again!' Edward laughed.

They travelled without incident, only slowing down to look for familiar faces as they passed through Tegey, and waving at a line of children as they left the school house with exercise books and bottles of ink balanced on their heads, pens and pencils thrust into the tight glossy fuzz of their hair.

'They'll probably be the civil servants of the new Facriwan government,' Heather mused.

Edward nodded. 'There will be a lot of changes here before long.'

When they reached the turn-off to the juju grove, he pulled in to the side of the track, switched off the engine, and repeated his offer. 'Do you want to go up there? D'you want to see the old burial ground for yourself?

Now's your chance to lay some ghosts if you want to.'

Heather hesitated. 'I'm not sure, Edward. I can't help feeling frightened of the place, but perhaps if I saw it in broad daylight with no drums to give the place a heart-beat of its own…Maybe that would help to kill off some of the dread and mystery that has grown in my mind despite trying to dismiss the superstitious beliefs. So many strange things have happened. I wonder if there is any connection between this burial ground and the body you found outside our bungalow? Is there really some mysterious aura about the place or is it all just a hoax to cover up a political intrigue or something illegal going on there?' Heather knew there were no answers to her questions, and probably never would be.

'It may have been abandoned by now. Musah told me that police and army patrols made several visits after Kovina was shot. It's obvious that something was going on that night, and I dare say he's got a good idea of what it was, but whatever happened, he's keeping it to himself,' Edward said.

'It's all these secrets that make me cross. There's neither rhyme nor reason to it – if everything is out in the open then the pieces fall into place.'

Edward switched on the engine.

'No, wait! Stop! We will go up and have a look. It's time I stopped half-believing these stupid juju stories,' Heather opened the car door and jumped out. 'Quick, Edward, before I change my mind again. If I stop and think about it I'll only lose my nerve.'

Before he left the car, Edward took the gun from its hiding place under the seat and slipped it into his pocket. Wanting to get it over as soon as possible, they made good progress up the incline towards the plateau, despite the punishing midday sun. It was immediately apparent to Edward that the route had been used many times since he made that first survey when he was caught by the driver ants. There was no longer need for a machete to hack a path through the scrub and they soon reached the level clearing.

'It's like a small stadium,' Heather whispered, out of breath from the climb. She put up a hand to shield her eyes from the glare as she gazed round. A large flat-topped rock stood on the far side of the clearing with smaller outcrops scattered about to form a ragged circle. They stepped into the circle and walked slowly towards the altar-like stone ahead of them. It was quiet and still and an eerie hush seemed to close round them;

no breath of wind, no rustle from the stunted scrub, no birdsong or hum of insects.

'God, what a spooky place! It's no wonder the locals say it's a sacred meeting ground of their forefathers,' Edward said, his voice barely audible. 'That rock looks as if it's waiting for a sacrifice to be laid on it.' He shuddered as he recalled the bloodcurdling scream he had heard the night he had come with Safo to rescue Kovina and take him to the hospital.

'I don't like it. Let's go back,' Heather's voice was hoarse. 'There's something evil about this place. I can feel it. There's nothing sacred or holy here. It's a place of horror, it makes my skin crawl.' She turned, her arms held tight across her chest as if for protection, needing to get away, to see the back of the burial place for ever. But before she could take a step, she froze, her eyes drawn towards something black and shining on the ground to one side of her. It was partly hidden by a wedge shaped stone and she leaned forward to see it better. Her eyes darkened, her hand flew to her mouth as she let out a scream of horror. As soon as Edward saw the cause of her distress he stepped in front of her, shielding her from the hideous sight.

At first glance it looked as if hundreds of small shiny black beads had been piled upon the ground, then the shape and the movement gave the unbelievable truth. A human body lay spreadeagled, pegged out on the ground beneath an invading sea of black ants.

'Don't look! Go back to the car,' Edward's voice was urgent, commanding.

'We must stop them. Get them off, the man might still be alive!' Even as she shouted the words, a faint gurgling, choking sound came from the pinioned body. Edward could see the man was beyond help. Heather tugged frantically at branches of prickly scrub, snapping them off, beating at the seething black sea of insects as they devoured the human sacrifice. Edward pulled her away.

'Get back, Heather! It's too late. Just leave it. Go back to the car.'

Heather turned her back, her shoulders heaving with great rasping sobs. As she stumbled away from the scene, a single shot rang out behind her. It echoed round and round the obscene wilderness, then re-echoed in her head again and again, like someone bouncing a ball inside her skull.

CHAPTER 19

'Of course I wanted him dead, but not like that. He was an evil man who caused a great deal of pain and sorrow, but no one could wish such a vile end to anyone's life,' Heather said. After several weeks of being unable to talk about the episode, she had finally come to terms with the scene she had witnessed at the burial ground. The harrowing nightmares that had plagued her, and the sound of the single shot which always woke her, cold and shaking, were less frequent now.

'I'm sorry the case is being so long drawn out,' the District Commissioner said sympathetically. 'Unfortunately these things always take time.' He shook his head. 'So much red tape, you know. If only Edward had left him there to die instead of putting him out of his misery, no enquiry would have been necessary and he would not be facing a charge of murder.'

'You see? Even though he's dead, he still has the power to hurt us. I sometimes think this whole thing will go on for ever, that we'll never be free of him.'

'Come now, my dear,' the Commissioner said, his voice gentle, but still grave, 'We'll try to get this unpleasant business dealt with as quickly as possible, then you and Edward should get away to the coast for a while.'

'Unpleasant business! I'd give it a stronger name than that,' Heather looked at the experienced diplomat with exasperation. 'Edward didn't know it was Komfo when he fired the gun. We'd never met him, we had no idea what he looked like, and anyway, it was impossible to recognise anyone under that seething black mass of ants,' she passed a hand over her eyes, trying to blot out the image.

'Yes, well, that has all been recorded in the statements made by you and Edward following the incident, and it will be taken into account at the next court hearing. I don't think you have anything much to worry about.

With luck, it should be pretty straightforward from now on.' He rubbed a mosquito bite on the back of his hand and added: 'Though I should warn you, some factions are trying to rock the political boat in all this.'

Edward had taken little part in the conversation; he'd heard it all before. The same things had been discussed from every angle over and over again during the past weeks. He knew what was coming next – it was like listening to a gramophone with the needle stuck in a groove, and the police seemed no nearer to finding the culprits who had pegged Komfo across a driver ants' train for the insects to eat him alive.

If only they hadn't been held up at the hospital, waiting for the rabies vaccine, they could well have arrived in time to save Komfo's life. Would it have been wiser to have walked away from the tribal execution, or, with hindsight, would it have been better not to have reported the fact that he had shot the man to prevent his slow and agonising death? Edward asked himself the same questions again.

The District Commissioner's voice broke into his troubled thoughts.

'You have to bear in mind, Edward, that such a way of dealing with miscreants is considered normal practice in this part of the world, so your intervention, even though with the highest possible motive, is not going to go down well with the tribal chief or whoever else it was who tracked down Komfo and authorised the sentence.'

Sick of listening, Edward got up and strode across the room.

'What's done is done. Nothing can be changed and I just have to live with it.' His statement was final, and delivered as if slamming shut the pages of a book. 'Come on, let's forget it now. Who's for a drink?'

The same subject was uppermost in the mind of nearly all the members of the expatriate community and was the main topic of conversation at the club and the British Council Library. While the majority believed Edward had done the only thing possible in the circumstances, a few still felt Komfo should have been left to die slowly. At all events, it would seem that Dr Flemballe's attempts to bring matters to a head had succeeded beyond all expectations, though not quite in the way anticipated. If only the person who tracked down the witch doctor had handed him over to the police, then the matter would have been dealt with in the courts. But who could blame that person for taking matters into his own hands when Komfo had already escaped prison on a previous occasion?

Musah, although showing some satisfaction at the turn of events, was well able to appreciate Edward's present doubts about the course he had taken, and knew it must now be galling for him to be accused of murder when he had only been doing his best to alleviate the suffering of another human being.

Kovina was the enigma. The one person they had all expected to be most elated by the death of their old adversary showed little reaction; in fact he appeared subdued. He barely spoke of the incident and carried on working as though it had never happened. Heather puzzled over his lack of interest, as she puzzled over so many things. She had never been able to account for the peculiar hypnotic affect Kovina had on her when she first arrived in the Colony. She tried to think back, to pinpoint the time when his compelling eyes ceased to throw her off balance. The more she thought about it, the more convinced she became that Kovina's strange influence had waned soon after Musah had given her the amulet for David's protection. Surely it was inconceivable that the fetish attached to the amulet could counteract the electric effect Kovina had once had on her?

It had been some months since she had last looked at the leather talisman. Perhaps now would be a good time to hold it in her hands once more. David had stopped wearing it some weeks ago and when she questioned him about it, the boy had told her that he had 'grown out of it'. He explained to her that he had talked to Musah about it and together they had agreed that it should be kept in a place of safety against the time when its strange powers might be needed once again. It didn't take her long to find the amulet in the top of the chest of drawers in David's bedroom. The boy kept it in an inlaid wooden box his grandmother had given him to house his small treasures. The amulet rubbed shoulders with his grandfather's war medals, a stone shaped like a snail, a shiny brown conker from their garden in England and a black and white dice from a Christmas cracker. Heather smiled as she looked at her son's cherished possessions, but her mood changed when she took the amulet from its hiding place. Pictures from the past returned, focusing on memories that would stay with her for as long as she lived. If Musah hadn't found David in the cave that day, would she ever have seen him alive again?

The amulet warmed the palm of her hand like a living thing. She touched the red eye of the fish with her finger, waiting for something to happen. She wanted to see the old man again, to feel his gentle reassurance – but there was nothing. Disappointed, she wound the leather thong round her fingers and returned the amulet to its resting place in the box. She felt cheated, though at the same time she chided herself for adopting the superstitious beliefs of black Africa which she claimed to deride, despite the fact that, were she strictly honest, a sneaking desire to accept them would always remain. She reasoned with herself: there was no excuse – she was just a pathetic study in contradiction. She sighed and took one last look, but before she could close the lid, a sound like a low moaning wind rose from the box, gradually becoming louder, swirling into a pattern of ethereal notes; forming a gossamer orchestral requiem. The music swelled faintly, enveloping her in a cocoon of perfect sound, one minute a lullaby, the next like waves lapping on a shore, going on and on for ever for as long as the moon and stars exist.

'What are you doing with my box?' David's voice brought Heather back to reality.

'Nothing. I was just listening to the music.' The words were out before she could stop herself.

'Oh, you hear it too,' the boy said, 'it's good, isn't it?' He took the box from her, holding it close to his chest. Closing the lid with care, he returned it to the back of the drawer and slammed it shut. He leaned his back against the drawer as if defending its contents, and turned to face his mother.

'Verity can't hear it. Why d'you think that is?'

'Perhaps it's something to do with the special friendship you and I have with Musah. Maybe it's a sort of bond between us.' Heather said weakly, unable to explain.

'I think it has something to do with electric currents…wavelengths.' The boy spoke with an adult authority that startled his mother. He was growing up and wouldn't accept black magic as a solution to anything out of the ordinary. He had reached the stage where he would search for more down-to-earth answers.

And very sensible too, Heather told herself. Yet still, a hint of regret lay like a feather, swept into a corner of her mind.

At long last a date had been set for the reins of government to be handed over in Facriwa. There would be a week of celebrations with many representatives attending from the United Kingdom and the United States.

Ministers from adjoining territories, as well as other African countries who had already been through this stage of rebirth, would turn out in full force to join in the ceremony. Dignitaries from all over the world would converge on this small West African Colony, offering congratulations and advice, seeking trade deals, making every conceivable proposal to enhance the economy and status of the emerging country, most of them lining their own pockets in the process.

An air of happy anticipation spread throughout Facriwa and the people were like children, excited in the build-up towards Christmas. They became intoxicated by great expectations, assured that all the promises made by their politicians would be fulfilled overnight. They had a lot to learn.

In Mampi and Sekari and other areas where Komfo had cast his shadow, there was an additional feeling of release, with a great deal of singing and dancing in the villages. The banter and barter in the marketplace was exuberant and on the surface, the political cliques seemed content to bide their time and play the waiting game. At Mampi Club there was speculation amongst the expatriates as to whether they should stay on in the Colony or hope for a posting elsewhere. Such placements were harder to come by since one territory after another became self-governing. Expatriates would be needed in these fledgling republics for a considerable time, but many colonials of the old school would find it difficult working under Africans who had, until recently, been their subordinates.

David was fast approaching the age when white children were sent home to boarding school for their education, a thought which filled Heather with dread. She had always put the inevitable separation from her children away at the back of her mind. Although she continued to work in her garden every morning and it still gave her a great deal of pleasure, she no longer felt able to make long-term plans. She shelved her ideas for a fish pond and water garden and concentrated on the rockery, which was now well established. Musah continued to accompany her on the morning tour of inspection as usual, closely followed by Eko, armed with trowel and watering can, ready to carry out any tasks asked of him.

'That young man should go to a horticultural college,' Heather remarked one morning. 'He's so keen to learn, it's a pity to waste such enthusiasm.'

'I think there's little chance of that,' Musah said. 'If you return to England and your bungalow goes to a Facriwan, it is unlikely that Eko would be kept on as a gardener.' He bent to tease a large green praying mantis with a piece of straw, watching the insect's enormous eyes follow the course of the dry grass, turning its head almost full circle as he waved it beyond vision. 'And even if he were kept on, it's doubtful as to whether he'd get paid. I shall try to get him into my old Mission School. He has changed so much since you took him to work in the garden, and as you say, he's eager to learn. We shall need plenty more like him if we are to survive.'

'I hope you are able to help him,' Heather replied, 'otherwise he'll probably end up working on a road gang or one of the new building sites that are springing up all over the place,' she stopped and turned to face him. 'And what about you, Musah? What of your future, what do you intend to do?'

Musah eyed her from beneath bushy brows and smiled broadly.

'I've been offered two alternatives.'

'Oh, and where did they come from?'

'Kovina, of course. He's going up in the world. I've no doubt he'll end up working in Government House before long.'

'He's certainly ambitious,' Heather agreed, 'but what did he offer you?'

'He suggests a position in the District Commissioner's office or a post at the Yabalo Botanic Gardens.'

'It looks as if you are going up in the world too!'

'It will happen to a lot of men as the expatriates leave,' Musah said thoughtfully. 'The problems will begin when some of us find we're not fully equipped to carry out what is expected of us.'

'I can't see that applying to you. Have you decided which post you'd prefer?'

'Not yet. Kovina said the DC's office job could lead to more responsible work because of my knowledge of so many of the different tribal languages and also their customs.'

'That's where all your earlier travels round the Colony would be most useful, I suppose.' Heather looked at her old friend with quizzical eyes. 'It's always puzzled me that you haven't got a well-paid desk job.'

'Perhaps I've not always been quite frank with you. There is a lot I've not been able to tell you, but the secrecy necessary at the time would not allow me to be otherwise. I have been working under cover for some time for the Police Department and the District Commissioner. Kovina has been doing much the same thing, but he had to cut down on most of his more dangerous underground activities after he'd been shot because it was suspected that someone had given the game away. Once it was known that he'd been spying, he had to change tactics.'

'So he was involved in that business when the man was shot outside our bungalow in Tegey?'

'Yes, but he didn't do the killing. I was responsible for that.'

Heather's eyes widened in disbelief. 'You killed him? I can't believe it! I know Kovina was there that night, but I saw no sign of you. I'd never even met you then.'

'I didn't stay around to pick up the pieces, Kovina's men dealt with that. The man I shot was on his way to meet Komfo at the old juju burial site,' Musah explained. 'He was not a local man, and was wanted for murder by the police of two other countries. He and Komfo were setting up the gun-smuggling business and arranging the storage of arms and ammunition in the cave where David was kept years later after he was abducted. Incidentally, the money Komfo was expecting you to pay for David's release was to have helped pay for guns and explosives. Kovina discovered a store of contraband goods, army uniforms and emergency food packs in an old warehouse at Sekari. Komfo was getting set to form his own private army as well as his Black Sword political party.'

'Does Edward know about this?' Heather asked, still trying to take it all in.

'I doubt if he knows anything for certain, but he probably had a pretty good idea what was going on. As you must know by now, it's difficult to keep anything secret for long in Facriwa.'

'Edward has always kept me in the dark. I suppose he wanted to protect me and spare me the worry,' Heather said, thinking back to her bad days. 'I can understand it now, but at the time I used to get ratty with him. I gave him a hard time, but I was annoyed that he kept everything to himself and treated me like a child.'

Musah smiled at her and nodded. 'Yes, and how right he was. You were only a child in the ways of Africa back then.'

'That may be so, but I grew up overnight when Komfo took David away. I won't ever forget my fear that I might never see him again. How I hated that man,' Heather said, with something of her old vehemence. 'It's odd, Musah, all this time I've been longing for that man to be caught and punished, but I have no feeling of satisfaction now that he's dead.'

'No doubt that is because of the way he died. You wanted it all to end tidily, with a court case and the due process of the law – the scales of justice and all that.'

'You may be right. I hate the way he died, but I still feel cheated in some way. I thought that one day I would confront him. I suppose I needed someone to shout at.'

Musah laughed, 'And he would have ignored you.'

'What possessed him to do all those brutal things to so many innocent people? Why were his followers so gullible?'

'His standing as a witch doctor was at the beginning of it, people looked up to him; then his desire for more and more power, and the wealth that came with it enabled him to manipulate people. All those who joined him expected high positions and financial reward in the new Facriwa.' Musah said.

'Well, thank goodness it's all over,' Heather said with a sigh of relief.

Musah made no reply, leaving her with the uncomfortable feeling that maybe it wasn't all over, and the final curtain had yet to fall.

She tackled Edward later, telling him of Musah's revelations, but he showed little surprise. She regarded him, her head on one side.

'So you did know what was going on, and that Musah was involved!'

'Not for sure, and even when I got wind of it, it could still have been rumour.'

'And do you think it's all over and done with?' Heather persevered, but she laughed, anticipating his reply, knowing he would avoid a direct answer.

'Who's to say? There are bound to be loose ends. Some of Komfo's men must still be about: they won't all have been rounded up. And who's to know whether they want to throw in the towel or take up where he left off ?'

'There's more to it than that. Something else is going on, isn't there?'

'I suspect so, and I think it has something to do with Kovina.' Edward said.

'What makes you say that?' There was an edge to Heather's voice as she posed the question.

'He's acting strangely these days. He's very quiet, as if there's something on his mind. There's something bothering him.'

'That's natural enough if he's now holding a position with much more responsibility.'

Edward didn't reply, he took a sheaf of papers from a file and sat down heavily at his desk. 'Look, I've got a lot of paperwork here that has to be sorted out. Let's just give it a rest.' He sounded weary and Heather leaned over the back of his chair and put her arms round his neck, kissing the top of his head. He had aged since his acquittal and she felt a sudden need to hug him, but the moment passed. She kissed him again and said, 'Okay, love. I'll leave you in peace.'

Guilt crept up on her as she walked out on to the verandah and leaned over the rail. Edward had known little peace since he had shot Komfo. He had been through day after day of interrogation, answering the same old questions, first at the District Commissioner's office, then at the police headquarters and finally in the law courts. It had gone on for months and she had hated every minute of it. She hated the relentless way it hounded him day in day out, but how much worse it had been for Edward, still plagued by self-doubt as to the wisdom of ending another man's life.

They were never to see Kovina again. A small gang of armed men were caught and surrounded while bringing arms and ammunition into the country, and Kovina was with the group of army personnel sent to bring them in. During the ensuing fracas, the gang leader took deliberate aim and shot Kovina through the head. The gunman was Kovina's son, Asokwa, who had been recruited by Komfo and had worked with him ever since he was a teenager.

Musah gave Edward the news not long after it happened, and told him that it was known that Kovina and his son had been having heated arguments for many months.

'We think Kovina knew what Asokwa was up to, but couldn't bring himself to arrest his own son and turn him over to the police.'

Heather felt sickened by the news. She would never again see the tall African who had once had the power to mesmerise her. Although she and Edward had believed Kovina's son had some sort of grudge, it was hard to believe that the young man could have harboured such hate that he would kill his own father. Or was Asokwa's desire to seize some of the power once carried by Komfo even stronger? The sooner they left West Africa, the better it would be for all of them, she thought.

And yet…when a year later, Heather stood at the stern of the ship taking them back to England, watching the country disappear over the horizon, there was a mourning sadness in her heart. She loved Facriwa, despite all that had happened during the years she'd spent there. The homesickness, the hardships and the fear had all been overcome with the passage of time. It was her son's birthplace, a place where she had learned to create a garden out of a wilderness, and where her love for Edward had grown deep and strong.

She had come to understand the people of Facriwa, to know a little of their ways and culture, their ability to be happy and content with very little material wealth. The majority of them lived hard lives with scant hope of ever changing their grinding day-to-day routine, yet still they sang and danced, and their laughter and the rhythm of their songs would continue to flow like life blood with their every heartbeat.